DATE

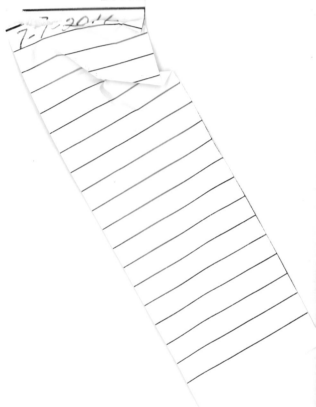

DEATH IN DISGUISE

A Selection of Recent Titles by Sally Spencer from Severn House

The Monika Paniatowski Mysteries

ECHOES OF THE DEAD
BACKLASH
LAMS TO THE SLAUGHTER
A WALK WITH THE DEAD
DEATH'S DARK SHADOW
SUPPING WITH THE DEVIL
BEST SERVED COLD
THICKER THAN WATER
DEATH IN DISGUISE

The Inspector Woodend Mysteries

DANGEROUS GAMES
DEATH WATCH
A DYING FALL
FATAL QUEST

The Inspector Sam Blackstone Series

BLACKSTONE AND THE NEW WORLD
BLACKSTONE AND THE WOLF OF WALL STREET
BLACKSTONE AND THE GREAT WAR
BLACKSTONE AND THE ENDGAME

DEATH IN DISGUISE

A Monika Paniatowski Mystery

Sally Spencer

This first world edition published 2016
in Great Britain and the USA by
SEVERN HOUSE PUBLISHERS LTD of
19 Cedar Road, Sutton, Surrey, England, SM2 5DA.
Trade paperback edition first published
in Great Britain and the USA 2016 by
SEVERN HOUSE PUBLISHERS LTD

British Library Cataloguing in Publication Data
A CIP catalogue record for this title is available from the British Library.

ISBN-13: 978-0-7278-8620-0 (cased)
ISBN-13: 978-1-84751-721-0 (trade paper)
ISBN-13: 978-1-78010-782-0 (e-book)

All Severn House titles are printed on acid-free paper.

Severn House Publishers support the Forest Stewardship Council™ [FSC™],
the leading international forest certification organisation.
All our titles that are printed on FSC certified paper carry the FSC logo.

Typeset by Palimpsest Book Production Ltd.,
Falkirk, Stirlingshire, Scotland.
Printed and bound in Great Britain by
TJ International, Padstow, Cornwall.

Mill owner murdered

Mr Wilfred Hardcastle (49), partner in the Hardcastle Bros. mill, and a leading figure in the Whitebridge and District Mill Owner's association, was found dead in his office last evening by Tom Clegg (17), his general factotum.

Given the nature of his injuries, it was clearly a case of murder, and the police were quick to arrest a twenty-four-year-old man who worked at the mill.

Mr Oswald Hardcastle (41), Mr Wilfred Hardcastle's brother, who has hitherto played no part in the running of the mill, will step in as the new managing director. He is quoted as saying, 'This was a cowardly attack on a man who always tried to be fair with everybody, especially his workers. My brother was looking forward to the birth of his first grandchild, and now this ungrateful monster has robbed him of that joy.'

The police have indicated that the arrested man, believed to work as a tackler in the mill, will be charged in the next few hours.

ONE

The Royal Victoria Hotel, Whitebridge, was widely considered to be a superior hotel for superior people, and most of the guests who stayed there would have thought it very bad manners to allow themselves to be murdered within its confines.

The American woman in the Prince Alfred suite had no such qualms, as was witnessed by the fact that she was sprawled in one of the armchairs with an open wound on her forehead, and was undoubtedly dead.

The body was discovered by the chambermaid, a girl of southern European peasant stock, who was thus well-used to both hard work and people dying before their time. She did not panic, but went straight to the floor supervisor. He, in turn, informed the general manager that a situation had arisen, and the manager immediately rang the police. The whole incident should have been a secret between the three of them, but, as if by osmosis, disquiet soon began to spread through the entire hotel, and long before the first policemen arrived, there was a generalised feeling that something had gone seriously wrong.

When Acting Chief Constable Keith Pickering received news of the murder, he felt much as a real-life mayor of New York City would have felt on being informed that a giant ape was perched on top of the Empire State Building – it wasn't his fault at all, but if he didn't manage the situation extremely carefully, it might as well have been.

The problem was that the Royal Victoria was not just any hotel. Successful local businessmen wined and dined their clients in its restaurant, and the town's solicitors, surveyors, accountants and councillors regularly met in the Prince Albert bar to perform the ancient rite of exchanging scandal. No father of the bride with any social pretensions would ever dream of holding his daughter's wedding reception anywhere else, and it had become *de rigueur* for the Masons to throw their Ladies' Nights in the Royal's ballroom.

Worse yet, it was the favourite haunt of the police authority, a body which (if George Baxter ever recovered enough of his mind to realise he could no longer do the job of chief constable properly) would either confirm Pickering in the post or bring someone in from outside.

He hit the intercom button on his desk.

'Which of the DCIs is available to take on a major case?' he asked.

'I don't think DCI Hawthorn has got much on at the moment, sir,' the secretary replied.

Ollie Hawthorn was solid, reliable, and totally lacking in the imagination that it takes to be a great detective, Pickering thought.

'What's DCI Paniatowski doing at the moment?' he asked.

'She's on a few days' leave,' the secretary said.

'Not any more, she isn't,' Pickering told her.

There had been a thin layer of ice on the pond in Corporation Park earlier in the day, but the combined efforts of several council workmen and a weak winter sun had been enough to ensure that the swans were not too inconvenienced.

Standing at the edge of the pond, Monika Paniatowski tipped the double trolley slightly, so that the twins – well wrapped up, with only their eyes and the bridges of their noses visible – could get a better view of the majestic birds.

'Our teachers used to tell us that a swan's wing could break a man's arm,' she told the boys. 'I wonder if that's true.'

She grinned. She really wasn't very good at talking to babies, she thought.

She tried again. 'Wook at the woverly wittle birdies,' she said.

Was that any better?

Probably not!

She was just going to have to rely on the twins sensing the love that emanated from her every time she was near them.

'We've got a woverly wittle murder on our hands, boss,' said a voice to her left, and when she looked, she saw DS Kate Meadows standing there.

'I'm on leave,' Paniatowski said.

'And the murder victim was a guest at the Royal Vic,' Meadows said, 'so all leave is cancelled.'

Joe Green liked to think of himself as an intelligent man who took an interest in what was going on around him, though many of the people who knew him preferred to call him a nosey parker, and there were even those who – uncharitably but not entirely without foundation – considered him to be one very short step away from becoming a peeping Tom.

Thus, it was not surprising that when he heard a car pull up on the opposite side of the street, he hauled himself out of his armchair and walked over to the window.

He was pleased to see that it was his neighbour, Monika Paniatowski, and as she transferred her two children from the back of her car to their trolley, he took the opportunity to carry out one of his periodic inspections of her.

She was, he guessed, edging ever closer to forty, but she still went in and out at the right places, and even if she was a few pounds overweight after giving birth to the twins, she carried it well. Her hair was a glorious blonde, and she had a central European nose which was rather large by Lancashire standards, but certainly did not preclude her from playing a regular part in Joe's fantasies.

A second car pulled up – a green Mini Cooper – and another woman got out. She was in her early thirties. She had a slim – practically boyish – figure, and wore her dark hair so short that it almost looked like a piece of rich smooth velvet just resting on the top of her head.

'Who's she?' asked a voice by his side, which was so unexpected that it made him jump.

He turned to face his wife.

'I don't know,' he admitted. 'Probably just another bobby.'

Paniatowski wheeled the trolley up to the front door, where Elena Ortega, her Spanish nanny, was waiting to take charge of the children.

'How would you describe her?' Angela Green asked.

'Who?'

'The woman with Monika.'

'I haven't really thought about it.'

'I'd say she was elfin or pixyish. No, that's not quite right. She's more like a delicate china doll, don't you think?'

'If you say so.'

'Do you fancy her?' Angela asked, and now there was a sharp edge to her tone.

'Me?' Joe asked. 'No, not really.'

But he did! By God, he did!

Once the children were safely inside, the two women walked to Meadows' Mini Cooper, and climbed inside.

As they drove off, Joe Green was back in the world of his fantasy, but this time Monika had brought a friend.

The quickest way to get from Paniatowski's house to the Royal Victoria was to take the Whitebridge bypass, and that was what they had done.

For the first half of the journey, the bypass was a dual carriageway, but they had now reached the point at which – the money for construction work having almost run out – it shrank into a three-lane highway, the middle lane to be used strictly for overtaking. Most drivers treated this middle lane with caution, because the last thing they needed when they'd pulled out was to meet a car coming at them from the other direction. Meadows had no such qualms – her philosophy being that there was no potential collision that couldn't be avoided with a little extra acceleration.

'So why me?' Paniatowski asked, after Meadows had successfully – but only *just* successfully – completed an almost heart-stopping overtake.

'Why you what, boss?' Meadows replied, scanning the on-coming traffic for someone else to play chicken with.

'Why does the chief constable consider it necessary to haul me in off leave, when there are at least three other DCIs who he could have assigned to the case?'

'You want me to say it's because you're the best, don't you?' Meadows asked, grinning.

'No,' Paniatowski replied, feeling slightly uncomfortable because she suspected that there was at least a small part of her that *had* wanted Meadows to say that. 'I was just wondering . . .'

'As a matter of fact, I think that *is* the reason,' Meadows said. 'A murder in the Royal Vic is a big event – especially when the victim was occupying one of the two suites on the top floor.'

'Which one?'

'The Prince Alfred suite.'

'Not *such* an important person, then – the real VIPs are given the Princess Beatrice suite.'

'Maybe the Princess Beatrice was already occupied.'

'Maybe,' Paniatowski agreed, and then, noticing the look of terror on the face of an oncoming driver, she added, 'Why are you driving so fast, Kate?'

'There's been a murder, boss,' Meadows replied. 'We need to get there as quickly as possible.'

'Then why don't you put your siren on, to at least warn other drivers that there's a maniac approaching?'

'Where's the fun in that?' Meadows asked.

'Put the siren on!' Paniatowski said firmly.

'If you're not careful, boss, you'll be slipping into grumpy middle age,' Meadows told her – but she switched the siren on, anyway.

A uniformed constable, posted just outside the hotel, was stopping anyone from entering the building, and standing next to him was a man wearing a smart business suit and a very worried expression.

'That's Mansfield, the general manager,' Meadows said, as she pulled into the curb. 'I think he's a pain in the arse.'

'From what I remember from the last time we had dealings with him, I'd say that's a pretty good assessment of the man,' Paniatowski replied.

The manager saw them climbing out of the Mini, and immediately rushed over to them.

'Thank God you're here, Chief Inspector Paniatowski,' he said. 'Of all the unfortunate things that I *could have* imagined going wrong, this has to be easily the worst.'

'Especially if you happen to be the victim,' Paniatowski said dryly.

'Yes, yes, of course,' Mansfield agreed, although he was still scoring minus one on the empathy scale. 'Shall we go inside?'

Paniatowski shrugged. 'Might as well, now we're here.'

The people who were cordoned off in the lobby offered no surprises. There were businessmen who had gone for a quick lunch, and then readily given way to temptation and made it into a long one. There were families, there to take advantage of the 'early bird' rates on the Royal Vic's cream tea. And there were hotel staff who had worked the first half of their split shift, and wanted to get home for a few hours' rest before they started the second half.

Paniatowski did a quick head count, and estimated there were around thirty of them. She guessed – based on previous experience – that until a minute or two earlier, they had been behaving like most of their fellow countrymen would have done in a similar position, which was to say that they would have been grumbling softly to themselves or exchanging grievances with their immediate neighbours, while all the time stoically accepting this was the way of the world, and they had no choice but to put up with it.

Now that situation had changed, and passivity had turned into active interest, as they watched a large, florid-faced man arguing with one of the constables by the door.

That had to be quickly nipped in the bud, before the others decided to join in, Paniatowski decided.

She walked over to the man and interposed herself between him and the constable.

'Is there a problem here, sir?' she asked.

'Who the devil are you?' the man demanded.

'I'm DCI Paniatowski, and I'm in charge here.'

'You can't be,' the man said, disbelievingly.

'I am.'

'Not just a woman, but a foreigner to boot,' the man said with disgust – and in a loud voice which was playing to his audience, he added, 'I really don't know what this country's coming to.'

'I asked you if you had a problem, sir,' Paniatowski reminded him, keeping her tone level and her voice low.

The man did not follow her example.

'Yes, I have a problem,' he said. 'I have an important meeting to attend right at the other end of Whitebridge, so will you please tell this idiot here –' flicking a fat thumb in the general direction of the uniformed constable – 'that I have to leave right now.'

Paniatowski regretfully shook her head, but only *slightly* regretfully.

'I'm afraid I can't do that, sir. And I would very much appreciate it if you could refrain from being abusive about my officers. In fact, I think I'm going to have to insist on it.'

'Do you have any idea who I am?' the man boomed.

'Yes, you're a potential witness in what may turn out to be a very serious crime.'

'I, Chief Inspector Whatever-your-name-is, am Sir Edgar Stott.'

'I'm duly impressed,' Paniatowski said, 'but it doesn't make you any less of a potential witness.'

'I'm going to leave right now,' Stott said, 'and I advise you not to try and stop me.'

'If you attempt to leave, I'll have you arrested.'

'You wouldn't dare,' Stott said.

'Have you ever been handcuffed?' Paniatowski asked. 'It's really not a very pleasant experience. But, I must admit, it might be useful to me in terms of crowd control, because once I've slapped the cuffs on you, I'm not going to get any trouble from anyone else in this lobby.'

'I'm a personal friend of Keith Pickering, your chief constable,' Stott blustered.

'Good for you,' Paniatowski said. 'Have you ever seen that trick he does with a cigarette packet?'

'What!'

'He takes an empty cigarette packet, makes a few tears in it, twists it round a bit and – hey presto! – you've got a model of a nun.'

'I don't see what that—'

'Or it may be a penguin. I don't think he's too sure himself which it is. Anyway, next time you see him, ask him to show you how it's done.'

'This is outrageous,' Stott said.

'Will you attempt to leave without my express permission?' Paniatowski asked.

'Well . . . no, but you've not heard the last of this,' Stott said, now speaking almost as quietly as she was.

'I expect I haven't,' Paniatowski agreed.

She turned to face the lobby. Most of the spectators hadn't heard what she'd said, but they'd read the body language of both participants, knew a knockout punch when they saw one, and were on the point of turning away.

'I appreciate that you'd all like to leave, ladies and gentlemen,' she said, 'but until we've taken your statements, I'm afraid that won't be possible.' She paused. 'We'll be as quick as we can be, but it will still take a while, and I'm asking you to be patient.'

Several people groaned, loudly and theatrically, as if in the spirit of Sir Edgar Stott, but much more tentative.

'You may think you have nothing to contribute to this investigation, and most of you probably haven't,' Paniatowski continued, 'but a few of you will – possibly unawares – be holding what might turn out to be a vital piece of information, which is why we have to talk to all of you. Justice can only be done when every single one of us strives to *see* that it's done. Thank you for your cooperation.'

There were a few moments of silence, then a number of people started nodding, and a few actually clapped. Even Sir Edgar Stott, the personal friend of the chief constable, looked a little abashed.

'When did you acquire gravitas, boss?' Meadows asked, as they followed the manager to the lifts.

'Dunno,' Paniatowski said. 'I think it must just have sneaked up on me when I wasn't looking.'

'And is it true that the chief constable can turn a cigarette packet into a penguin?'

'Or a nun.'

'Or a nun?'

'I don't know – but it's always a possibility.'

Meadows grinned. 'Nice one, boss!'

'Thank you,' Paniatowski replied.

As they stepped into the lift, Mansfield said, 'Sir Edgar is both the president of the golf club and the master of the Mid Lancs Hunt. You wouldn't really have arrested him, would you?'

'What can you tell me about the dead woman?' Paniatowski asked, ignoring the question.

'She's an American lady,' Mansfield replied. 'She's been a guest here for the last two weeks.'

In which case, she'd already spent a packet on hotel accommodation, Paniatowski thought.

The suites were on the sixth floor, but the lift stopped at the third.

'Has something gone wrong?' Paniatowski asked.

'No,' the manager said, 'but the chief constable would like a quick word with you before you begin your investigation.'

'And he's here?'

'Yes, I've put him in room 316.'

The lift doors slid open.

'Do you know what it's about?' Paniatowski asked.

'I haven't got a clue,' the manager said.

You're a bloody liar! Paniatowski thought, as she stepped out of the lift.

Room 316 was a single room, with a single chair, and the moment Paniatowski entered the room, the chief constable stood up, indicated that she should take the seat, and perched himself on the edge of the bed.

It was a nice gesture, she thought, and, in fact, Keith Pickering was a nice man. But he was also the chief constable, who thought in terms of overall crime figures, while she was a chief inspector who thought – sometimes obsessively – about catching specific murderers. They were from two different worlds, and when those worlds touched – be it ever so briefly – it was wise to tread carefully, while grabbing every advantage from the situation that you possibly could.

'I didn't want to make my presence in the hotel too obvious, but I thought we should have a chat before you began your investigation, Monika,' Pickering said. 'You know what this is about, don't you?'

Rule number one in the chief inspectors' survival handbook: don't let the brass get away with putting *their* words in *your* mouth – make them spell out what they want said themselves.

'No, sir, I really *don't* know what it's about,' Paniatowski said.

Pickering frowned. 'Most of the people who matter in this town use this hotel,' he said. 'They use it because of its high standards of comfort and service, and because it is . . . discreet.'

'You mean, they use it when they fancy having a bit on the side?' Paniatowski asked.

The frown deepened.

'There are a number of reasons why they might not wish their presence here to be public knowledge,' Pickering said evasively.

Paniatowski said nothing.

'It is possible that your investigation will uncover some of these . . . these . . . shall we call them assignations?'

'Yes, let's call them that by all means, sir,' Paniatowski said.

'And if any of these . . . err . . .'

'Assignations?'

'Assignations are relevant to the investigation, I would naturally expect you to follow them through.'

Another pause.

Another chance for Paniatowski to say something.

She decided not to avail herself of it.

'But if these assignations prove to have no relevance to the case, I would not like to see matters go any further.'

'In other words, having dug them up, you'd like me to drop them back in the hole from whence they came,' Paniatowski said.

Pickering studied her for a moment – as if suspecting her of taking the piss – then said, 'You've got it in one, Monika.'

She could see his point, especially since members of the police authority – which held his future in its hands – were likely some of the 'people who mattered' using the Royal Vic for their dalliances.

'Well?' Pickering asked.

'I'm not in the morality police, sir,' Paniatowski told him. 'If it's not illegal, then it's none of my business.'

'That's very understanding of you.'

'And I hope you'd be equally understanding, sir, if one of my team was ever in a similar situation.'

'Are you thinking of anyone in particular?' Pickering asked.

Yes, Paniatowski thought, I am thinking of Kate Meadows who, sooner or later, is bound to be a guest in an S&M club when it's raided by some overzealous superintendent from the uniformed branch.

'No, sir, I'm talking hypothetically,' she said aloud.

'Well then, *hypothetically*, I promise to be very understanding,' Pickering said.

Mansfield and Meadows were waiting for her by the lift. The manager looked relieved to see her finally appear, as if he had found his time alone with the sergeant to be something of a strain – which was quite a common reaction among people Meadows had taken a dislike to.

They rode the lift to the sixth floor, and when the lift doors opened, they stepped out into a corridor in which the carpeting was thicker than that on the third floor and the paintings on the walls much more valuable.

A uniformed constable, on duty outside the suite, saluted when he saw the chief inspector.

Paniatowski turned to the manager. 'Thank you, Mr Mansfield, you can go now,' she said.

'Go?' Mansfield repeated, 'but don't you want me to . . .?'

'No,' Paniatowski said firmly. 'But I would appreciate it if you made yourself available in case we do need you.'

The manager turned reluctantly to the lift.

'He's really shitting himself, isn't he?' Meadows said, as the lift began its descent.

'Wouldn't you – in his situation?' Paniatowski asked.

'No,' Meadows replied.

And that was probably true, Paniatowski thought, because Meadows had a certainty and self-assurance that she herself could only envy.

'Shall we go and look at the body?' she suggested.

'Seems like a good idea to me,' Meadows replied.

*   *   *

The Princess Beatrice suite (where Paniatowski had once spent a gruelling hour of bluff and double-bluff with a hard-faced member of the intelligence service) was based on the decor of Osborne House, Queen Victoria's home on the Isle of Wight.

The Prince Alfred suite, named after her younger son, had taken its inspiration from quite another source – Balmoral Castle, the queen's residence in Scotland – and here there was a definite Highland theme.

Pictures of the Scottish glens hung at intervals on the walls, punctuated by bagpipes, claymores and kilts. A stag's head stared – glassy-eyed – at the fireplace across the room.

The fireplace itself was made up of large blocks of granite, and had been cunningly and painstakingly constructed to suggest that the whole thing had been hastily cobbled together by one of the queen's Scottish ghillies. It was intended to dominate the room, and most of the time it would, no doubt, do just that. On this occasion, however, the centre of attention was unquestionably the dead woman in the wing-backed armchair near the writing desk.

At first glance, Paniatowski thought, the woman could easily have been taken for a drunk who had simply collapsed backwards into the chair, and then been unable – or unwilling – to shift into a more conventional position. But drunks did not stare out at the world through eyes as cold and glassy as those of the dead stag on the wall. Nor did their chests show absolutely no sign of movement. And – usually – drunks did not have large indentations on the foreheads, around the edge of which splinters of the frontal bone were coyly peeping out.

She examined the wound clinically and without emotion. Unless the victim was a child, it was always easy to be unemotional at the beginning, she thought. It was only later – when you'd filled in some of the details of the corpse's personality – that you ceased to regard what you'd been looking at as just a piece of meat, and started to see a real person who had been robbed of his or her precious life.

Paniatowski took a step backward. The dead woman was in her late thirties, she guessed. Her hair was light brown, and set in tightly permed curls, but it was skewed – slightly oddly – to the side.

'She's wearing a wig,' Meadows said.

'Yes,' Paniatowski agreed, 'she is.'

The corpse was dressed in a brown skirt and white blouse.

'Have you got anything to say about her clothing, Kate?' Paniatowski asked Meadows.

'It's reasonable quality, but not too expensive,' Meadows replied. 'It's very respectable.'

Paniatowski gave a half-grin. Of all the people she worked with, only Meadows could make 'respectable' sound almost an insult, she thought.

'They're the sort of clothes an office worker might buy,' Meadows continued. 'My guess is that she picked them up at Marks and Sparks, or one of the local chain stores.'

'You'd think a woman who could afford this suite would spend more on her clothes,' Paniatowski mused. She turned her attention to the corpse's face. 'Does anything strike you about the way she's applied her make-up?'

Meadows thought about it. 'She's not made the best of herself,' she said finally.

'Exactly,' Paniatowski agreed. 'She's got oval eyes and cheekbones most women would kill for, but she hasn't highlighted either of them. In fact, she's gone in just the other direction.'

'It was the absolutely the wrong thing to do – but she didn't do it because she knew no better,' Meadows said. 'She achieved exactly the look she wanted – and that took considerable skill.'

Paniatowski nodded. She'd thought much the same herself, but it was good to have it confirmed by her sergeant, because, in her off-duty hours, Meadows became Zelda, an S&M goddess – and she *really* knew about make-up.

'So why did she do it that way?' Paniatowski asked.

'Because she wanted to disguise herself.'

'Is she on the run, do you think?'

'I'd very much doubt it. People on the run like to keep themselves well below the radar – and you don't do that by booking into the second most expensive suite in the best hotel in Whitebridge.'

'But if she's *not* on the run, why bother with a disguise at all?' Paniatowski asked.

She walked over to the large Victorian desk which dominated one half of the sitting room, and which, unlike the examples of Victoriana on the lower floors, was the genuine article.

Someone – almost definitely either the dead woman or her killer – had placed a large brown handbag in the centre of the desk, and Paniatowski began carefully unpacking it and laying the contents on the desk.

There were the usual things they might have expected to find: compact, mascara, nail file, lipstick, cigarettes, matches and tampons. In addition, there were several pens in a variety of colours and A.C. Brownley's *A Short Guide to the Historic Mills of Whitebridge*.

'No rubbers,' Meadows said.

'Would you expect there to be?'

'I think so. Most women who are promiscuous carry sheaths around with them, because you can't rely on the men to provide them.'

'How do you know she was promiscuous?' Paniatowski asked.

Meadows shrugged. 'I just do. I can feel it. It's a gift I have.'

Paniatowski examined the wallet next. It contained a hundred and ten pounds and some loose change – and that was all.

'What do you keep in *your* wallet, Kate?' Paniatowski asked.

'Driving license, credit cards, photographs—' Meadows began.

'Photographs!' Paniatowski repeated.

She hadn't meant to interrupt like that, but the idea of Meadows carrying something as personal as photographs of other human beings around with her was almost incredible.

'Not me,' Meadows said, hastily backtracking. 'I don't carry photos myself, but I believe that most people do.' She paused. 'Maybe the silly girl kept all her documentation together, in the desk drawer.'

Paniatowski tried the desk drawer, half-expecting it to be locked, but it slid open easily.

A quick examination of the contents was enough to explain why Mary Edwards hadn't bothered to lock it. The drawer contained paper clips, rubber bands, a number of pens (each one with a different coloured ink), and a notebook.

What is this thing she had with multicolours? Paniatowski wondered, as she flicked through the notebook, only to discover that it had never been used.

'See if you can find the wall safe, Kate,' she said.

Meadows – who would have made an excellent criminal – quickly located the safe. It was behind a large painting of Whitebridge Moor in the pale moonlight, the work of a local artist who was becoming quite fashionable in London and New York, but who the sergeant – who had once had a modest art collection of her own – considered to be grossly overrated.

The safe, like the desk drawer, was not locked, and contained nothing at all – not even a coloured pen.

'Maybe she put everything in the main hotel safe,' Meadows suggested.

Maybe she had, Paniatowski agreed silently, though her gut was telling her that the killer – for reasons of his own that she couldn't even begin to guess at yet – had removed all the victim's documentation. Her gut further added – almost by way of a footnote – that this was going to be one of those cases that twisted and turned right in on itself, and that until the case was solved – if it *was* ever solved – most of the information that they managed to collect during the course of the investigation would make no sense at all.

'Go and ask your mate the manager what – if anything – she's handed in to him for safekeeping,' she told her sergeant.

'Will do,' Meadows said – and as she stepped into the corridor, she saw Dr Shastri getting out of the lift.

Dr Shastri was dressed in one of the colourful saris which she wore throughout the year – whatever the outside temperature – and the only evidence that she was a doctor at all was the stethoscope around her neck and the rubber gloves she was holding in her hands.

'Ah, another day, another victim,' she said chirpily to Paniatowski, 'and once more, my dear Monika, you will be expecting me to take one brief glace at the victim and then immediately tell you the murderer's height and weight, his colouring – and what he had for breakfast.'

Paniatowski grinned. 'His name and address would be even better, doc,' she said.

'And how are your two darling boys?' Shastri asked.

Paniatowski marvelled at the light tone to the doctor's words. It was almost as if she knew nothing at all about the violent, brutal way in which the twins had been conceived, though the fact was that – as far as Paniatowski was aware – Shastri was the only one who *did* know the truth.

'The boys are fine,' Paniatowski said, certain that, although she did not appear to be, Shastri was listening very carefully to the nuances in her words and reading her facial expression as she said them.

'Good,' Shastri said, so briskly that Paniatowski had no idea what her assessment might have been. The doctor glanced across at the armchair. 'Is this the victim?'

Paniatowski grinned again, partly with relief at getting off the subject of the twins and back to business.

'Is that the victim?' she repeated. 'You're supposed to be the medic – *you* tell *me*.'

Shastri walked over to the chair. 'Well, the cause of death looks simple enough,' she said.

'Was she standing when she was attacked?'

'From the position in which she now rests, I would say that she almost definitely was.'

So the victim had been looking at her killer, and must have seen the weapon in his hand – but she hadn't been frightened, otherwise she would have tried to escape. And what that suggested was that she knew her murderer, and had been confident that he would never carry out the threat which the weapon he was holding had implied.

Well, she'd certainly been wrong about that!

Shastri slipped on her gloves, placed one hand each side of the victim's face, and moved the head slightly to the left and then slightly to the right.

'Rigor mortis has not even begun to set in yet,' she said, 'which means, given the ambient temperature, that she was killed not more than three hours ago – and possibly much less than that.'

In other words, Paniatowski thought, she had been killed

towards the end of lunchtime, which was probably the point in the day when there were most non-residents in the hotel.

'Was the victim killed by a single blow?' she asked.

Shastri laughed. 'And so it begins,' she said. 'Even before I get to work with my dinky little scalpel, you are demanding information.' She sighed, and gave in to the inevitable. 'It is *likely* it was a single blow. It is also likely – given the force of the blow – that the killer was a man, although, as I always caution, an outraged woman can draw on formidable reserves of strength.'

'Any idea what the murder weapon might have been?'

'The proverbial blunt instrument. I would guess that it was metal and rather heavy.'

'Like an iron bar?'

'Exactly like an iron bar,' Shastri said. 'Would you like to take another look at the body before I remove the wig?'

'No,' Paniatowski replied. 'You go right ahead.'

Shastri put one hand behind the dead woman's head, tilted it forward slightly, and took off the wig with her free hand. She made it look so easy, Paniatowski thought, though, from her own experiences of handling dead weight, she knew just how difficult it could be to manipulate a corpse.

Shastri removed the wig to reveal the dead woman's real hair. It was golden and very fine. It seemed almost to shine.

'Is it dyed?' Paniatowski asked.

Shastri placed a gloved hand on the dead woman's head, and parted the hair so she could examine the roots.

'No, it appears to be totally natural,' she said.

So the victim had used make-up to make herself look less attractive than she was, and had covered up her wonderful blonde hair with a nondescript wig, Paniatowski thought.

Now why should she have done that?

Shastri lifted the victim's hand.

'There is a tattoo on her wrist,' she said. 'Come and look.'

The tattoo was of a butterfly. Its wings were mostly brown, but there were red markings near the edges of the wing, and the edges themselves were white.

'It's a nice piece of work,' Paniatowski said.

'Very nice,' Shastri agreed. 'Did you know that there is a

new – but growing – field of psychological study which examines the reasons that people acquire tattoos and the significance of the particular tattoos they choose?'

'No, I didn't.'

'I am sure it is all very fascinating, but unfortunately, since people will keep on dying, and you, for your part, will keep insisting that I cut them up, I have not yet had time to look into the subject.'

'Could you get your technicians to take a couple of photographs of that tattoo?' Paniatowski asked.

'Most certainly. When would you like them?'

'As soon as possible.'

Shastri sighed. 'I don't know why I even bothered to ask,' she said. 'It is always "as soon as possible" with you.'

TWO

The office was located just behind the Royal Vic's reception area, and was both spartan and utilitarian.

This wasn't really Mansfield's office – the place where he spent most of his working day – Meadows guessed. That office, tastefully decorated and lavishly furnished, would be somewhere else in the building, but he didn't want his little oasis polluted by the police, so they were doing the interview here.

Time to start.

'So what can you tell me about the stiff in the Prince Alfred suite, Mr Mansfield?' she asked.

The manager shifted uncomfortably in his leather chair. He saw himself as a man with a definite – and defined – place in Whitebridge society. Within the confines of the hotel, he was a virtual monarch, issuing proclamations at will, and watching – with not some little satisfaction – as his minions scurried around enacting them. Outside the hotel, he bowed his head to no man (except, of course, his regional manager), and rubbed shoulders with the crème de la crème of the town.

And as far as his relationship with the police went, he regarded officers of the rank of superintendent and above as his equals, but expected those below that rank – like Detective Sergeant Meadows – to treat him with the deference due to his position. So why was it that when their paths crossed – and this had happened twice before – he always felt he was being bullied, and came away from the encounters with a sense of defeat and exhaustion?

'Well?' Meadows said, commandingly.

'As I told you earlier, Miss Edwards has been our guest for the last two weeks,' the manager said. 'She is – she *was* – an American lady.'

'How did she book the room?' Meadows asked. 'Was it through a travel agency?'

'No, she booked the *suite* personally, by telephone,' Mansfield said, before adding, in almost a hushed tone, 'from New York.'

'From *New York*! Gosh, how exciting!' Meadows said. 'Who did she talk to, when she called from (gasp) *New York*?'

'Initially, she spoke to the booking clerk, but then she asked to be transferred to the general manager's office.'

'And you didn't mind being disturbed by someone who was, after all, but a mere client?' Meadows asked.

'Of course not. Being of service to our clients is the raison d'être of everyone who works at the Royal Victoria.'

'Jolly good,' Meadows said, encouragingly. 'Do you have a home address for Miss Edwards?'

The manager consulted his ledger. 'Lurting Avenue, Bronx, New York,' he said, and once again, he infused magic and significance into the last two words.

'Hmm,' Meadows mused, 'it's not exactly Tribeca, is it?'

'I beg your pardon?'

'Doesn't matter,' Meadows said. 'What did Miss Edwards entrust to you for safekeeping?'

The manager turned a page in the ledger and scanned the columns.

'Nothing,' he said.

'You're sure of that?'

'Absolutely. If a guest wishes to deposit anything in the main safe, we assign that guest his or her own safety deposit box – and we always keep a record of it. There is no record of Miss Edwards being given one.'

'But at the very least, you'll have her passport.'

More scanning.

'No, we haven't.'

'I thought you always held the passports of foreign guests.'

'No, we sometimes do, as insurance that they won't leave without paying their bills – not that there's much chance of that with the quality of guests we attract, ha ha!'

'Ha ha!' Meadows echoed.

'But if a foreign guest is prepared to give us some other form of surety, we're perfectly happy to return the passport once we've checked it.'

'Some other form of surety,' Meadows repeated. 'Like what? Their firstborn child as a hostage, for example?'

The manager, who was never quite sure whether Meadows was sharing a joke with him or simply using humour to beat him over the head, laughed uncomfortably.

'Scarcely that,' he said. 'We usually just get them to sign a blank credit-card slip.'

'And that's what happened here?'

'Probably. But I don't have the details myself—'

'Of course you don't – you're far too important to bother about details.'

'So you'll have to ask the clerk who booked her in.'

'What a good idea,' Meadows said.

The corpse had been taken away to the police mortuary, and the Scene of Crime Officers – with their sterilised pouches, dusting powder and infinite patience – had not yet arrived.

Paniatowski picked up the phone, and when the operator answered, she said that she wanted to make a transatlantic call.

In the movies, switchboard operators were both super-efficient and positively bursting with eagerness to help the police. The girl on the Royal Victoria switchboard, it soon became apparent to Paniatowski, was not of that ilk.

'Who should I charge for the call?' she asked.

'You do know that I'm a police officer, and that I'm investigating a brutal murder in this very hotel, don't you?' Paniatowski countered.

'Only, we're supposed to bill all the calls, especially if they're long distance,' the operator continued, as if Paniatowski had never spoken. 'And the one you want to make is *very* long distance, if you know what I mean . . .'

'I do know what you mean.'

'Because you want to call *America*.'

The way she pronounced the last word suggested she couldn't imagine why anyone in their right mind would ever seriously want to place a call to the other side of the Atlantic.

Paniatowski sighed, and gave in. 'Send the bill to police headquarters,' she said.

'Right-y-ho,' replied the switchboard operator, as if, now that little difficulty had been cleared up, they could go back to being on best mate terms again. 'So who would you like me to connect you to?'

'I'd like to speak to Captain Fred Mahoney, 14th Precinct, the Bronx,' Paniatowski said.

'Precinct? What's that?'

'It's a police station.'

'Well, why didn't you say so?'

It would be nice to talk to Fred again – if this idiot girl ever managed to make the connection – Paniatowski thought.

She had met him at an international policing conference in Denmark. He was a big, beefy, no-nonsense cop. She'd liked him immediately, and if she positively *had to* hand over part of her investigation to someone in the States – and she obviously did – then she was glad it was Fred.

Miracle of miracles – Mahoney came on the line.

'Hi, Monika, how the hell are ya?' he asked.

'I'm fine. And you?'

'Great! Top of my game. So how long is it since we made beautiful music together in Copenhagen?'

Paniatowski grinned. 'It's three years since we were *in* Copenhagen, Fred,' she said, 'but we never made beautiful music because I'm practically a nun, and you're a ridiculously happily married man who would never even think of looking at another woman.'

'Shit, that's right, especially the second half,' Mahoney said, with a groan. 'So what can I do for ya?'

Paniatowski told him about the dead woman.

'As soon as the mortuary's done its best to make her look presentable, I'll be faxing you her photograph,' she said. 'When you get it, I'd like you to send someone round to her house and get her family to make an identification. I'd also like to know what she was doing in Whitebridge, and I'd be grateful for any other information they're able to collect.'

'You got it,' Mahoney told her. 'You want me to call you when my boys have visited Lurting Avenue?'

'Yes, please.'

'OK then, you'd better give me a number I can reach you at.'

Paniatowski recited the number, and Mahoney wrote it down.

'So where is that?' he asked, when he'd read it back to her. 'Whitebridge Police Plaza?'

Whitebridge Police Plaza! Fred Mahoney really did live in a different world, she thought.

'No, it's not a police plaza,' she said. 'It's the public bar of the Drum and Monkey.'

Mahoney nearly choked with laughter.

'You Brits,' he said. 'You're so . . . so quaint.' He paused for a second. 'You know, sometimes, when I've been dreaming, I wake up convinced we *did* sleep together, Monika.'

'And . . .?'

'Are you absolutely certain that we didn't?'

Paniatowski laughed. 'Positive – though I have to admit, it took a lot of self-discipline to stop me throwing myself on a hunk like you.'

'Well, that's something, I suppose,' Mahoney said.

And then he hung up.

Paniatowski looked around the suite in which Mary Edwards had been killed, and felt a sudden, unexpected shudder run through her body. Her gut was playing her up again – warning her this wasn't going to be a simple case with a simple motive, and that if she didn't tune into the rhythm of the investigation pretty damn quickly, the murderer would slip though her fingers.

'But at the moment, there simply isn't anything to tune into,' she said aloud.

'Talking to yourself, boss?' said a voice from the doorway. 'That *is* one of the first signs, you know.'

Paniatowski grinned. 'It's a risky business – accusing your boss of being doolally,' she said, 'because there's always a chance that before she goes completely off her chump, she might have you transferred to traffic.'

'There's no danger of that,' DI Beresford replied. 'You'd be lost without me – and we both know it.'

It was true, Paniatowski thought. Colin Beresford would never be a brilliant detective – he simply did not have Meadows' flair – but he was hard-working, dependable and loyal, the latter having much to recommend it in the snake pit that was the Mid Lancs police. Besides, they'd worked together since he was a constable and she was a sergeant, and, though neither of them would have put it in quite those terms, Beresford was her best friend, and she loved him like a brother.

Beresford looked around the room.

'This is the perfect setting for one of them old-style whodunits,' he pronounced. 'Lord Muckety-Muck is found dead, and you know from the start that the murderer just has to be either the spendthrift nephew or the betrayed wife. And then it turns out that, despite all the clues pointing to them, they're both completely innocent, and the real murderer is, appropriately enough, someone from the lower orders who talks a very common sort of English.'

If only it could be like that in real life, Paniatowski thought. Look for the one person who couldn't possibly have done it, and he's your killer.

Simple!

'Brief me on what's happening in the world outside the Royal Vic bubble,' she said.

'Word's come down from the top brass – and beyond – that this is a priority case, that we should use all available manpower, and that there'll be no quibbling when we put in the overtime sheets.'

'And what manpower have we got at the moment?'

'There are five detective constables waiting downstairs for instructions, and I'm expecting another half a dozen within the hour.'

'Good,' Paniatowski said. 'We'll need an incident room. I think we'll use the hotel ballroom-stroke-conference room.'

'The manager won't like that,' Beresford said.

'Then get Sergeant Meadows to deliver the bad news. He's frightened of her.'

'And which of us hasn't been – at one time or another?' Beresford said, with a slight shudder.

'Once you're up and running, I want statements taken from everybody who was in the hotel between one o'clock and four o'clock. After that, I want anybody who was in the immediate area questioned. And finally, I want door-to-doors conducted, starting in the immediate vicinity and working outwards.'

'What will we be looking for?' Beresford asked. 'Are we trying to track Mary Edwards' movements and associations?'

'Exactly,' Paniatowski agreed. 'She's been here for two weeks. I want to know what she's done and who she's seen, and then maybe we'll be able to work out *why* she was here.'

'Shall I get Jack Crane to set up a press conference for you?' Beresford asked.

Paniatowski shook her head. 'Not yet. We've nothing to say. But as soon as her face has been made presentable, see that a photo of Mary Edwards is in all the local papers and on television. I'll draft the usual vague appeal for information.'

'Got it,' Beresford said, turning to go.

'Wait a minute,' Paniatowski said. 'I'd like to have a poke around before the SOCOs get here, and if I'm doing that, I want a witness.'

The desk clerk's name was Jimmy Bentley. He was a good-looking lad of twenty-three, who, if he'd been prepared to make the effort, could probably have bedded a fair number of girls of his own age after only a relatively short courtship. He had, however, chosen to go another way, targeting older women on the grounds that they made far fewer demands on him, were so much more grateful, and – because they'd been half-expecting it all along – did not kick up too much of a fuss when he dumped them.

Generally speaking, he was not really bothered if they were plain (or even ugly), because, as the old saying went, you didn't look at the mantelpiece when you were poking the fire. But that was not to say he didn't have standards, he reassured himself. For instance, he insisted that the women he slept with had good bodies, unless, of course, there were no women with good bodies around, in which case he would make do with what was available.

The older woman sitting opposite him now – Detective Sergeant Meadows – had a good body, though she was slimmer than most of the women he seduced. She was also prettier – in an innocent, fairy story sort of way – than his usual quarry, but he saw no reason why that should be any barrier to her experiencing the Jimmy Bentley phenomenon, and he had promised himself that he would hunt her down and have her in his bed before the week was done.

He didn't realise he was daydreaming until Meadows tapped him lightly on the skull with her knuckles, and asked, 'Anyone at home?'

'Sorry,' he said.

'I was wondering if you remember checking in Miss Edwards at reception,' Meadows said sweetly.

He was in here, he told himself. That gesture with the knuckles had been so intimate that he was sure she really fancied him. But best not make it easy. He could encourage her, certainly, but it should also be made plain that she was going to have to work at it.

He gave her a smile which he felt conveyed *just* that message.

'Yes, I do remember,' he said, 'I remember it *very well.*'

'Really?' Meadows asked, looking vaguely troubled. 'Now that does surprise me.'

'Why?'

'Well, I would have thought that you register so many guests over the course of a week that they all blur together.'

'Most of them do,' Bentley admitted. 'But a few of them have special qualities that make them stand out.'

'Like what?'

He is used to dealing with women who half-heartedly – or incompetently – model themselves on Hollywood stars, but this woman is the genuine article. She sweeps into the foyer dressed like an exotic bird of paradise, with a caravan of porters carrying the luggage in her wake, strolls boldly up to the desk and says, 'Hi, I'm Mel . . . Mary Edwards.'

A lesser man would have been struck speechless, but Jimmy merely gives her one of his special smiles and says, 'Welcome, Mrs Edwards.'

'That's Miss Edwards,' she replies, with her American direct-ness. 'Is my suite ready?'

'Yes, Miss Edwards, it most certainly is.'

'Did the manager – Mr Mansfield, that's his name, isn't it?'

'That's right, Miss Edwards.'

'Did Mr Mansfield fix it?'

He doesn't know what she means – and says so.

'Mr Mansfield said that the best suite in the hotel was already booked, but he'd see if he could arrange it so that it became available,' the woman explains. 'He sort of made it sound as if it was a done deal.'

Jimmy glances down at the register, and sees that the Princess Beatrice suite is very firmly occupied by Sir Grenville Todd, a local property magnate.

He sighs. Bloody typical of Mansfield, he thinks – dodging the bullet himself and leaving his underlings to take the impact.

'I'm . . . err . . . afraid that the Princess Beatrice suite is still occupied, but the Prince Alfred is almost as good,' he says.

The woman seems to inflate – a bird of paradise no more, she has become an aggressive peacock, intent on getting its way.

'Almost as good?' she said imperiously. 'Almost as good! Do you have any idea who I . . .'

She stops suddenly, as if she's realised she was about to say something she'd regret later, and slowly she deflates, until she is an outraged peacock no more, but instead his mild-mannered mate.

'I'm sure the Prince Alfred suite will be just great,' she says lamely.

'So the reason you remember her is partly because of the way that she was dressed, and partly because she looked like she was about to throw a wobbly with you?' Meadows asked.

'Yes,' Jimmy admitted, 'but even without those two things I would have remembered her, because she was beautiful.'

'Really?' Meadows said. 'Of course, I've only seen her dead, but even so, I don't think most men would have said that about her.'

'But I'm *not* most men,' Jimmy said. 'When I look at a woman, I can see the beauty that shines through from the soul.'

It suddenly occurred to him that he didn't need to use his standard line of patter with Meadows, because she genuinely was good looking.

'Of course,' he continued, 'some lucky women have it all ways. Like you, for example – you have a beautiful soul, but you also have a beautiful face.'

He could see that the compliment had flustered her, and that she was trying her hardest not to blush. This was going to be easy, and it might be wise to check that he had an ample supply of rubber johnnies in his wallet.

'So, Jimmy, could you tell me what happened when she checked in,' Meadows suggested.

Bentley shrugged. 'Nothing particularly happened. I registered her, and that was about it.'

'But you didn't take her passport off her, did you? I know that for a fact, because it's not in the hotel safe.'

Jimmy Bentley began to get a vague, slightly uncomfortable, feeling that something was going wrong.

'No, I didn't take it,' he said. 'There was no need to.'

'Why was that – because she signed a blank credit-card slip?'

'No, because she paid in cash – a month in advance.'

'Isn't that unusual?'

'It is, rather, but she explained that was the way she preferred to do business, and since that came within the hotel's guidelines . . .'

'But you had a look at her passport, didn't you? That's a legal requirement when you're dealing with aliens – and I would imagine that it's company policy as well.'

'Err . . . yes, well naturally, I did take a good look at the passport,' Jimmy said, unconvincingly.

'You're lying to me, Jimmy,' Meadows said – and her tone was suddenly exactly like his bloody mother's had been, that time she'd caught him in his bedroom, looking at pictures of semi-naked women and experimenting with his semi-erect penis.

'I . . . err . . .' the clerk said.

'I . . . err . . .?' Meadows repeated. 'Would you like to be a little more explicit, Jimmy?'

'I just need to see your passport, Miss Edwards,' Jimmy says. 'It's one of the hotel's rules.'

The woman – Mary Edwards – smiles at him.

'Of course,' she says.

She opens her handbag – it is a rather large one – and rummages round inside for nearly a minute.

She is still smiling when she looks up again.

'It isn't here,' she says, 'and now I come to think about it, I remember putting it into one of the suitcases after I'd cleared immigration. I thought it would be much safer there, you see.'

'Then perhaps you can open the suitcase in question, and take it out,' Jimmy suggests.

Miss Edwards frowns. 'The problem is, I can't remember which suitcase it was, and,' she chuckles, 'there are rather a lot of them to check on, as you can see for yourself. Couldn't it wait until I've unpacked? Then maybe you could come up to my suite, and I could show it to you there.'

He can already feel her heels – crossed behind his backside – digging into his spine.

'Yes, I suppose it could wait,' he says.

'She didn't ask you up to her suite, did she?' Meadows asked. 'Not that first day – not ever?'

'No, she didn't,' Jimmy Bentley agreed, staring down at the desk in what might have been shame, and what might have been embarrassment – and was possibly both.

'And you didn't like to remind her of it, because she might have taken any reminder as an indication that that you were gasping for her body, instead of it being the other way round – and you're far too proud to have any woman think that.'

'I really don't know what you're talking about,' the booking clerk said, reddening.

Meadows laughed – loudly and uninhibitedly.

'She played you, Jimmy-boy,' she said. 'She wrapped you around her little finger, and you didn't even know it was happening.' She paused for a second. 'And by the way, the answer is no.'

'I don't even know what the question is.'

Meadows laughed again – and this time there was a Shakespearean bawdiness to it.

'Of course you do – and just to make the situation as clear

as can be, I want you to know that you've as much chance of getting me into bed as a one-legged man has of winning an arse-kicking competition.'

The bedroom in the Prince Alfred suite was twice the size of Paniatowski's own bedroom, but then she was only a detective chief inspector, and the woman who had rented this suite had been a . . .

Had been a *what*?

Paniatowski had absolutely no idea.

She slid back the sliding door on the long wardrobe to reveal Miss Edward's collection of dresses and coats.

'Jesus!' Beresford said. 'How long do you think she was planning to stay here? A year?'

There certainly were a lot of clothes, Paniatowski agreed, but what interested her more was how they had been organised. She wondered if Beresford would spot it too.

'I'm no expert on women's clothes, boss,' he said, showing that he had noticed, 'but it seems to me as if the clothes on the left-hand side are different to the ones on the right.'

'In what way are they different?' Paniatowski asked.

'Well, the ones on the left-hand side are the sort of clothes women wear if they've got dolled up for a Saturday night out in the best room in the Drum and Monkey. Don't get me wrong, they're smart enough in their way, but unless the woman wearing them was an absolute stunner, I'd probably not even notice them – if you know what I mean.'

'I know what you mean,' Paniatowski agreed, remembering that Meadows had said that the clothes the dead woman had been wearing – and which had undoubtedly come from this side of the wardrobe – were 'respectable'.

'The ones on the right-hand side would grab my attention right away, even if the woman wearing them wasn't much to look at,' Beresford continued. 'I don't know whether that's because they're expensive, or because of the way they're cut, but they look different somehow.'

Paniatowski inspected the labels on two of the dresses on the right-hand side. One said Saks Fifth Avenue, the other said Bergdorf Goodman.

Now why would a victim have two different – and completely contrasting wardrobes, she wondered.

She was beginning to suspect they were the tools of her trade.

THREE

The Drum and Monkey was the pub that progress had passed by with barely a glance. Other pubs in Whitebridge had had all their walls knocked down and become one large room, but the Drum still maintained different rooms for different sorts of clients: the vault, where only men went, and foul language was not only permissible but almost *de rigueur*; the public bar, where darts were thrown and dominoes played; and the best room, where married couples who no longer had much to say to each other went to celebrate their nights out together in uneasy silence, and courting couples – who knew that *they* would never be like that – went to plan their future. Other pubs had garish carpets laid throughout; the Drum had bare boards in the vault, linoleum tiles in the public bar, and a plain dark brown carpet in the best room. It was a slightly scruffy place, but it was comfortably scruffy – and it served the best pint in Whitebridge.

It had been the combination of scruffiness and alcoholic excellence which had caused Charlie Woodend, when he first returned to Whitebridge as a chief inspector, to select the Drum as his base. Woodend believed that a good detective needed to be able to make the occasional imaginative leap in his thinking, that these leaps were best fuelled by several pints of Thwaites bitter, and the ideal location for such a process to take place was the corner table of the public bar in the Drum. That was the table at which he and his team sat from his very first case to the day he retired – and his successor, Monika Paniatowski, had maintained the tradition, because it had worked for Charlie and it seemed to be working for her.

There were four of them – the core team – at the table that night, though not all of them were following Woodend's maxim that bitter was the brain's natural lubricant. Paniatowski was a vodka drinker – Polish vodka through choice, though the Iron Curtain restrictions meant that was not always possible. Meadows, who, but for her bizarre night-time activity, was almost a puritan, neither drank nor smoked, and seemed to derive a deep pleasure from sipping bitter lemon which left the rest of the team baffled. The two men, however, followed faithfully in Woodend's footsteps, though the younger of them – DC Jack Crane – had only met the legendary Charlie once.

'First things first,' Paniatowski said, when the waiter had deposited the drinks and gone away again. 'Have all the guests and employees of the Royal Vic been interviewed?'

Beresford glanced at his watch. 'Probably not, but by the time my lads knock off for the night, they will have questioned everybody we *know* was there around the time Mary Edwards was killed. The problem is there was at least a three-hour gap between the murder and the discovery of the body, so there are bound to be dozens of people who passed through the hotel that we *don't* know about.'

'Some of them – hopefully, all of them – will come forward when they find out we want to talk to them,' Paniatowski said.

But the television and newspaper appeals would also bring any number of sad and delusional people crawling out of the woodwork and making false claims. Many of these claims would sound so plausible – the lonely and the deranged knew that to get what they wanted, they needed to be cunning – and dozens of man-hours would be wasted in exposing their statements for what they were. Still, it had to be done – there really was no other way.

'Any promising leads?' she asked.

But there was not much hope in her voice, because the members of her team were not like the ones on half the other teams operating out of Whitebridge Central – *they* didn't hold back information until they could see a way to use it to their own maximum benefit.

No, if Colin had had something juicy, he would have told the rest of them about it the moment they sat down.

Confirming her suspicions, Beresford shook his head. 'If she'd been staying on a lower floor, where there are lots of rooms, then she – or her killer – might have been noticed by other guests leaving or entering *their* rooms, but, as you know, there are only two suites on the penthouse level, and the occupant of the other one was away for the day.'

'She made it so easy for him, didn't she?' Paniatowski said, and, without waiting for an answer, she continued, 'The murder weapon has still to turn up, but there's a notable gap on the fireside companion in the Prince Alfred suite, so I think we know what we're looking for.'

'What's a fireside companion?' Crane asked.

'What's a fireside companion!' Beresford repeated, incredulously. 'Didn't you have to light the fire when you got home from school, so the house would be nice and warm by the time your mum and dad arrived from work?'

'No,' Crane said. 'I didn't.'

'Well, you certainly have led a charmed life,' Beresford said.

In addition to thinking that Crane was a good bobby, Colin also liked him as a man, Paniatowski thought. But he did sometimes feel threatened by him, too, because Crane was an acknowledged high-flyer with an M.A. from Oxford University, and there were occasions when Beresford could not resist taking a pop at him.

'So who *did* light the fire, young Jack?' Beresford continued. 'It surely wasn't your poor grey-haired old granny, was it?'

'No, it wasn't,' Crane said. 'We didn't have fires in our house.'

'So what did you do when it got cold?'

'The same as I do now – turn the central heating on.'

'Oh,' Beresford said, sounding deflated.

If Colin had a weakness, Paniatowski thought, it was that he sometimes found it difficult to project himself into other people's lives, and – the other side of the same coin, this – he didn't *quite* believe that his own experiences weren't universal. Jack Crane was young, highly educated and clearly middle class. It should have come as no surprise to Beresford that the path Crane had followed was different to the one trodden by a working-class, secondary modern boy like himself, who, in addition to everything else, was almost a generation older.

Do I do that? she wondered. Do I say things which make me seem old and naïve about the wider world?

'*You can't blame the boss if she doesn't always get the point,*' she heard an imaginary Crane say to an imaginary Meadows in her head. '*I mean, she's not exactly old, but she was born before the war.*'

Dear God – *that* was a chilling thought!

'A fireside companion is a stand from which hang a hearth brush, a small shovel, a pair of tongs and a poker,' she explained to Crane. 'It's the poker that's missing.'

'I'm just trying to picture the scene,' Beresford said. 'Given that Mary Edwards was knocked into her chair, they must both have been standing in the centre of the room, talking to each other. Right?'

'Right,' Paniatowski agreed.

'And then she says something which drives him into a sudden rage. He looks around for something to kill her with—'

'To threaten her with,' Meadows interrupted. 'I think at that point he only wanted to threaten her.'

'What makes you say that?'

'You don't think logically when you're in a rage – and you don't take your time. You just lash out. Now, if the fireside companion had been right beside him, he might have used it. But it wasn't. So if he felt the sudden urge to kill her, he'd have strangled her. What he wouldn't have done was walk over to the fireplace, bend down, pick up the poker, and walk back to where she was standing.'

'What do you think about that, Colin?' Paniatowski asked.

'Makes sense,' Beresford said.

'If, on the other hand, you're only going to threaten to kill someone, you need a prop to be really effective,' Meadows continued. 'So he goes and gets the poker and waves it in front of her. Which means that at this point he might be angry, but he's still in control of himself.'

'But that doesn't scare her, because if it did, she'd make some effort to escape,' Paniatowski said. 'So *why* doesn't it scare her?'

'She thinks she knows him well enough to be sure he's not going to go through with it,' Crane said, 'either because he's too nice to kill, or because he hasn't got the balls.'

'The argument continues, he sees red, and the next thing

he knows, she's sprawled in the chair with her head caved in,' Beresford said.

The barman leaned over the bar counter. 'There's somebody on the phone wants to speak to you, chief inspector,' he called across the room. 'Will you take it on the corridor phone, as usual?'

'Yes, that'll be fine,' Paniatowski called back.

She rose to her feet and made her way to the corridor, in which – midway between the stacks of beer crates and the ladies' toilets – the public telephone was located.

The first thing Fred Mahoney said when she picked up the phone was: 'What kind of establishment was this Mary Edwards of yours staying in? Was it what you Brits call a boarding house?'

'No,' Paniatowski replied, with a sudden feeling of fore-boding. 'It was the best hotel in Whitebridge.'

'So it's expensive?'

'Very, especially if you took a suite, like she did.'

'Gee, I wish you'd told me that before I sent my boys over to the address you gave me,' Mahoney said.

'She doesn't live there, does she?' Paniatowski asked – but it was not really a question.

'They're good, hard-working people on Lurting Avenue – but they're not the kind of folks who stay in first-class hotels,' Mahoney told her. 'There was no Mary Edwards at the address you gave me – it's the home of a couple from St Louis, who have lived there for ten years – and the name wasn't familiar to any of the neighbours, either.'

'I see,' Paniatowski said.

'I might as well give you the rest of the bad news,' Mahoney continued. 'I sent a couple of guys over to the DMV to check out the driving licences. There are dozens of Mary Edwards in the tri-state area, but none of them looks anything like your stiff.' He paused. 'If you want me to, I can go public with it – get the picture in the papers and on the news.'

'That would be good,' Paniatowski said, 'but it's not that photograph of her I'd like you to use.'

'You got another one?'

'Not yet.'

'Now you've got me confused.'

'It will all make sense when you see the photograph,' Paniatowski promised. 'I really do appreciate your help, Fred.'

'It's my pleasure,' Mahoney assured her. 'Tell me, are you really in one of your olde English pubs right now?'

'Well, it's a pub, certainly,' Paniatowski replied.

'And does it have a thatched roof, and horse brasses on the wall? Are there yokels in smocks, sipping cider and sucking on straws?'

Paniatowski smiled weakly. 'Yes, there's all that. And in the car park, I can see a knight in armour slaying a dragon.'

'Excellent!' Mahoney said.

Some of Dr Shastri's staff claimed (only half-joking) that she only ever left the mortuary when there was a full moon, and while that was patently untrue, she was certainly the first person to arrive in the morning and the last to leave at night, so Paniatowski was not the least surprised when it was the doctor herself who answered the phone.

'You again!' Shastri said. 'Can't you leave a girl and her corpses alone together for even a few hours?'

'Sorry about that,' Paniatowski said, grinning.

'I have completed my report on Mary Edwards,' Shastri said, 'and apart from one or two nagging – though probably minor – questions, it is very straightforward, so if you care to drop by the mortuary tomorrow morning—'

'Who would you say is the best cosmetic technician in Whitebridge?' Paniatowski interrupted.

'Bunny Thomas,' Shastri replied, without any hesitation. 'The man is a positive genius, and if I ever needed make-up applying to my own face – which, of course, I don't . . .'

'Of course not,' Paniatowski agreed. 'Why would anyone mess with something which is already perfect?'

'Just so. But if I did need that kind of artificial aid, I would keep Bunny in constant attendance.'

'I want Bunny to give Mary Edwards a make-over, as soon as possible – by which I mean tonight,' Paniatowski said. 'Money's no object. I want him to lose the wig and make her look as attractive as he possibly can.'

'That is a rather bizarre request, if you don't mind me saying so,' Shastri told her.

'Murder tends to be a rather bizarre business,' Paniatowski replied.

The rest of the team did not need to ask Paniatowski how her conversation with Mahoney had gone – they could read it in her face.

'I had my doubts when I saw the address,' Meadows said, 'but then I figured that maybe things had changed since the last time I visited the Big Apple.

'If she lied about her name, she could have lied about other things, too,' said Beresford. 'She might not be from New York at all. She might not even be an American.'

'She's a New Yorker,' Meadows said confidently.

'How can you be so sure?'

'I've seen the good side of her wardrobe.'

'OK, so she bought her clothes in New York,' Beresford conceded, 'but lots of people from all over America – from all over the world – go to New York to buy clothes.'

'But they don't buy them with a New Yorker's eye,' Meadows said. 'Anyone from anywhere could have bought any one of those outfits, but only a native would have bought all of them, and combined them in that particular way.' She took a sip of her bitter lemon. 'You're going to have to trust me on this.'

'I do,' Paniatowski said.

'Me, too,' Crane agreed.

'Aw, what the hell do I know about women's clothes anyway?' Beresford said.

Paniatowski told the team about her conversation with Shastri.

'There are two Marys,' she said, 'the naturally blonde Mary, who we'll call Model Mary, and the one who wears a wig and will be known as Mousy Mary. Since she was Mousy Mary in Whitebridge, that's the picture we'll be giving to the local newspapers and television stations. The Americans, on the other hand, get the Model Mary pictures, because that's probably how she would have looked when she was over there.'

'The question is, why was she wearing a disguise?' Beresford said. 'Because a disguise is definitely what it was.'

'Maybe she's famous, and didn't want to be recognised,' Crane suggested.

'I've thought of that, and I've tried to imagine how she would look with her own hair and different make-up, but unless she looks dramatically different after Bunny's finished working on her, I don't think I'll recognise her even when she's Model Mary,' Beresford said. 'Does anybody else think they might recognise her?'

Nobody did.

'So, as far as we know, she's not famous,' Beresford continued.

The others nodded. If none of them – a disparate group of people with widely differing tastes and only their work in common – recognised the woman, then the chances were that her face was not well-known.

'But if she's not famous, and she wasn't running away from someone . . .' He paused. 'We are all agreed she *wasn't* running away, aren't we . . .?'

'Yes,' Paniatowski said. 'If she'd been running away, she'd have chosen somewhere much less conspicuous to hole up in.'

'Then why did she bother with a disguise at all?'

'Perhaps she dressed like that for professional reasons,' Meadows suggested. 'Perhaps she was on the game.'

'You think she might have been a common prostitute?' Beresford asked, incredulously.

'Not a common one, no, but it's certainly a possibility that she was a prostitute of some sort.'

'But if she was on the game, wouldn't she have done all she could to make herself look as attractive as possible?'

'I don't think so. Not everyone wants to sleep with the latest Hollywood star, you know.'

'Don't they?' Beresford asked.

'No. There are some men who like to screw women dressed as chickens. There are some who only want to go to bed with amputees. I can give you even more extreme examples, like—'

'I'd much rather you didn't,' Beresford interrupted.

'And maybe this woman specialised in men who fantasized

about having sex with their first primary school teacher – or even their nanny.'

'It's a nice theory,' Crane said, 'but the numbers don't add up. Say one man in a thousand wanted to sleep with his dowdy teacher. Given that most of them wouldn't even dream of going to a prostitute, and quite a number who would couldn't afford it – because if Mary Edwards *was* a hooker, she was a *high-class* hooker – you're left with a very narrow customer base which could never be economically viable in a place the size of Whitebridge.'

'Economically viable,' Meadows said, rolling the words around in her mouth. 'I love it when you take dirty, Jack.' She sighed. 'But you're right – the prostitute theory is a non-starter.'

'How about this as an explanation of why she wore a disguise,' Paniatowski said, with a slight hint of excitement in her voice. 'It wasn't the person she was when she *came* to Whitebridge that she was worried about being recognised, it was being recognised later as the person who'd *been* in Whitebridge.'

'Clever!' Meadows said admiringly. 'Very clever!'

But the two men merely looked baffled.

'Model Mary has nothing to fear,' Paniatowski explained. 'It was Mousy Mary who was supposed to disappear without trace.'

'You're saying she came to Whitebridge to do something criminal,' Beresford said.

'Exactly.'

'Like a bank robbery, for example?'

'No, not a bank robbery. If that had been her intention, she'd have kept a low profile, just as she would have done if she'd been running away. So why *did* she make herself so conspicuous? She did it because she had to do it – because the suite in the Royal Victoria is as much a part of her disguise as the wig!'

'What do you mean?' Crane said.

'The wig and make-up say she's dowdy – and probably lonely – and the suite says that she's a wealthy woman.'

'You think she was a con artist?' Crane asked.

'That would certainly make a lot of sense, wouldn't it?' Paniatowski countered.

'And you think that the con trick went wrong, and whoever she was trying to pull it on killed her.'

'We certainly can't dismiss the possibility.'

'I have a question, boss,' Meadows said.

'Yes?'

'If the point of the suite was to suggest she was rich, as part of the con, then why didn't her clothes—?'

'I've already explained that,' Paniatowski interrupted, crossly. 'For some reason, which was no doubt to do with another part of the con, she wanted to look dowdy.'

'Yes, but you can look dowdy and rich just as easily as you can look dowdy and poor.' Meadows grimaced. 'Sorry, boss – I know that's not what you want to hear, but I thought I had to say it.'

'Perhaps it was a much more elaborate con than we've realised,' Paniatowski suggested, with a hint of both exasperation and desperation in her voice. 'Perhaps the suite was meant to suggest money, while the clothes – which were not only dowdy but cheap – were meant to suggest a lack of self-confidence.' She groaned. 'Shit, I don't know! I'm just babbling, aren't I?'

Nobody contradicted her.

'Moving on,' she said, 'Mary had this tattoo on her wrist.' She handed round photographs for them all to examine. 'Does it suggest anything to anyone?'

'What you want one of us to say is something like, "This tattoo is only displayed by the inner circle of the Daughters of the American Revolution"?' Crane suggested.

'That's right,' Paniatowski agreed.

'Just looks like a butterfly to me,' Crane said.

It just looked like a butterfly to Beresford and Meadows, too.

'There must be a butterfly expert at the university,' Paniatowski said. 'I want you to take this photograph to him first thing in the morning, Kate, and see if he can identify it.'

'Any particular reason, boss?' Meadows asked in the flat tone she employed when she was being asked to do something she didn't want to do.

'Yes,' Paniatowski replied. 'You say she's a New Yorker, and I accept that, but isn't it possible that she *became* a New Yorker, maybe in her twenties, rather than being *born* one?'

'It's possible,' Meadows conceded.

'So maybe she comes from some other state, and maybe this is the official butterfly of that state.'

'Seems like a bit of a long shot,' Meadows said dubiously.

'At the moment, long shots are all we've got,' Paniatowski reminded her. She looked up at the bar clock. 'Right, that's it for tonight. Maybe by tomorrow morning we'll have some more tangible evidence to work with – and we can put all this speculation back in the box.'

'Maybe we will,' Beresford said.

But all of them – including Paniatowski – were thinking, And maybe we won't.

JOURNAL

I wonder if, when time has dulled the memory of writing these notes and I look back on them, I will be expecting to find a well-ordered narrative. If that *is* what I expect, then I am doomed to disappointment, because I will not be presented with a tightly structured argument, but instead will have to accept a collection of random thoughts which have built up behind the barriers of my mind and then, like a dam which can hold no more water, spilled unchecked out onto the page.

If I believed in omens, I would have taken the incident in the international terminal at JFK as a bad one, and would not be here now. What happened (I am reminding my older self who is reading this who-knows-where-and-when) was that I was recognized.

The man was middle-aged — maybe around forty-three or forty-four. His shoulders sloped — not naturally, but as if they could no longer bear the weight of existence — and his eyes were dull and tired and hopeless.

But those eyes came alive when he saw me.

Oh yes!

He said he knew who I was, and there was no point in me denying it.

His voice was low — almost self-deprecating — at first.

'Do you know what you've done? Can you even imagine the amount of damage you've done to innocent people?'

But as he continued to speak — as he laid out for inspection all the crimes against humanity of which he said I was undoubtedly guilty, as he harangued me for all the lives I have allegedly destroyed merely for my own profit — the voice gradually grew louder and more fanatical.

People — busy people, *travelling* people — stopped rushing around the terminal and formed a loose circle around us.

I tried to get away, but the man grabbed me by the arm and insisted I listened to the rest of his vitriol. I could, of course, have stopped him if I'd really wanted to — could have hurt him quite badly, in fact — but that, I had already decided, would only have made matters worse.

The other voyagers did not know this – as far as they were concerned I was just a helpless woman forced to listen to this barrage of abuse – but none of them tried to help me. Perhaps they felt I deserved what I was being subjected to – or perhaps there is simply a dark seed deep within the human soul which needs to feed on the humiliation of others.

Eventually, three or four uniformed airport officials came and restrained my tormentor (the fact that someone as precise as I am does not know whether it was three or four is indicative of the state I was in by this point). I would like to think they did it to save me more misery, but the truth – I suspect – is that this thing that was happening to me was impeding the smooth running of the airport, and that could simply not be tolerated.

The man was taken away to I know-not-where, and when it became plain to the lingering crowd of emotion vultures that I wasn't going to put on a show for them by breaking down in tears, they slowly drifted away.

There was a part of me – standing alone in that vast airport – that wished I'd had Brad or Chuck around, because with one of them by my side, the incident would never have been allowed to happen. I almost called them then – almost told them that I'd made a big mistake and I really, really needed them – but forced myself not to, because I knew that if the journey was to be made at all, I had to make it alone.

I told myself it had been a brave decision not to call Brad or Chuck, and that I should be proud.

But I could not be brave twice in one afternoon.

I could not bring myself to walk up to the check-in desk then, and risk a second onslaught from someone else who despises me for what I do.

So instead, I caught a taxi back to the city. It was the most expensive cab ride I've ever taken, because it not only cost me what was on the meter, it also cost the price of a first-class ticket to Manchester, England.

Once I was back on home ground, I bought a wig and the sort of make-up I would not normally even think of using. When I looked in the mirror, I hardly recognized myself. It was at that point that I decided to stick to my disguise even when I'd reached my destination, because it was just possible that someone in Whitebridge might recognize me, and if they did, the whole thing would be blown.

I booked another ticket, but this time it was for the person I'd seen in the mirror, so I made it tourist class. And guess what – the seat was cheaper than my excess baggage charges!

And now here I am in England, a tiny country when compared to the USA, a speck on the map that is not even as big as the state of New York.

I do not need to look around to see how different Whitebridge is to the places I am used to. It is only necessary to sniff the air. Here there is none of the crispness that you smell around Lake Tear of the Clouds, nor the aroma of Manhattan – that strange, exotic mixture of Chinese food, diesel fuel and energy.

Here, the air is full of clinging dampness and thick industrial smoke – and history. This town – and a few others like it – kept the world supplied with spun cotton for nearly two hundred years. Whitebridge was more real – and more necessary – to the nineteenth-century planters of Virginia and Alabama than was Chicago or St Louis. My ancestors lived here, smelling almost the same air as I am smelling now – and that is both awesome and frightening.

My project is still in its early stages, but already I have made mistakes. I should have learned from the encounter at the airport and ditched all my baggage. Physical baggage, I mean, not emotional (ha! ha!) – although that could have gone too.

I should not have arrived in such grand style at this little provincial hotel which the natives set such great store by. But I was still thinking in New York terms – in terms of the 'me' who lives in Manhattan. I see that now, and have taken steps to correct my errors, because if the project is ever to succeed, I will have to become a completely different person (or, at least, appear to have become a completely different person).

I am not sure what I am any more. In New York, I understood myself – or at least thought I did. And anyway, I was too busy to worry about such matters. But here, on the edge of the bleak moors which the locals describe as vast – but which could be dropped into the Adirondack Park and never found again – there is too much time to think.

Am I a parasite – a miner of human misery – as the man at JFK suggested I was?

Am I a seeker of truth – an uncoverer of secrets that have been long hidden?

Am I worthy – or just greedy?

I don't know – I really, honestly don't – but perhaps the answer lies somewhere out there, behind the abandoned mills and the decaying chimneys.

If they knew what I was doing, my friends back in Manhattan would say that I was a fool.

But do I care what they think?

And are they really my friends – or just the friends of the woman I am trying to leave behind me?

There are times when I myself think I am a fool, because only a fool would take such risks – would gamble so much on an uncertain future. And yet I know that I have no choice in the matter – know that if I had carried on as I was, I would have begun slowly dying from the inside.

FOUR

Paniatowski had imagined that once the twins had begun to take a more active part in life – thoroughly examining every inch of the carpet in the search for things to put in their mouths, for example – they would sleep more.

'Which just shows how little *you* know about bringing up kids,' she told herself ruefully.

In point of fact, they seemed to be waking up earlier with each successive day, and she was happy they did – because, though it meant she got less sleep than ever, she was able to spend more time with them.

That morning, after turning down Elena's offer of help, she had bathed them, changed their nappies, and explained to them the possible complexities of the Mary Edwards' case in an experimental baby language (she really *was* trying to be a conventional mum) that her team would not have been able to follow but her children seemed to find acceptable enough. Finally, she placed them on the floor, and instructed them, in a stern mummy voice, to entertain themselves in ways which would not inevitably lead to her having to perform a Heimlich manoeuvre. Her conscience clear – for at least three minutes – she turned on the television at low volume for the local news, and forced herself to eat a bowl of the revolting muck that her adopted daughter Louisa insisted would provide her with much-needed fibre.

As she ate, she kept glancing down at her babies. The twins were the product of a brutal act which had more to do with power and fear than with sex, and though Paniatowski's newly rediscovered religious convictions had not allowed her to have them aborted, she had never really believed that she would love them.

But she did. She loved them so much that she knew it would kill her if anything happened to one of them.

And yet . . .

And yet sometimes, as she fondly watched them constantly discovering new aspects of life beyond the cradle, she found herself wondering if she had made the right decision – wondered if they had in them a seed of evil which would grow as they grew, and would one day be unleashed on an unsuspecting world.

She wouldn't let it happen, she promised herself. Her church taught her that God was merciful and love would overcome all – and her faith commanded her to accept that.

So why, when she caught a certain look in Thomas's eye, or saw Philip snatch something away from his brother's hand, did she feel a shudder run through her whole body?

Would she have felt like that if dear sweet Colin Beresford had been their father?

Was she seeing things which were perfectly normal and putting a dark interpretation on them?

She could not wish she had never had her twins – but she sometimes wished she had never gone into the woods that night.

Best not to think about it!

Best to watch the news, especially since the screen was now filled with the image of the Royal Victoria hotel, making it likely that the police appeal would be next.

The picture of Mary Edwards in her Mousy Mary persona appeared on the screen.

'This woman, believed to be called Mary Edwards, was found dead in a Whitebridge hotel yesterday,' the newsreader said. 'Anyone who has information on the whereabouts and activities in the last two weeks should contact the police immediately at the number now showing on the screen.'

Paniatowski nodded her head with satisfaction. She and the news editor had carefully worked out the wording between them, and the result was just what she had wanted – a message which gave just enough information to underline the serious-ness of the inquiry, but contained little to inflame the sensation junkies who lived for this kind of shit.

Louisa walked into the lounge, dressed in her school uniform.

Three more months, and then she'll never wear it again, Paniatowski thought, perhaps a little sadly.

'You're up early,' she said aloud.

'I've got a study group before class,' Louisa replied.

Yes, three more months, and Louisa would have the choice of going to university (several of which had already expressed a keen interest in her) or becoming a police cadet (which was what she had had her heart set on for years). Paniatowski had no intention of trying to stop her exercising the latter option, but prayed nightly that she would change her mind and plump for the former.

Louisa gave both of her stepbrothers a cuddle, then sat down at the table opposite her mother and ate, with obvious relish, some of the muck she'd made her mother eat.

When she'd emptied her bowl, she looked up said, 'I'm a little bit worried about Elena.'

'Why?' Paniatowski asked, alarmed. 'Isn't she looking after the twins properly?'

'No, it's not that – she's doing a marvellous job, but, you see, I feel responsible for her.'

Paniatowski did her best to hide her smile. She could see where the idea came from, even though Elena was a good three years older than Louisa. The Spanish girl came from the village where Louisa's family had their roots, and it had been while reconnecting with those roots that the two had met. And yes, it had been Louisa who suggested Elena as a nanny when Paniatowski had unexpectedly become pregnant, but even so . . .

'I think we're exploiting her,' Louisa said bluntly.

'Do you?' Paniatowski asked, surprised. 'I pay her much more than she could ever earn in her village.'

And rather more than I can really afford, she added mentally.

'Yes,' Louisa agreed, 'but we're not doing anything much to help her get on in life.'

'So what do you suggest?'

'She could enrol in a few evening classes at the technical college. I've been down there myself, and there are several courses which might be useful to her when she eventually goes home.'

'And if she was down at the technical college, who would look after the twins when I have to work late?'

'I would.'

'What about your own studying – I'm not having that suffer.'

'Come on, Mum, we both know that if I took the exams today, I'd pass with flying colours.'

'Ah, but if you really believe that, why do you need to go to study sessions before school starts?' Paniatowski asked, then sat back and waited for Louisa's attempt to counter her logic.

'I don't need them – but I'm the head girl, and I think I should set an example for those who do by going myself,' Louisa said.

Paniatowski shook her head in wonder.

'When did you become so middle-aged?' she asked, half-humorously.

'Years ago,' Louisa said. She grinned. 'Let's face it, Mum, there needs to be at least one adult in this house, and since you're clearly not up to the job . . .'

'Cheeky devil,' Paniatowski said. 'I'll tell you what I'll do – I'll ask Elena if she wants to study in the evening, but I'm not going to force her.'

'Perfect!' Louisa said. She stood up, kissed Paniatowski on the forehead, and headed for the door. 'Got to run. I love you, Mum.'

'And I love you,' Paniatowski said – but by then Louisa was already in the hallway.

As the front door closed, Philip suddenly started crying. Paniatowski picked him up, rested his head on her shoulder, and began to gently massage his back.

'What's the matter, my little darling,' she cooed. 'Is it wind?'

And through her head ran a prayer which she had not consciously composed, but which seemed to have written itself.

'Please let nurture overcome nature in my babies. Please let them be a joy to me – and not a curse.'

Largely as a result of having to care for his mother when she had developed early-onset Alzheimer's disease, Colin Beresford had not lost his virginity until he was in his early thirties. Since then, he had been making up for lost time, and when he had learned that his nickname around headquarters was Shagger Beresford, he'd been over the moon about it.

And hadn't he the perfect right to be over the moon? he'd asked himself at the time.

Wasn't it only fair that a man who had carried his virginity around as a heavy, guilty secret for so many years should finally come into his own?

Now, increasingly, he was coming to see the nickname as a curse, rather than as an accolade. He did not want to be remembered as the man who had slept with the largest number of attractive girls in Whitebridge – though that *was* an ambition he was still pursuing relentlessly – but rather as a bobby who, while he never rose above the rank of detective inspector, had been a *bloody good* detective inspector.

These thoughts flashed through his mind as he mounted the podium which had last seen use at a regional awards ceremony for DigRight garden implements salesmen.

He looked down at the rows of detective constables, each with his own small desk and telephone.

'Welcome to the Royal Victoria Hotel ballroom,' he said. 'Will you all please take your partners for the invitation foxtrot.'

The line got him a laugh, but then he was an inspector, so that was almost guaranteed.

'You'll get a lot of calls this morning, and most of them will be a complete bloody waste of time,' he continued. 'That's why you've got your scripts – to help you to weed out the nutters from the genuine articles. The first thing that you'll notice, at the top of your scripts, is a number of facts – that the dead woman had a tattoo, that she smoked Tareyton cigarettes (which are not available in this country) et cetera, et cetera.'

Detective Constable Mark Simcox sat at the back of the ballroom, doodling what had started out as a series of random lines, but was rapidly becoming a sketch of Shagger Beresford. He was pretty good at drawing, he thought. Actually, he was pretty good at quite a lot of things, and while the others might need this talk, he certainly didn't – because he could spot a fake at fifty paces.

'If someone claims to have seen Mary Edwards, you might ask them if she was smoking,' Beresford continued. 'If he tells you that Mary was, you ask what brand. If he says he didn't notice, that doesn't necessarily mean he hasn't seen her. If he says they were an American brand, but he can't remember the name, that's promising. If he can remember the name – and it's the right name – you can move onto the next stage. But if he says they were Benson and Hedges Special Filter – and insists that's what they were when you ask him a second time, then you're on a hiding to nothing, because that's what a lot of nutters do – fix on something real, insert it into their fantasy world, and stick to it like glue.'

The sketch of Beresford was coming along rather well, DC Simcox thought. He particularly liked the fact that he had drawn the inspector's head in the shape of a penis tip.

'Once you've established that the caller is not a timewaster, you should go to the questions in the lower half of the page. They're all basically "who", "where", "why" and "how" questions. They're there to help you ask the caller the right things. What they are *not* is an instruction to be followed slavishly. You've all been trained to use your own judgement, so bloody well use it.' Beresford paused. 'Are there any questions?'

None at all, DC Simcox thought. As far as he was concerned, the last fifteen minutes had been a complete waste of time.

It had not been confirmed until the early evening that murder had been done in the Prince Alfred suite, and by then it had been too late for the guests to even contemplate changing hotels that night. The next morning was a different matter entirely, and by a quarter past eight – while the travelling salesmen were stuffing their faces with the Royal Vic's complimentary breakfast – a fairly long queue of the more timid guests was already building up at the reception desk.

The manager watched their departure without undue distress. He normally hated guests leaving, not because he was particularly hospitable – he tended to see them as figures on a balance sheet, rather than people – but because that meant empty rooms, and the battle to avoid under-occupancy (which head office regarded as the most obscene word in the English language) would have to begin again. This time, however, there would be no such battle, because there had been a stream

of calls asking if there were any available rooms. He understood why his hotel had suddenly become so popular – the
ghoulish instinct which lives in everyone was particularly close
to the surface in these early-morning callers – but he did not
care, and despised these potential guests only a little more
than the ones who were in the process of abandoning him.

The only dark cloud on his horizon was that he had had to
cancel a booking he had taken for a conference of local small
businesses, since the ballroom was occupied by Inspector
Beresford's lads. He wondered, briefly, if he should chance
his arm and send a bill to police headquarters for loss of
income. And then he thought of Sergeant Meadows, and
decided it was not a good idea.

Elena had taken charge of the children, and Paniatowski was
just about to leave home when the call came through.

It was Meadows.

'We've dangled our bait in the water, and we've had our
first nibble, boss,' the sergeant said.

'Who from?'

'It was a man called Arthur Tyndale. He says that he's a
solicitor.'

'Hi ho Silver, away!' Paniatowski said, almost automatically.

'What was that, boss?'

'Sorry, Kate. Yes, he's a solicitor, but he's not just *any* old
solicitor. We call him the Lone Ranger, because he rides the
wide plains of Lancashire in his white Jaguar, supporting the
underdog and fighting injustice wherever he encounters it. I'm
surprised you haven't heard of him.'

Although, now she came to think about it, she wasn't really
surprised at all, because Meadows hadn't been in Mid Lancs
that long, and she herself couldn't remember seeing Tyndale
in court for two or three years.

'He sounds like an ambulance chaser to me,' Meadows said.

'Oh, he's much more than that,' Paniatowski said. 'The man
has an ego the size of a double-decker bus, but there's a savage
earnestness about him which terrifies most magistrates. And
if the case gets as far as trial, he doesn't brief the *best* barrister
available – he briefs the barrister *best able* to present the argu-

ment that he's come up with. You should see him in Crown Court – the judge is watching him, the jury is watching him, and defence counsel doesn't dare make a move unless he raises an encouraging eyebrow.'

'You're talking as if you've come up against him yourself.'

'I have – a couple of times.'

'And what was the result?'

'He got one client off, and the other was sent down.'

'And was the one that he got off guilty?'

'We thought so, but we also thought the convicted one was guilty, too – but he was released on appeal, in the light of new evidence.' She reached into her handbag for her packet of cigarettes. 'What does Tyndale want, anyway?'

'He says he has some information about the murder. Do you want me to ring him, and tell him to report to headquarters?'

'No, the Lone Ranger really doesn't like being summoned. He'd turn up eventually, of course, but there'd be a lot of foot dragging before he did, and since his office is on my way to headquarters, I might as well do what he wants, and drop in on him.'

Paniatowski paused for a moment to light a cigarette.

Filthy habit, she told herself.

'Anything else to report?' she asked.

'Shagger's—' Meadows began.

'Kate!' Paniatowski warned her.

'Sorry, boss. Inspector Beresford's got the incident room up and running – rather well, it seems to me – and there's a whole bunch of uniforms on the streets, handing out pictures of Mousy Mary.'

'Good,' Paniatowski said. 'Keep me informed.'

'You've got it, boss.'

George Clegg owned a television set, but he never switched it on now, because that would only have reminded him of the many happy evenings he'd spent in front of the screen with his beloved late wife, Ellie, and that would have made him feel the loss even more than usual.

Thus, he did not catch the evening news bulletin which had shown the image of Mousy Mary.

He didn't take the evening paper, either, so it was not until his kindly next-door neighbour pushed his copy through the letterbox that George even realised that the woman calling herself Mary Edwards was dead.

The effect on him was instantaneous. Pain shot through his left arm, and he felt a band tightening across his chest. He walked back – staggered back – to his kitchen, and plopped down helplessly in his armchair.

She was dead; his head pounded.

She was *dead*.

That lively, beautiful girl who had visited him only a couple of days earlier had been murdered.

He needed to talk to the police, he told himself – he needed to talk to them *now*.

But now was not an option, because, feeling as he did, he'd never even make it to the front door.

He wished he had a phone, but he and Ellie had never seen the need for one, because anyone they ever needed to talk to lived only a few doors up or down from their own home.

He tried to work out who might pay a call on him during the course of the morning.

Not the milkman, he collected his money on Saturdays.

Not that nice social worker from the town hall – since the cutbacks, she only came once a fortnight.

There was no one – but he had to get to the police, because they seemed to know nothing.

They didn't even know what Mary's real name was, or they'd have used it in the article!

All his neighbours were out at work, and wouldn't be home until evening, so he couldn't rely on them.

He had to do this himself. He had to somehow gather the strength to walk to the phone box at the end of the street.

Because although he could not be positive, he was *almost* certain he knew who had killed the woman in the Royal Vic.

The man's name was Walter Spinks, and he was resident lepidopterist at the confused complex of red brick and plate glass buildings which was known as the University of Mid Lancs.

He was a tall, thin man with very long fingers, curly brown hair and thick glasses. He wore a bow tie, and was the first man Meadows had met in a long time who – she was sure – hadn't wondered, even for a moment, what it would be like to take her to bed.

'The butterfly is the most fascinating and inexplicable creature,' Spinks enthused. 'Take the monarch as an example. The generations that stay in one place live for only three to five weeks, but the generations that migrate – and imagine anything as tiny and delicate as a butterfly migrating – live for much—'

'That's all very interesting, but I'm here as part of a murder investigation, Dr Spinks,' Meadows interrupted.

'Some of them have been recorded to have flown over 4800 miles,' Spinks said, as if he thought that he only needed to hit the *right* fact to capture her whole attention.

'I'd like you to look at this,' Meadows said, sliding a photograph of Mary's tattoo across the desk.

'This isn't a butterfly – it's a tattoo,' Spinks said.

'I know,' Meadows admitted, 'but it's all we have to work from at the moment, and we were hoping that it resembled a real butterfly closely enough for you to make a judgement.'

'Actually, it's a rather fine piece of work,' Spinks said, examining the photograph through a magnifying glass. 'It's almost like a watercolour painting, don't you think?'

'Almost,' Meadows agreed. 'Can you identify it?'

'I think so. It looks like a northern brown argus. There are sub-species of this particular butterfly spread all over the world – Scandinavia, Russia, North Korea – but I think this is the genuine article. Of course, to be really positive, I would need to see more. Some of the sub-species have white spots on the underside of the wings, for example, and—'

'What part of America is it common in?' Meadows asked.

'America?' Spinks exploded, with something akin to horror. 'America, you say!'

'Isn't it . . .?'

'This is a *northern* brown argus. We don't share it with the *Americans*. We don't even share it with the Midlands or the Home Counties. It's *ours*.'

'Ours?'

'You find it in Lancashire and Cumbria – and you don't find it anywhere else.'

DC Simcox was still stuck at his desk in the ballroom of the Royal Victoria, taking calls from people whose main motive in ringing up was that they just wanted someone to talk to.

It was all Shagger Beresford's fault, he told himself. A better boss than Beresford would have instantly spotted his potential, given this tedious task to some poor drudge, and thus freed him to make a substantial – perhaps *the* substantial – contribution to the investigation.

The latest caller he was being forced to deal with was a woman called Janet Dobson, who said she worked as a librarian at Whitebridge Central Library. He'd been surprised when she announced her occupation, because, up to that point, he had thought from her voice that she was quite a young woman. Now, of course, he realised his mistake, and a picture formed in his mind of a thin woman with a pinched face, who had her grey hair tied in a severe bun, and wore spectacles with lenses as thick as jam jar bottoms.

'Exactly what is the nature of your information, Miss Dobson?' Simcox said, sticking – for the moment, anyway – to the script he had been given.

'It said on the news that you wanted to hear from anyone who had seen the woman who was murdered,' Miss Dobson said.

'And do you think *you've* seen her?' Simcox asked, softening his voice to a tone he felt was appropriate for talking to old ladies.

'Well, of course I do,' Miss Dobson said tartly. 'I would never have called if I hadn't. And, by the way, there's *no* think about it.'

Vinegary old hag, Simcox thought.

'So where do you think – I'm sorry, where do you *know* – you've seen her?' he said aloud.

'Where do *you* think I'm *likely* to have seen her? Do you imagine that I walked into my living room one night and there she was – sitting in my favourite armchair with her feet up, and reading the evening newspaper while she slowly supped at a gin and tonic?'

'No, I—'

'Or maybe I was in my bath when I noticed her crouched evilly behind the taps, like some kind of malevolent hobgoblin.'

'I don't *know* where you might have seen her, madam – that's why I asked,' Simcox said, in a harder, more impersonal voice which was intended to remind the dried-up old spinster that she was talking to an officer of the law, who was therefore entitled to her respect.

Miss Dobson sighed. 'I saw her in the library.'

Bollocks! Simcox thought. Absolute cock!

There were people who went to the library, and people who simply didn't. He himself was a member of the latter group, having never crossed the library threshold since he was forced to do so at school, and so – it was obvious to him – was the dead woman.

'What was she doing in the library?' he asked, starting to doodle a picture on his notepad which could well turn out to be Miss Dobson. 'Was she borrowing a book? That's what most people do in libraries, isn't it.'

'Is it?' Miss Dobson asked. 'I never realised that. Do you know, thanks to this wonderful knowledge that you've just imparted to me, I'm going to adopt a whole new approach to my work from now on.'

'There's no need at all for you to take that attitude, Miss Dobson,' Simcox said stiffly.

'And there's no need for you to talk to me as if I were mentally deficient,' Miss Dobson countered. 'But in answer to your question, no, she was not borrowing a book. In fact, since she was not a rate payer, a member of a rate payer's family or someone who paid her rates indirectly through rent to her landlord, she was not *entitled* to borrow books.'

She was a right stroppy old cow, this one, Simcox thought, giving her image on his notepad a pronounced squint.

'How do you know she wasn't a rate payer?' he asked.

'Firstly – because she was an American; and secondly – because she told me that she was just visiting Whitebridge.'

'So why was she in the library?' Simcox asked, mystified.

'She wished to consult the archives.'

'The what?'

'The archives.'

'Oh, I see,' said Simcox, who would have died rather than admit he had no idea what she was talking about.

'She was specifically interested in the local newspapers from one year in the early 1920s – 1924, in point of fact.'

'And you keep them in the library, do you?' asked Simcox, half suspecting that she was taking the piss out of him.

'Yes, we do. We have all the newspapers since 1876.'

'They must take up a lot of space,' Simcox said, his suspicions mounting by the second.

'We store them on microfiche.'

'Oh, I see,' Simcox said. He glanced down at his script, and realised how far he had veered away from it.

'When did all this happen?' he asked.

'On Monday and Tuesday of last week.'

'Monday *and* Tuesday!'

'Yes.'

'You're saying that she didn't just read the newspapers one day, but came back for second helpings?'

'Obviously.'

To do it once seemed, to Simcox, to be crazy. To repeat the action seemed . . . well, he just didn't know *what* it seemed.

'Thank you for calling, Miss Dobson,' Simcox said, returning to his script. 'The Mid Lancs police force values any and all the help it receives from members of the general public, and—'

'Is that it?' the librarian asked.

DC Simcox pencilled in a bushy moustache under his librarian's prominent nose.

'I don't know what else you were expecting,' he said.

'I was expecting you to say that someone will be coming to the library to interview me.'

'And so they will, madam, in the fullness of time,' Simcox said, balling up his picture and dropping it into the battleship grey regulation police waste-paper basket next to his desk.

The man had insisted on seeing Beresford personally. He was around sixty years' old, with broad shoulders and a square head. He was wearing a heavy check jacket, cavalry twill trousers, and what were probably very comfortable – if somewhat battered – suede shoes.

He looked to Beresford like either an ex-bobby or a pub landlord, and when they had shaken hands, he said, 'My name's Terry Carson. I used to be on the force myself, but now I'm the manager of the Rising Sun.' The inspector couldn't resist giving himself a mental pat on the back.

'So what can I do for you, Mr Carson?' Beresford asked.

'It's like this,' said Carson, sounding perhaps a little nervous and *definitely* very cautious. 'I've been running the Sun for a couple of years now. It was a bit of a rough pub before I took it over – and that's probably why they decided to put an ex-bobby in. Anyway, the first week I was there, this feller from the brewery paid me a call. He was one of them men with a sharp blue suit and a five quid haircut. You know the type I mean.'

'I know the type you mean,' Beresford agreed.

'So this feller gives me a ledger with "Incident Book" written on the front. He said it was part of a general statistics gathering process, and every time there was a disturbance in the pub, I was to write it up.'

'But you didn't?'

'Did I hell as like! "General statistics gathering process", my arse. The only statistics they'd be collecting were on me. It was like asking a condemned man if he wouldn't mind providing his own rope – and that book is as virginal and unsullied now as it was the day he handed it over.'

'But there have been fights in the Rising Sun in the last two years, haven't there, Mr Carson?'

The landlord hesitated. 'This is where it all starts feeling a bit uncomfortable for me,' he admitted. 'This is where I get the impression that I'm skating on very thin ice.'

'As an active officer talking to an ex-officer, let me see if I can help you with this,' Beresford suggested.

'All right.'

'The Rising Sun is a lot quieter than it used to be, but it's still in the centre of Whitebridge, and it's still a pub used mainly by working men, so it would be a bloody miracle if there wasn't a fight every once in a while, especially late on Friday or

Saturday nights. Now, as a private citizen, you're only allowed to use physical force when you need to defend yourself. Right?'

'Right.'

'So when a fight breaks out, what you're supposed to do is call the police. The only problem with that is that by the time we get there – even if we're quick – the whole pub could be smashed up.'

'That's right,' Carson agreed. 'And who gets blamed for it? The poor bloody landlord – that's who!'

'So what you actually do is wade into the fight yourself,' Beresford continued. 'And before the troublemakers know what's happening, they're lying in the gutter outside the pub with aching jaws and black eyes, and you're standing over them, telling them their custom is no longer welcome in the Rising Sun. Right?'

Carson frowned.

'Maybe,' he said reluctantly.

Beresford laughed. 'You overlooked that sort of thing when you were on the beat, didn't you, Mr Carson?'

'Well, yes.'

'And so did generations of bobbies before you – so why should you assume it's any different now?'

'Well, you know, times change,' Carson said dubiously. 'There's a new breed of bobby around these days – the cousins of that feller from the brewery with the five quid haircut.'

'I can assure you that I'm not one of the new breed,' Beresford said. 'Why don't you just tell me what it was that you came in to tell me?'

'It was last Thursday night,' Carson said. 'I noticed these two women in the snug who'd I'd never seen before.'

'And you think one of them was Mary Edwards?'

'I'm certain she was.'

'Go on.'

'They were sitting very close together, and they were giggling a lot, like mates do when they're out on the razzle. Then suddenly the door burst open, and this big bugger came in. He saw them together, and he went crazy. He said something like, "What are you doing here, Sheila?" She said, "I'm talking to my friend." "It's Doris what's your friend, not this *thing*," he screamed at her. The other woman – Mary – got up. I think she wanted to reason with him.'

'What were you doing at this point?'

'I was just watching and waiting – because, very often, the landlord stepping into an argument only makes things worse, and what might well have died of its own accord – if he'd left it alone – rapidly turns into a punch-up. Besides, if it had been Sheila that stood up, I would have been more worried, but I never thought he'd hit a woman who wasn't his wife.'

'But he did hit her?'

'He certainly did. He gave her a real back-hander across her face. That's when I started to move – and if I'd reached him in time, I'd have made him very sorry that he ever hit a woman in my pub.'

'What do you mean – if you'd reached him in time?'

'Before I was even halfway there, Mary had handled it. It was very fast, so I'm not entirely sure what happened in what order, but what I *think* she did was first kick him in the nuts and then – when he was half doubled up – follow it through with an uppercut to his jaw. I tell you, whoever trained that woman – and there's no doubt in my mind that she was trained – did a bloody good job.'

'So it would seem,' Beresford said.

'Anyway, the feller went down like a sack of potatoes. Mary dusted off her hands – calm as you please – stepped over him, and left the pub. After a few seconds, Sheila stood up and left as well.'

'Was she following Mary?'

'I don't think so. I think she just wanted to get away from the feller while he was still down.'

'And what happened to the feller?'

'I picked him up and eased him gently into a chair. Then I got him some ice for his balls, and brewed him a nice cup of tea with brandy in it.'

'What happened to the feller?' Beresford repeated.

Carson grinned. 'I took him by the collar, and dragged him to the door. Once I had him out on the street, I may have accidentally kicked him a couple of times – because I really don't like fellers who hit women.' He paused. 'I know I should have reported it, but if I had, it would have gone down in the incident book, and I didn't want to give that smarmy bastard from head office the satisfaction. Besides, Mary might have had a bruise for a day or two, but after what she did to that feller, he won't be able to ride his bike for a month.'

'Could you give a description of Sheila and the man to the police artist?' Beresford asked.

'Absolutely,' Carson replied. 'It's what I was trained to do.'

FIVE

Tyndale & Comstock (Solicitors and Commissioners of Oaths) had occupied a house in the centre of Alexandra Row for as long as Monika Paniatowski could remember, but she had never – until that morning – had cause to pass through the dark blue front door.

Beyond the outer door was the general office/waiting room, which would have looked like every other old-fashioned solicitor's waiting room but for the framed newspaper front pages hanging from the walls.

The grey-haired receptionist smiled at her and said, 'It's Chief Inspector Paniatowski, isn't it?'

'Yes, it is.'

'Mr Tyndale is engaged just at the moment, but he should be free soon. Would you like to take a seat?'

The chair the receptionist had indicated was perfectly positioned to give her a clear view of most of the framed newspapers. That was no accident, Paniatowski thought, but – more than likely – Tyndale's idea of a good joke.

All the front pages were from local papers, all had been blown up to at least three times their actual size, and all of them had a headline relating to criminal proceedings.

Local man freed! said one of the headlines.

John Hodges' sentence overturned, screamed a second.

And in case there was any doubt why these papers were being displayed in this office, a third proclaimed: **Another triumph for Tyndale**.

That kind of ostentation was probably frowned on by the Law Society, but she doubted that bothered Tyndale, because he was a big boisterous character, and, like the real Lone Ranger, slightly larger than life.

The door to one of the offices opposite her opened, and a man stepped out. She could not put a name to the face, but she knew he was no stranger to the custody cells in Whitebridge police headquarters.

On the threshold, the man turned.

'Thank you, Mr Tyndale,' he said. 'Thank you *so much*.'

'Do your best to stay out of trouble, won't you, Harry?' said a voice which sounded like it belonged to a very old man.

'I will, Mr Tyndale,' Harry promised. 'I swear I will.'

Harry moved away from the door, and Paniatowski got her first look at Tyndale.

It was a shock! He had aged at least twenty years since they had last met. His skin had grown slack, his complexion was almost yellow, and he was leaning heavily on an ebony walking stick with a silver handle. If she'd seen him out on the street, she doubted she'd even have recognised him.

'I see you're admiring my walking stick, chief inspector,' he said in the same thin voice she had heard earlier.

'Yes, I . . .' she said – because she *had* been looking at it, if only to avoid looking at his face.

'The stick originally belonged to my father,' Tyndale said. 'When he died, I kept it as a memento. I certainly never thought that there'd come a time when I'd be needing it myself.'

It was hard to know what to say – so she said nothing.

'Please come through,' Tyndale said.

He led her into his office, gestured towards the visitor's chair, and – with obvious effort – installed himself behind his old mahogany desk.

'It seems very strange to be volunteering information to the police,' Tyndale said. 'It feels like – no, to hell with "feels like", it actually *is* – breaking the carefully acquired habits of a lifetime, but on this occasion, I really feel I have absolutely no choice in the matter.'

'Does your information concern Mary Edwards?'

'It does, and ever since I telephoned the Kremlin—'

'The what?'

'The Kremlin. That's what I call Whitebridge police head-quarters. It's sort of a joke.'

'And sort of not,' Paniatowski said.

'And sort of not,' Tyndale agreed. 'Anyway, ever since I

made that call, I've been giving serious consideration to the question of what I could tell you – and what I could not – about what passed between myself and my client.'

'You're saying she was your client?'

'Yes.'

'Since when?'

'Since early last week, I think. My secretary will have the exact details. As I said, I have given the matter serious thought, and have decided that since our conversation was so general in its nature, I can reveal almost all of it.'

'So not *absolutely* all of it?'

'That is correct.'

'I'll settle for what you're willing to tell me for the moment,' Paniatowski said. 'Later on, it might be a different matter.'

'Later on, you'll get no more from me than you're getting now,' Tyndale said firmly.

'I'm listening,' Paniatowski said.

'Mary Edwards told me at the start of our meeting that she had some business to conduct in Whitebridge, but we didn't actually discuss that at all.'

'So what did you talk about?'

'How can I best describe it, I wonder?' Tyndale mused. 'She seemed to want me to brief her.'

'On what?'

'On the town of Whitebridge in general, and the local police force in particular.'

'What did she want to know about the police?'

'She asked me what I thought of them. I said that on an institutional level, the corruption was endemic, though not – thankfully – too widespread. I added, perhaps a little immodestly, that I myself had played a small part in preventing that corruption from growing. I went on to say that within the police you'll find the good, the bad and the ugly, the intelligent, the average and stupid, much as you'd expect to find in any organisation.'

'Was she happy with your answer?'

'No, she wasn't – not at all. She listened to my explanation – which was, in the original, much longer and much wittier than the brief summary I've given you – but when I'd finished, the only thing she could think of to say was, "But they're not *armed*, Mr Tyndale".'

'Had she expected them to be?'

'Yes, I believe she had. She came from New York, where all the police are armed, and I think she assumed that to be the norm around the world, which – by and large, you know – it is. At any rate, I explained to her that there were some officers trained in the use of firearms, and when the situation calls for it, those firearms will be issued to them. That didn't seem to reassure her at all, because what she said next was, "It might be too late by then." So I further explained that there was very little gun crime in this country, and she said that that was no consolation to someone who'd been shot.'

Tyndale suddenly began to cough violently. As his body shook, he fumbled in his pocket for a handkerchief, and when he spat into it, Paniatowski was sure he was spitting blood.

She had to say something, she told herself. She simply couldn't ignore it any longer.

'Is there anything that I can do for you, Mr Tyndale?' she asked.

He shook his head, and when he had stopped coughing, he said, 'It isn't always like this, you know. Some days I almost feel like my old self. But that, the doctors tell me, is the nature of the disease.'

'Are you *very* ill?'

'I'm dying.'

'Then are you sure you should be at work?'

Tyndale laughed. It was a throaty laugh – and seemed to Paniatowski almost like a death rattle.

'After the death sentence had been passed on me by my doctor, I spent a year and a half at home – and that *did* nearly kill me,' he said. 'Working may speed up the inevitable process, but at least I'll have the satisfaction of dying in harness.' He examined the handkerchief, folded it neatly, and put it in his pocket. 'Now where was I? Oh yes. She asked me how easy it would be for a foreign criminal, arriving in this country, to smuggle his gun in with him.'

'And what did you say?'

'I told her that with enough determination, nothing was

impossible, but it was difficult enough to deter most people from even trying. So then she asked me how difficult it would be for him to get one here, because she'd looked in all the pawnbrokers' shops in Whitebridge, and they didn't seem to have any. Do pawnbrokers' shops in America really sell guns, chief inspector?'

'I believe they do.'

'What an extraordinary country it must be. At any rate, it was at that point that I asked her if she was a crime novelist, because if that was what she was, she'd be better off talking to the police, who both know more about the subject than I and wouldn't charge my extortionate fees.'

'How did she respond?'

'She assured me that she was no kind of novelist at all, and then she asked me what I could tell her about safe houses. Safe houses, for God's sake! I said I assumed such places existed, and that the police had access to them, but that was as far as my knowledge went. And with that, the meeting came to an end. She paid me for my time – in cash – and added a retainer to cover any future services that I might perform for her. She did not specify what those future services might be.' Tyndale paused, perhaps to catch his breath. 'When she left, I gave serious consideration to calling the chief constable, but one does not like to engineer a situation in which one's clients are almost certain to be questioned by the police.' He chuckled again. 'That, I think, smacks too much of drumming up business for oneself.' A look of pain flashed across his face. 'That's about all I have to say. I'll show you to the door.'

'There's no need to get up,' Paniatowski said.

'I *want* to show you to the door,' Tyndale insisted. 'It's the gentlemanly thing to do.'

He rose stiffly, and – leaning on his stick even more heavily than he had earlier – made his way to the door.

'How's Charlie Woodend getting on these days?' he asked, as they both stood on the threshold.

'He's living in Spain, and doing fine,' Paniatowski said. 'He had a bit of a scare a while back, when they discovered he had cancer, but . . .'

She stopped, horrified at herself.

How could anybody be so stupid? she wondered.

'But . . .?' Tyndale prompted.

She had to finish the sentence. There was no other way.

'But he's recently been given the all-clear,' she said.

'Hmm, they're obviously much more generous with their drugs in Spain than they are here in England,' Tyndale said. He shook his head in what looked like self-disgust. 'I'm sorry, that came out wrong.'

'No, it's understandable,' Paniatowski said. 'It's all my fault. I should have thought before I sp—'

'I asked you a straight question and you gave me a straight answer,' Tyndale interrupted her. 'You've nothing to feel guilty about, and I've no reason to feel aggrieved. There isn't any point in being bitter about the hand that fate has dealt you. That only serves to sour the little time you've got left.'

'You're right about that,' Paniatowski agreed, 'but it's still a brave thing to say.'

'There's nothing brave about accepting the inevitable,' Tyndale said, brushing the compliment aside, 'and I wish Charlie Woodend nothing but well.'

He was hit by a sudden coughing fit and reached for his handkerchief. When it was over, he examined the blood with almost clinical detachment, then took a plastic bag out of his pocket and dropped the handkerchief into it.

'I know what I've got isn't catching, but I don't really see why anyone else should have to deal with the results,' he said. He paused again. 'I miss Charlie, you know, or rather, I miss the chats we used to have.'

'You had *chats* with Charlie Woodend?' Paniatowski asked, almost incredulously.

'Yes. We had them on a regular basis – and some of them could go on for hours and hours.'

'He kept very quiet about it, then.'

'And so did I. We were from opposite sides of the fence, and neither of us wanted to be seen to be consorting with the enemy. But, in fact, we weren't really consorting at all. When we had our meetings, he wasn't a detective chief inspector and I wasn't a solicitor. We were simply two men who had been drawn together by a mutual passion.'

'You're a fan of Charles Dickens!' Paniatowski said, with sudden understanding.

'Indeed I am,' Tyndale agreed. 'I've read all Dickens' novels three or four times – my favourites much more than that – and Charlie Woodend is the only man I've ever met who's done the same. He is quite wrong about Martin Chuzzlewit, of course, but other than that his views are quite sound and his knowledge is both broad and deep.'

Paniatowski checked her watch.

'I have to go,' she said apologetically.

'Of course you do, my dear,' Tyndale replied. 'You have a busy life, full of challenges, and you can't afford to waste too much of your valuable time talking to a dead man.' He smiled. 'That came out wrong, as well. I've appreciated our chat, Monika, but now I'm tired and need to rest, and you need to get about your business.'

They shook hands – Tyndale's grip was very weak – and Paniatowski was about to leave when the solicitor said, 'Looking back, I really wish I *had* phoned the chief constable after Miss Edwards' visit. I feel I have failed her as a client, and a dying man already has enough regrets, without adding to them.'

'What you're saying is that, though she didn't state as much explicitly, she genuinely believed her life was in danger,' Paniatowski said.

'Yes, and given the way events have transpired, it seems that she was right to be afraid.'

DS Graham Yates – twenty-four years in the service, and not a single blemish on his record – understood incident rooms in much the same way as a skilled surgeon understands the workings of the human body, or a talented motor mechanic knows what makes a complex engine tick. He was sensitive to their dynamics and moods, and he knew, as the big hand on the clock on the wall ticked round towards twelve o'clock, that soon the calls would start to taper off, because everybody – nutters and earnestly concerned citizens alike – got hungry.

At noon, he banged his fist on his desk to get the attention of the detective constables.

'You'll all get a break, but we'll have to do it on a shift system,' he explained. 'You'll each have forty minutes – and not a second more. On the first break –' he pointed with his index finger – 'will be you, you, you, you, you, and that lad at the back of the room – Simcox is it?'

'Yes, skipper.'

'And Simcox, who, as you can all see for yourselves, is currently engaged in the complex task of trying to push his tiny brain out through his right ear by inserting a pencil in his left.'

'I'm just cleaning the ear, skip,' Simcox protested.

'You should try soap and water, lad,' the sergeant told him. 'It's always worked for me. Off you go then – and remember, you've got forty minutes.'

The Royal Victoria Hotel's doorman stood – as might be expected – in the doorway of the hotel. He was dressed resplendently in a scarlet carriage coat, top hat, and black leather gloves.

Beresford thought he looked vaguely familiar, but was that because he had a criminal past – or for some other reason entirely?

He decided on the direct approach.

'I know you from somewhere,' he said.

The doorman grinned. 'Then, my friend, you must be a follower of the pugilistic arts,' he said.

That was it!

'You're Wally White, the Accrington Whirlwind!' Beresford said. 'I saw you fight in the Memorial Hall, when I was a nipper.'

'Did I win?' White asked.

'Yes, you most certainly did. I think your opponent was Mac Danvers—'

'Aye, I fought Mac a few times.'

'And you gave him this amazing uppercut to the jaw in the third round and got a technical knockout.'

The doorman sighed. 'Them was the good old days,' he said. 'These days I'm not so much Wally White, the Accrington Whirlwind as Wally White the Accrington Gentle Breeze.'

Beresford shook his head in wonder. White had seemed a

giant of a man back then, and it was because he wanted to grow up to be just like him that the young Colin had started body building, so it was something of a shock – edged perhaps with a little sadness – to find that he was now looking down at the man.

'Of course, the advantage of these days over the old ones is that nobody tries to play ping pong with my brain anymore,' White continued. He paused for a moment. 'Is there something I can do for you, inspector?'

'What?' Beresford asked, as if he had no idea what the doorman was talking about. 'Oh, yes,' finally remembering why he was there. He unfolded the sketch he had in his hands and held it up for inspection. 'Have you seen this man?'

It was a good sketch, he thought while the doorman examined it, a credit to both the artist's ability and Terry Carson's observational skills. There was real character in it – real, but not necessarily good – and whilst an impartial observer might not automatically have said that he looked like a man who had no qualms about hitting women, that observer would probably not have been surprised to learn that he had done just that.

'Well?' he asked.

'Yes,' the doorman said, 'I'm almost certain I have – but not since the murder.'

No, you wouldn't have seen him since – not if he's the feller we're looking for, Beresford thought.

'So when did you notice him?' he said aloud.

'Saturday – a couple of days before Miss Edwards was killed.'

'Tell me more,' Beresford said eagerly.

It was no great distance from the Royal Victoria to Whitebridge police headquarters, but most of the constables leaving the ballroom on the first break felt like a change from the regulation stodge served up in the police canteen, and so headed for a nearby pub, the Spinner and Bergamot, where they ordered stodge of an entirely different kind in the form of Hopkinson's Celebrated Meat Pies with Brown Gravy (famous since 1911) which they washed down with pints of best bitter.

Thus it was that when the appeal for information on Mary Edwards was broadcast by the regional television station for perhaps the tenth time that day, DC Simcox happened to be sitting at the bar in the company of DC Rowley.

'How's it gone this morning, Rollo?' Simcox asked. 'Did any of the people you spoke to have anything useful to tell you?'

Rowley shrugged. 'Not really. A couple of them thought they might have seen Miss Edwards, but when I started questioning them, it turned out that the woman they'd seen was the wrong height or the wrong age – or just plain *wrong.*'

'What a load of tossers they all are, aren't they?' Simcox asked, as some of the famous brown gravy slithered down his chin.

'I wouldn't put it quite like that,' Rowley countered. 'Most of them are concerned citizens who just want to help us do our job.'

'Quite right – that's exactly what they are,' Simcox agreed, wiping the gravy away with the back of his hand.

'Mind you, there are some nutters about,' Rowley continued. 'I had this one woman who seemed hopeful at first – she got the description down to a T – and then she went and spoiled it all by saying she'd seen Miss Edwards being beamed up from the Boulevard into a UFO.'

Under normal circumstances, that would be a hard story to top, Simcox thought, but fortunately he had one which, if not so dramatic, was even weirder.

'One of mine was a librarian,' he said. 'She *claimed* that Miss Edwards had spent two whole days in the library. Two whole days! And guess what this batty bitch said Mary was doing there. Not that you *could* guess – even if I gave you a million chances.'

'If I'd never guess, I might as well give up now then,' said Rowley, who was starting to find Simcox irritating.

'She said that she was reading old newspapers – on something she called microfiche!'

'And did you report it to the skipper?' Rowley asked.

'Do I look like an idiot? Of course I didn't report it. The librarian was either mistaken, or she was making the whole thing

up in the hope that some handsome young police officer, much
like myself, would go round to the library and question her.'

'What makes you say that?' Rowley wondered.

'Makes me say what?'

'That she was making it up.'

'I should have thought it was obvious. A woman with a
suite in the Royal Vic – which means a woman with a lot of
money – isn't going to waste her time in a musty old library,
is she? And even if that *is* how she gets her kicks – because
I do accept that there are some bloody funny folk about – there
must be places like that in America, so why would she bother
coming over here?'

'Maybe she was doing research into her ancestors,' Rowley
suggested. 'That's the sort of thing Yanks do.'

'And maybe, like I said, this Miss Dobson just wanted a
bit of glamour in her life,' Simcox countered, confidently
unyielding.

'Even so, I wouldn't have taken the chance myself,' Rowley
said, 'because if she is telling the truth, and he finds out you
knew and didn't pass it on, Shagger Beresford will have your
balls for breakfast.'

A picture of the victim appeared on the screen.

'This woman, believed to be called Mary Edwards, was found
dead in a Whitebridge hotel yesterday,' said the newsreader's
voice. 'Anyone who has information on her whereabouts and
activities in the last two weeks should contact the police
immediately, at the number showing on the screen.'

'They've changed the message since they first broadcast it
this morning,' Simcox said, suddenly sounding vaguely troubled.

'No, they haven't,' Rowley disagreed. 'It's exactly the same
as it's always been.'

'There were more details this morning,' Simcox said, now
with a hint of desperation entering his voice.

'That's where you're wrong,' Rowley said firmly. 'All details
have been kept to an absolute minimum. Like DI Beresford said,
it's one of the ways we have of judging from the start whether
the caller actually knows anything. It's all there in your script.'

'Oh shit!' Simcox said. He put his pint down on the counter,
almost untouched. 'I have to go.'

'We're due back in the incident room in ten minutes,' Rowley reminded him, 'and if you're not there, DS Yates will skin you alive when you *do* turn up.'

'That's nothing to what will happen if I don't get down to the library right away,' Simcox said, heading for the door.

On the map, it looked as if the mortuary shared a site with the Whitebridge General Hospital, but due to the actions of a thoughtful town council in the sixties, they were now separated by a line of trees, so that while they were not exactly two separate worlds – how could they be, when the less fortunate of the hospital's patients continued to make the one-way journey from warm bed to cold slab? – they were at least distinct from each other.

Once upon a time, Monika Paniatowski had regarded the mortuary as nothing more than a very ugly building – a swollen concrete carbuncle in fact – that her friend, Dr Shastri, was strangely fond of.

All that had changed the morning after the rape, when she had gone there so that Shastri – the only medic she could trust with her secret – could examine her and assess the damage.

Now whenever she entered the mortuary, it was like entering a time machine, and she had no sooner crossed the threshold than she was back in the woods, lying in the damp earth and being violated.

She did not have to go there.

She realised that.

She could easily have sent one of her minions instead.

Yet she continued to visit the mortuary herself – continued to step inside the nightmare time machine – because not to have done it would have been to accept that the rapists had won and her life had lost.

On this visit, she found Shastri in her office, looking, if not troubled, then at least puzzled. 'I am finding the inside of my latest guest's head a little perplexing, Monika,' Dr Shastri admitted. 'What happened to her may not be as straightforward as it at first appeared.'

'Are you saying that she wasn't killed by the poker after all?' Paniatowski asked.

'No, it was undoubtedly the poker – or some other metal bar – which dealt the fatal blow.'

'Then what's the problem?'

'There had been further damage to the brain that I have not yet been able to account for.'

'Could you explain that?'

'Certainly. The blow which killed her was an almost horizontal one, but there is a second contusion – a diagonal one – which runs from near the top of the right-hand side of the frontal lobe to near the bottom of the left-hand side.'

'Did the poker do that, too?'

'No, that's what makes it so interesting. The pattern of the damage is entirely different.'

'So what weapon was used?'

'There you have me,' Shastri said. 'Since the damage is nowhere near as extreme, I would have to say that this weapon was not as hard.'

Paniatowski pictured the murderer standing there – facing Mary – with the poker in one hand and something else – as yet unknown – in the other. Not only would he have looked slightly ridiculous, but it would have been awkward for him, because few people are ambidextrous enough to wield a weapon in each hand. Besides, a second weapon would have been unnecessary – the poker alone was enough to rob the poor woman of her life.

'You are wondering why he needed two weapons,' Shastri said.

Paniatowski grinned. 'I hate it when you can read my mind,' she told the doctor.

'The truth is, Monika, that I cannot say, with any degree of certainty, that the first injury – the diagonal one – was even the result of an attack.'

'Are you saying it could have been an accident?'

'Absolutely. She might, for instance, have tripped, and fallen against a shelf. If that shelf had had a rounded edge – as many do, for safety's sake – it would have left just such an impression as we see here.'

'But since the two blows were delivered at the same time, then surely . . .'

'Ah, but, you see, we cannot say for certain that they *were*. The brain had not had time to begin repairing itself, so it is *possible* that the blows were simultaneous. On the other hand, the first blow could have been at least several hours old when Miss Edwards died.'

Great, Paniatowski thought. Bloody great!

'How much damage would the first blow have done?' she asked.

'Again, I am unable to give you a clear-cut answer. It may have rendered her unconscious, or it may have just given her a headache. In cases like this, each individual is different, and, of course, chance always plays a part.'

Paniatowski took out her packet of cigarettes, then, remembering that the taste of formaldehyde did little to enhance the smoking experience, she put them away again.

She had already ruled out the idea that the murderer had two weapons in his hands when he killed Mary, but had he been responsible for the diagonal injury?

No – because if he had hit Mary earlier, she would not have just stood there while he waved the poker in her face.

'You are quite right, Monika,' Shastri said. 'Though my scientific training tells me that I can reach no firm conclusion, my common sense tells me that the first injury was accidental.'

'You're doing it again,' Paniatowski told her.

The woman behind the desk at the Whitebridge central library was around twenty-five years' old. She had blonde hair and a firm bosom, and even though they weren't visible below the desk, anyone looking at her would have known instinctively that she had a pretty sensational pair of legs.

But sensational legs were – for once – the last thing on DC Simcox's mind, as he burst into the library, having run all the way from the pub.

'I need . . . I need to speak to Miss Dobson,' he gasped. 'Is she in?'

The blonde smiled.

'I'm Miss Dobson,' she said. 'How can I help you?'

She was Miss Dobson? She couldn't be! Yet she seemed to have the same voice as the woman who'd rung the incident room.

'I'm DC Mark Simcox,' he said. 'If you remember, we spoke earlier this morning.'

The smile froze, and then drained completely away.

'I spoke to someone,' Miss Dobson said, 'but I don't know whether it was you or not, because *whoever* it was didn't have the common courtesy to tell me his name.'

'I'm . . . I'm sorry about that,' he said.

And he was thinking, Why didn't I believe her? Why didn't I pick up on the fact that if she knew the victim was American, she must have actually met her – because one of the details that had been held back had been her nationality?

'The thing is, Miss Dobson, I should have reported your phone call, and I didn't,' Simcox confessed.

'And why was that?'

Why *was* that – a very good question to which the truth was the worst possible answer.

'Straight after your call, I got another one from a woman who was threatening to kill herself,' Simcox lied. 'She was serious – I could tell she was serious – and I knew that if I put the phone down, she'd really do it. So I kept talking to her. I must have been on the phone for nearly an hour, but by the time she rang off, she was really sounding much better.'

He saw with relief that Miss Dobson was smiling again.

'So you're a bit of a hero,' she said.

'I wouldn't go that far,' he protested.

'No,' she replied, 'neither would I.'

'The thing is, when I do report what you've told me, my inspector will want to know why it took me so long,' Simcox said.

'Yes, I expect he will.'

'And since an hour or two isn't going to make much of a difference to the progress—'

'It's more like three hours since I called you.'

'Isn't going to make much of a difference to the progress of the investigation, I was wondering if I could ask you to say that you didn't actually phone until much later.'

'I don't want to get in trouble myself,' Miss Dobson mused.

'You won't. I swear you won't.'

'Well, since you've spent the morning doing a good deed,

I suppose there'll be no harm in me stretching the truth for once,' Miss Dobson said.

'Thank you, thank you,' Simcox said, with relief. 'Well, I'd . . . uh . . .' He started to back away from the counter. 'They'll be expecting me in the incident room.'

Miss Dobson's smile broadened. 'I'm sure they will,' she said. 'I'm sure they'd be quite lost without you.'

As Simcox made his way down the library steps, he was starting to feel better. By his quick thinking, he had managed to snatch victory from the jaws of defeat, he told himself.

God, he was good in a crisis!

Back inside the library, Miss Dobson was wondering whether or not she'd done the right thing. Simcox obviously wasn't a very good policeman, and the sooner he and his superiors realised that, the better all round. On the other hand, he had looked so pathetic, and refusing to do what he wanted would have been a little like sticking a hat pin in the paw of a small sick puppy.

The first thing that George Clegg became aware of when he came round was the cold, which had wrapped itself around him in an icy shroud, chilling his bones and making the tips of his fingers tingle.

The second thing was that he was sprawled in his old familiar armchair, in front of a fire which had long since burnt itself out.

How long had he been there?

How much time had passed since he'd seen the young woman's picture in the newspaper, and understood that something dreadful – something almost unimaginable – had happened?

The discomfort was still there in his chest, but he was going to have to learn to ignore it, because there was something vital he had to do.

Slowly and painfully, he eased himself out of the chair and made his way shakily to the front door.

When he stepped outside, he realised immediately how bitterly cold the air was, but he did not go back into the house for his heavy overcoat, because that would have taken too much time – and anyway, he was not sure he could summon up the strength for all the twisting and turning that would be required to put the coat on.

The street was deserted, and there was no smoke coming out of the chimneys of any of the houses.

In the past, he had considered himself very lucky to be surrounded by neighbours who were thoroughly decent people – people who wanted nothing from the state, as he hadn't when he'd been younger, and expected to work for what they had.

Now, he wished there had been at least a few scroungers living on the street, because even scroungers, on seeing the shape he was in, would have helped him – even scroungers would have made sure that, even if he could not deliver it himself, the police would get his vitally important message.

He could see the bright red telephone box – almost like a beacon – at the end of the road.

A few years earlier – perhaps even as little as twelve months earlier – it would not have seemed very far away at all.

But things were different now. Ellie's death had robbed him of his vitality. It was as if his body, responding to his grief, had begun to shut down. And that phone box – though it could not have been more than a hundred yards away – seemed as distant as Tibet.

He took a deep breath, tried not to think about the ever-tightening band of pain around his chest, and took a tentative step towards the box.

He did not notice the black ice until he stepped on it, and by then it was too late.

He felt his legs fly from under him, and then the jarring of his spine as it made contact with the hard pavement.

JOURNAL

You simply can't buy a copy of the *New York Times Review of Books* in Whitebridge.

It's no loss. The *Review* is staffed by loathsome creatures with college degrees and a serious humanity deficit. They are like those men in bars who watch women come in, then turn to their friends and say, 'Jeez, I wouldn't date her – she's a dog.' And it doesn't ever occur to these pot-bellied drinkers that while the women they're dismissing so easily are not exactly Jane Fonda, the face that greets *them* in the shaving mirror each morning would make Woody Allen look like a real hunk.

Critics! They are slavering beasts who sink their teeth into a living thing and tear it to shreds. They are wreckers who send their sledgehammers smashing into the cornerstones of delicate structures that other – more worthy souls – have put their hearts into.

People change, and situations change, and, in twelve months' time, I might have quite a different opinion of the yellow-teethed rodents who inhabit the Times Tower. I doubt it, but I suppose it is a slim possibility.

In the meantime, rats are rats, and I want nothing to do with them.

Question: if all the above is true, then why did I spend the entire morning scouring every newsagents in Whitebridge for a copy of the *Review*?

SIX

The team had ordered a late lunch of sandwiches from the Royal Vic's justly famous kitchen, and sat eating them at a table in the corner of the incident room. Paniatowski had chosen roast pork, Crane had plumped for Bavarian ham, and Beresford had asked for a corned beef sandwich in which both the bread and the corned beef must be thickly sliced. Meadows, always one to do things differently, had gone to the kitchen to prepare her own sandwich, and so far none of the others had plucked up the nerve to ask her exactly what was in it.

'The first thing I want to deal with is the tattoo, so that we can get it out of the way,' Paniatowski said. 'If you remember, I saw it as a possible way of finding out which state Mary was from, but it turns out that the expert thinks it's a butterfly that only lives in Lancashire and Cumbria. So either the expert's mistaken – which is more than possible, considering it was only a tattoo he was working with – or her family originally came from Lancashire, and she had it done as a reminder of her roots. But I don't really see how that helps us, either.'

'Can I say something, boss?' Crane asked.

'Of course, Jack.'

'It could be there as a reminder of her roots, but it could also be the symbol of a promise that she made to herself.'

'What kind of promise?'

'That one day she'd make the journey – the pilgrimage, if you want to call it that – to Whitebridge. There are lots of similar examples in literature, and—'

'Oh, come on now, Jack,' Beresford said. 'This isn't literature, lad – it's real life.'

'The thing you don't seem to appreciate, sir, is that literature isn't something that's totally distinct from real life,' Crane countered. 'On the contrary, it both draws on real life and influences it.'

'I'm sure that theory would go down very well with your clever mates in Oxford . . .' Beresford began.

Then he noticed that Paniatowski was glaring at him, and dried up.

'You may be right, Jack,' Paniatowski said. 'Possibly she had been planning to come to Whitebridge for a long time – and possibly the tattoo was a symbol of her commitment. But I don't see how, for the moment at least, that contributes anything to the investigation. Do you see a way in which it might?'

'No, boss, I don't,' Crane admitted.

Paniatowski turned to Beresford. 'So what have your lads come up with, Colin?'

'We still have a lot of Mary's time in Whitebridge unaccounted for,' Beresford confessed, 'but we are making progress. We've talked to all the shop assistants who sold Mary her clothes . . .'

'How can you be sure you've spoken to *all* of them?'

'Because we've matched all the clothes hanging in the bedroom closet with the assistants who sold them to Mary.'

'Fair enough. Carry on.'

'One of the assistants wondered why anyone who dressed so nicely would want to buy any of the tat that her shop had on offer – she didn't phrase it quite like that, of course, but it's what she meant. The other assistants didn't make any comment on how she was dressed, so I think we can assume she only bought one Mousy Mary outfit wearing her Model Mary clothes, and she did the rest of her shopping wearing that.'

'Yes, it's looking like she abandoned Model Mary as quickly as she could,' Meadows said. 'But in that case, why didn't she check out of the Royal Vic and book into a modest boarding house?'

It was a question that they simply didn't yet have enough information to answer, so none of them even tried.

'We also know that she spent two whole days last week in the microfiche section of Whitebridge Central Library, going through old newspapers,' Beresford continued.

'She was obviously doing research – but what exactly was it she was researching?' Paniatowski said. 'And to what end?'

The rest of the team shrugged.

'But at least it explains all the coloured pens you found in her suite,' Crane said.

'Does it?' Paniatowski asked. 'How?'

'When you're doing research, not everything you find is of equal importance,' Crane said. 'In addition, some of the material may relate to one side of the problem, and some to another. And of course, it's sometimes necessary to draw a connecting line between two sets of data. You can end up with a really confused mess, and colour coding just helps to make everything a little bit clearer.'

'So we know she was approaching her research in a serious – maybe even professional – manner,' Paniatowski mused. 'Have you got anything else for us, Colin?'

'Yes,' Beresford said. 'And I think that this is the best lead we've come across so far.'

George Clegg had often seen beetles on their backs – kicking their legs in the air in a futile attempt to right themselves – but he had never thought he would ever be like them.

And I'm not like them, he told himself. I'm a man, and when I die, I'm going to die like a man.

He managed to roll over onto his side, and then – by making a huge effort – to get onto his hands and knees.

What next?

He needed some support if he was ever to stand upright again, but the closest lamppost was several yards away, and even if he managed to crawl to it, there was nothing he could really hold onto.

He turned, with all the slowness and lack of grace of a manoeuvring tortoise, until he was facing the nearest house. It, like all the other houses on the street, had long sash windows which stopped less than two feet from the pavement. If he could get one hand on the window sill, and then the other, he might just be able to lever himself up.

If he had the strength!

You have to have the strength, he thought. You owe it to that girl to find the strength.

And suddenly he realised that it was not only the girl he

owed. He also had a debt – though he couldn't even begin to explain the connection – to his long-dead uncle.

Beresford unrolled the artist's impressions of the man who had attacked Mary in the Rising Sun, and the woman who had been with her at the time, and then filled the rest of the team in on the background.

'Mary humiliated him,' Beresford said, 'and he doesn't look to me like the kind of man who'd be willing to let her get away with it. Anyway, I showed this sketch around the hotel, and the doorman, who struck me as a very reliable witness, definitely recognises him.'

The wind is blowing in from the snow-covered moors, and carries with it a ferocious cold that that seems capable of cutting through to the bone, which is why, instead of standing outside the Royal Vic, as he usually would, Wally White has positioned himself in the lobby.

He keeps his eyes firmly on the street, because if a taxi pulls up, bringing new guests, those guests will expect the doorman to be there to open the taxi door for them and make arrangements for their luggage.

Cars go past, but there is little pedestrian traffic, because the only people out in this weather are the ones who have to be.

The first time the man walks past, Wally registers no more than the facts that he appears to be a real rough bugger, and that instead of looking ahead of him, at where he is going – as most folk would – he keeps taking sideways glances at the hotel.

The second time he appears – walking in the opposite direction – Wally hardly looks at him, but the third time, the doorman starts studying him more closely.

'He walked past the hotel ten times in total,' Beresford said.

'Why didn't the doorman challenge him?' Meadows asked.

'On what grounds could he have done that? The man wasn't annoying the guests – because there were none out there to annoy. He could easily have arranged to meet somebody outside the hotel, and was just waiting for them to turn up. But I'm convinced that what he was really doing was watching the hotel – or, more precisely, he was watching for Mary Edwards.'

'Then why run the risk of drawing attention to himself?' Paniatowski asked. 'Surely the best way to carry out surveillance would be to select a spot in which he could see the hotel, but – because of the angle – the people in the hotel wouldn't notice him unless they were specifically looking for him. And once he'd found that safe spot, why wouldn't he simply stay there?'

Beresford smiled with what might possibly have been a little self-congratulation.

'Under normal circumstances, what you've just said is quite true,' he agreed. 'In fact, it's a standard surveillance technique. But remember, boss, it was brass monkey weather out there that day, and if he'd stayed in one spot he ran the risk of coming down with a serious case of hypothermia.'

'Do we know who he is?' Paniatowski asked.

'No, we don't.'

'So he doesn't have a record?'

'I've had one of my lads going through criminal records, but so far he's come up with no match, so I've arranged with the television stations and newspapers to run the pictures this evening, with the usual gubbins about police being anxious to talk to them, etc, etc, and I'd be more than surprised if I didn't have a name by tomorrow morning.'

'Anything else?' Paniatowski asked.

'No,' Beresford admitted. 'That's about it.'

'But you're still doing door-to-door?'

'Yes.'

'Good,' Paniatowski said.

'I . . . I want to tell you who killed that woman in the hotel,' said the strangled voice at the other end of the line.

DC Holland, manning one of the phones in the Royal Vic ballroom, wondered if the caller really was as old and distressed as he sounded.

Probably not, he decided, as he pictured a group of teenagers standing around a phone, with one of them doing the voice while the others were working hard at containing their laughter.

Still, there was a laid-down procedure to be followed, whether or not the caller was a hoaxer.

'Before we go any further, I will need your name and address, sir,' the detective constable said.

'Good God, man, didn't you . . . didn't you . . . hear what I just said?' the caller asked.

'I'm afraid I must insist, sir.'

'My name's George Clegg, and I live at 33 Hope Terrace.'

'Are you ringing from your home?'

'No, I don't have a phone at home. I'm calling from the box at the end of the street.'

Most hoaxers would have rung off by then, but maybe this one was brighter – and sneakier – than the average, and, urged on by his mates, was prepared to take the game as far as he could.

'That's fine, Mr Clegg,' Holland said. 'Now the next step is for you to tell me something about Mary Edwards which will prove to my satisfaction that you have actually had some kind of contact with her.'

'Her name wasn't Mary at all. It was Mag—'

'Can you provide me with such a detail, Mr Clegg? Remember, it must be verifiable.'

'I don't know what you want,' said the caller, who sounded like he was really fighting for breath now. 'I'm not sure what you mean by verifiable detail.'

'Well, for example, you could tell me that she had a scar across her left cheek, or that she spoke with a French accent.'

'She . . . she had a butterfly tattoo on her wrist. She said it were a northern brown argus.'

Jesus, Holland thought, this feller wasn't just genuine – he was a hundred per cent gold-plated genuine.

'You said you had information about who might have killed Mary Edwards, sir,' he said.

'I . . . uh . . .' George Clegg replied.

And then Holland heard the sound of a heavy object falling.

'Can you hear me, Mr Clegg?' he asked.

There was no response.

'Help is on its way,' Holland promised. 'We'll get there as quickly as we can, so you hold on.'

'Let's move on to the American angle,' Paniatowski said. 'It's possible – even probable – that Mary Edwards isn't our victim's real name at all, and that's why, according to Kate, she went out of her way to avoid showing the desk clerk at the Royal Vic her passport.'

'It would also explain why she paid for everything in cash,' Crane said. 'Her credit cards will be in her real name.'

'Exactly,' Paniatowski agreed. 'She didn't want anyone to know who she really was, and since we can assume it was the killer who took away her passport, it seems he didn't want it to be known, either. I've asked the Home Office for the details of any American women of roughly the right age who entered the country round about two weeks ago, but it's a massive job collating the information, because we don't know what her point of entry was, and we don't know for sure if it *was* two weeks, or if she'd been here much longer.'

'Shit!' Beresford said.

'So we're going to try and get the information from the other side of the pond,' Paniatowski continued, 'which is why we have these.'

She showed them the photographs of Mary after Bunny had finished working on her.

'She looks like a completely different person in this picture,' Beresford said, astonished.

'Yes – but only to the untrained, masculine eye,' Meadows muttered softly to herself.

'Fred Mahoney's going to blitz the local New York papers and television with this,' Paniatowski said. 'He's also asked for a set of Mary's fingerprints.'

'Which won't be of much use at all, unless she has a criminal record,' Beresford said.

'That's where you're wrong,' Paniatowski told him. 'If she's ever had a civil service job, or applied for a driving license, the authorities will have her prints on record.'

Beresford shook his head in admiration. 'Why can't we

have a system like that?' he asked. 'It would make our jobs a hell of a lot easier.'

'And less fun,' Meadows said.

Paniatowski related her conversation with Arthur Tyndale.

'From what the Lone Ranger told me, it's obvious that she saw the threat as coming from the USA,' she said. 'So what theories can we put on the table? One: Mary was a con artist – false name and disguise – who came to Whitebridge to pull a scam, and was killed by her intended victim.'

'Two,' Meadows said. 'Basically the same as One, except that her victim was caught in a previous scam, and sent a hit man across to kill her.'

'Three: Mary got into a fight with a feller in a pub, and he killed her for revenge,' Beresford said.

'The problem is, they're all plausible,' Paniatowski said, 'and they're not even comprehensive. Maybe the man in the pub wasn't the only person Mary pissed off. Maybe there were half a dozen of them, and it was one of the others who killed her. We need to narrow down the field, and we can only do that by establishing *why* she was here, and what she did *while* she was here. So, Colin, I want the door-to-door intensified, because she couldn't have stayed in her room for most of those two weeks, so somebody must have seen her.'

'Got it,' Beresford said.

'Where are her notes?' Crane asked, out of the blue.

'Her notes?' Beresford repeated.

'She spent two whole days in the library, doing research. No one can absorb that much information in their heads – and anyway, she had all those coloured pens – so she must have taken notes.'

'Maybe she decided the notes were no good, and threw them away,' Paniatowski suggested.

'When you've invested two days of your life in research, you don't throw your notes away,' Crane said. 'You might tell yourself that, from a logical viewpoint, they'll never be any use, but there's always a nagging voice in your head that warns you they just *might* be. In fact, you almost convince yourself that the moment you've chucked them out, fate will arrange it so that you *do* need them.' He smiled. 'Trust me on this – trust someone who's got a trunk full of notes he just can't bring himself to dump.'

'If you're right, then the killer took the notes as well as the passport,' Paniatowski said. She pushed her sandwiches to one side, and reached into her handbag for her packet of cigarettes. 'Jack, I want you to go down to the central library and find out what fascinated Mary about newspapers that were published over fifty years ago, in 1924.'

Crane's face fell at the thought of being stuck in the library when he could have been out on the street.

'I really talked myself into that bloody job, didn't I, boss?' he said, mournfully.

'No, I was always going to send you to the library, because it's a part of the "why" she was here,' Paniatowski said. 'All you've just done is to make this particular task seem even more important.'

'I don't see how I go about it, boss,' Crane admitted. 'The average newspaper is probably about thirty pages long, and there are six of them every week for fifty-two weeks a year.'

'True,' Paniatowski agreed.

'If it had been actual physical newspapers she'd been looking at, there might be some evidence of that. She might have underlined something, or made a note in the margin. You're not supposed to, but a lot of people do. But it's not paper, is it? It's microfiche – so how am I supposed to work out what, in particular, she was interested in?'

'Fair point,' Paniatowski agreed. 'Let's see if we can narrow things down. If Mary was collecting small, isolated pieces of information – recipes, say, or births, marriages and deaths – then you're never going to find out what she was looking at. But my guess is that she didn't come all this way, spend so much money, and don a disguise, for that sort of thing. She came to look at one big story – which she may have intended to use in her scam, if there was, in fact, a scam – and it took her two days to look at it properly. So find that big story – there can't be many of them.'

'What if your supposition is wrong?' Crane asked. 'What if she came here to check her ancestry, so births, marriages and deaths were exactly what she was looking at?'

'It's not ancestry,' Paniatowski said.

'Are you sure?

'I'm sure. If it had been tracing her roots, she wouldn't have confined herself to just one year. But you're quite right, Jack, it could all be a dead end. That's police work for you – like the princess has to kiss a lot of frogs before she finds her handsome prince, we have to sift through a lot of shit before we uncover the nugget of truth.' She took a drag of her cigarette. 'Right, that's it. As soon as you've finished your sandwiches, you can get back to work.' She stood up – leading by example. 'Oh, there is just one more thing – what's in your sandwiches, Kate?'

'It's cucumber,' Meadows replied, 'sliced so finely you could read a 1924 newspaper through it.'

Yes, Paniatowski thought, it would have to have been something like that, wouldn't it?

Paniatowski and Beresford were sitting in the cafeteria of Whitebridge General hospital. The tea they were sipping was no better than that served up in the police canteen, but at least it was a different sort of awful.

'There are two things that make George Clegg a credible witness,' Paniatowski said. 'The first is that he not only knew about the tattoo, he knew it was a northern brown argus – and he could only have got that information from Mary Edwards. The second is that he knew that wasn't her real name.'

'Did he say what her real name was?' Beresford asked.

'Sort of,' Paniatowski told him.

She took a small tape recorder out of her jacket pocket, and pressed the play button.

'*Now the next step is for you to tell me something about Mary Edwards which will prove to my satisfaction that you have actually had some kind of contact with her,*' said a tinny voice belonging to DC Holland.

'*Her name wasn't Mary at all. It was Mag . . .*'

'*Can you provide me with such a detail, Mr Clegg? Remember, it must be verifiable.*'

Paniatowski pressed rewind for a second, then hit the play button again.

'. . . *that you have actually had some kind of contact with her.*'

'*Her name wasn't Mary at all. It was Mag . . .*'

'He was obviously in some physical distress when he was making the call, but it sounds like "Mag" or "Marg", which could mean that he believes she's called Margaret,' Paniatowski said.

'If Holland had just cut through the bloody procedure . . .' Beresford said, angrily.

'You can't have it both ways,' Paniatowski told him. 'You can't bollock them when they *don't* follow procedure, and bollock them when they *do.*'

'True,' Beresford agreed. 'Do you think he really does know who killed Mary?'

'I don't know. But what I do know is that he was having a heart attack, yet he battled his way to the phone box. And when he got there, he didn't ring for an ambulance for himself – he rang us to tell us what he knew. So, at the very least, we have to think that *he* believes he knows who the killer is, don't we?'

'I suppose so,' Beresford said. 'What condition is he in?'

'Not good. He was unconscious when the ambulance reached the phone box, and he still hasn't come round. The doctor thinks he may *never* come round, but they're not talking about switching off the life-support system quite yet. I want a detective constable in twenty-four-hour attendance at his bedside, just in case he does regain consciousness. And make sure you only use good people, Colin – I don't want anyone in there who thinks it's a soft option.'

JOURNAL

I am building up a picture in my mind of both the time and the place, and the group photograph of the mill's annual day trip to Blackpool has been invaluable to me.

There is Tom Clegg. He has a thin face and a gawky body, but there is something gentle – almost feminine – about him. His eyes are big and round, like those of a frightened doe. All those around him have abandoned their cares for the day – cast aside thoughts of the miserable existence that awaits them at the end of the charabanc (bus) ride home. But not Tom! He cannot forget the hostile world he inhabits because – so his expression in the photograph says – it travels around in his head.

Wilfred and Oswald Hardcastle are wearing top hats and are standing a little apart from the group, because though they are *with* their workers, they are not *of* their workers.

It is clear that they are brothers, though they are very, very different.

Wilfred looks stern and unbending – the sort of man who may get satisfaction out of life, but will never know pleasure. His expression says that there are no second chances with him. He does not know – how could he? – that he has only a few days to live, but I know, because I have seen the date on the back of the photograph.

Oswald is – as they say in Lancashire – a different kettle of fish entirely. A photograph is a static thing, and so I cannot claim with any degree of certainty that his eyes are constantly roving across the scene, but I *sense* that they are.

Wilfred, the down-to-earth businessman is, it seems to me, always on the look-out for opportunities, but Oswald, his dissolute brother, is always searching for chances, which is a different thing altogether.

And then there is John Entwistle – solid, square, with a moustache the size and thickness of a small yard-brush (a yard in Lancashire, I have learned, is not like a yard in the States, but is a small enclosed area at the back of the house, where formerly – and sometimes still – the toilet facilities are located). John has chosen to wear neither the cloth cap of the workers nor a top hat of the bosses, and instead stands bareheaded, close to the charabanc, as if he feels it is his responsibility to see that no one steals it. He looks dependable, and he would have to have been, since both the workers and the bosses do depend on him.

It could be said that this is all conjecture. It could be said that I went into this whole thing with foreknowledge, and that everything I read in the photograph is a result of that foreknowledge.

But I think there's more to it than that. I feel a *connection*. These men are not just frozen images in an old faded photograph. To me, they are real people – and I understand them.

SEVEN

Harvey Morgan was sitting in the back of a limo, reading the *Washington Post* book section and smoking his first cigar of the morning. (Cuban, and hence supposedly unavailable in the USA, but hey, when you knew people, you knew people). He was not aware that though it was only nine-thirty in New York City, it was already early afternoon in Whitebridge, but then he wouldn't have *wanted* to be aware, any more than he would have cared what time it was in Moscow or Tokyo, because the only time that really mattered was Manhattan time.

He loved Manhattan Island with what was, for him, a totally uncharacteristic and almost Disney-like fancy, and he sometimes thought of it as a sort of magic kingdom, bounded by a moat called the East River on one side and by a second moat called the Hudson River on the other. On this island, he was King Arthur – or, at least one of many King Arthurs – and his writers were his Knights of the Round Table. For him, the outside world existed only to pay his knights their rightful tribute – in the form of royalties on book sales – a generous percentage of which, as their monarch, he would skim off for himself.

There were two kinds of literary agents, he would tell anyone who asked him for an insight into the business. There were those who discovered brilliant new writers and nurtured them like the delicate flowers they were, and there were those who handled authors who sold books by the truckload. He was one of the latter kind, because he had decided early in his career that while it probably felt great to be lionised by the literati at artistic cocktail parties, it was even better to have a four-bedroom cabin overlooking Lake George, and a car collection that had been featured in enough glossy men's magazines for him to have lost count of how many it actually was.

Yet though he was in the business for the money, he did genuinely care about his authors, and rarely dropped them from his list when their sales began to dip. He cared about his staff, too (within the limits imposed by the laws of the jungle that was the New York publishing world, naturally), and when, having completed the journey from the limo to his office, he noticed that his secretary, Linda Kaufmann, was crying, he felt a compassion which was only mildly tinged with irritation.

'Has Jack been at it again?' he asked. 'Jeez, why can't that douche bag of a husband of yours learn to keep it in his pants?'

'It's . . . it's not Jack,' Linda told him. 'It's this.'

She held a copy of the day's *New York Times* to him, opened at page forty-two.

'Hundreds of dead fish found in the Hudson?' Morgan asked, scanning the headline.

'No, not that – below it.'

Morgan looked at the picture of the blonde woman, and read the short text underneath.

'This is a corpse,' he said. 'What's it got to do with us?'

'It's Melissa Evans,' the secretary sobbed.

'No, it isn't,' Morgan said. 'Listen, Linda my dear, just because Melissa happens to be in England, it don't necessarily follow that any corpse that turns up there has to be her.'

'It is her,' the secretary said. 'Look again.'

And because he sometimes allowed his secretary to bully him – or rather, *told* himself that he allowed it – he did take a second look.

'I still don't see it,' he confessed.

'That's because of the way the make-up's been applied,' Linda said, addressing him now almost as she would talk to a very young – and not particularly bright – child. 'Whoever did it—'

'Did what?'

'Whoever made up her face after she'd been killed.'

'Do people really do that to people?' asked Morgan, looking slightly sick. 'I mean, do *live* people really do it to *dead* people?'

'Of course they do! Haven't you ever wondered, when you've gone to funerals, why the deceased person looks so good – sometimes even better than he looked in life?'

'I don't look at corpses,' Morgan said. 'I go to funerals, but

I don't look at corpses. Once they're gone, they're dead to me.'

'The thing is, some faces are so limiting that there's only one way you can go with them to make them as attractive as they can be. But Melissa had great bone structure. There's two or three different ways to get her looking good, and whoever made her up chose a different way to the one she herself chose in life. But it's her. I'm sure of it.'

'You want me to ring this Captain Mahoney whose number is in the paper, don't you?' Morgan asked, ready to bow to the inevitable.

'Yes, I do,' the secretary confirmed.

'And when I've done that for you, do you think you might be able to get back to work?'

'I can try.'

Miss Dobson greeted Jack Crane from the librarian's desk with a broad – if somewhat pre-programmed – smile, but that quickly faded away when he showed her his warrant card.

'You're here about that poor woman's murder, aren't you?' she asked.

'That's right,' Crane agreed, pushing to the back of his mind that she was a very attractive young woman. 'What can you tell me about the victim?'

'Surprisingly enough, not a great deal,' Miss Dobson said regretfully.

'Why is it surprising?' Crane wondered.

'Because normally, I could give you a thumbnail sketch of anyone who spent any amount of time working in the stacks. Would you like an example of what I mean?'

'If you wouldn't mind.'

'Take this woman who started coming in here a few months ago. I know that her name is Elsie, she's in her early sixties, and she lives on Sycamore Street. She has two grown-up children – the son's a motor mechanic and the daughter's a hairdresser – and she's a widow. She'd never have thought about tracing her ancestry if her husband hadn't died, and she only took it up *then* because she was feeling lost, and knew she had do *something*. But it's opened new worlds for her.

She's made tons of friends, and now she's studying for a certificate in genealogy in the extra-mural department of the University of Mid Lancs.'

'Most impressive,' Crane said.

'Yes, I thought she was, too.'

'I mean *you're* impressive,' Crane told her. 'How did you manage to learn all that about Elsie?'

'Everybody has to take a break from study now and again, and if I was free when she was taking one of hers, she'd come over and chat to me. People find it easy to talk to librarians. I think we're a bit like priests in that way – except that we're less imposing and judgmental.'

'Yes, I can see that most people would find it *very* easy to talk to you,' Crane said.

Miss Dobson smiled.

'You're not flirting with me, are you?' she asked.

Damn, Crane thought, that's exactly what I'm doing.

'No, I'm not flirting,' he said seriously. 'I'm making a professional assessment of your approachability.'

'Well, that's all right then,' Miss Dobson said, still smiling, but now rather mischievously.

'I take it from what you've said that Mary Edwards wasn't in the habit of chatting to you,' Crane answered, pumping as much officialdom into his tone as he could muster at that moment.

'No, she wasn't,' Miss Dobson agreed. 'Oh, don't get me wrong, she was polite enough. She'd say hello when she arrived, and goodbye when she left, but there was no real feeling of human contact. And she never asked for my help, which most of the researchers do. She seemed to have a very *professional* approach to her research – and that's a novelty in here, too.'

'She wanted to study the local papers from 1924, didn't she?'

'Yes, that's right.'

'Are you sure it was 1924?' Crane asked – because the last thing he wanted to do was plough his way through the wrong year.

'Yes, I'm certain,' Miss Dobson said.

'Is there some special reason you remember?'

Miss Dobson frowned. 'No, I don't think so. And there's no real reason why I *should* remember it, is there?'

'Close your eyes,' Crane said.

'Why?'

'Because doing it will help you to drag up memories from your subconscious mind.'

Miss Dobson giggled. 'That sounds almost kinky,' she said, but she closed her eyes anyway.

'You're standing behind your desk when she walks in,' Crane said softly. 'Can you see her?'

'Yes.'

'What's she wearing?'

'A blue dress, like the one I saw in the Marks and Spencer's window, and thought of buying for myself.'

'Is she carrying anything?'

'Yes, she's got a leather briefcase in her hand. It has brass buckles, and you can tell it must have cost a bomb.'

There was no briefcase listed on the crime scene inventory, so the killer must have taken that, too.

'So there's Miss Edwards in her blue Marks and Spencer's dress,' Crane said softly. 'What do you say to her?'

'I say something like, "Good morning, madam. Is there anything I can do to assist you?".'

'And how does she reply?'

'She says, "Have you got copies of the local newspapers from 1924?" And I say, "We haven't got the actual papers, but we do have them on microfiche."' Miss Dobson opened her eyes. 'Now I know why I remember the date so clearly – it was the expression on her face!'

'What about the expression?'

'Do you remember a couple of minutes ago, when you said you thought most people would find it easy to talk to me, and I asked if you were flirting?' Miss Dobson asked.

'Yes,' Crane replied, uneasily.

'Well, the expression on your face then was the exact twin of the expression on Miss Edwards' face when she said she wanted to look at the newspapers from 1924. It was a "Gosh-I-wish-I-hadn't-said-that-because-now-I've-given-the-whole-game-away" face. I think she was wishing she hadn't been so specific, and had just said "the 1920s". And *I* thought, What's so special about 1924? That's why it stuck in my mind.' She smiled again. 'You are clever, aren't you – getting that out of me when I didn't even know it was in there.'

'I was just employing a standard investigative technique, Miss Dobson,' Crane said.

'Sometimes, it doesn't really matter if you give the game away, you know,' the librarian said. 'And by the way, you can call me Janet if you want to.'

Fred Mahoney was on the phone from New York City.

'I've finally got a name for you to fit to that cadaver of yours, Monika,' he said.

'Are you sure about that?'

'Hell, yes – sure enough to bet the farm on it. As soon as we got a tentative identification from her agent – and a stone cold certain one from his secretary, Linda – we matched the prints you sent me against the ones in the DMV, and there's a perfect fit.'

'What's this about her agent?' Paniatowski asked. 'What did she need an agent *for*?'

'Oh yeah, you don't know about him yet, do you?' Mahoney said. 'She needs an agent because her name's Melissa Evans, and she writes the sort of sensationalist biography that makes my old lady stand in an all-night queue just so she can get her hands on one of the first copies off the press.'

Then what the hell was she doing in Whitebridge – where there really wasn't anybody famous – Paniatowski wondered.

'Have you read any of them yourself?' she asked

'Shit, Monika, I'm an as-hard-as-nails, old-style Noo York cop,' Mahoney said. 'I don't read anything but the sports pages.'

'So have you?' Paniatowski insisted.

'Yeah, yeah, I may have dipped into one or two of them,' Mahoney confessed. 'Hell, if Martha's gonna squander most of my pay on hardbacked books, I might as well get something out of it.'

'And what are they like?'

'Racy and pacy. And if even half the things she says are true . . . Well, let's just say I seem to have led a very sheltered life.'

'What happens next?'

'I'll be sending out some of my people in the next hour or so to talk to her family and friends.'

'Could I go public with the name?'

'When?'

Paniatowski did a quick calculation. 'I'd like to hold a press conference at six. That's about three and a half hours from now.'

'No problem. By then, it should have been broken gently to everybody close enough to her to need it breaking gently.'

'Another thing – would it be OK with you if I talked to Mary Edwards' . . . I mean Melissa Evans' . . . agent?'

'I don't see why it wouldn't be.'

'Then could you please give me his telephone number?'

'Sure thing.'

The first editions of the evening papers – with the artist's impressions of the man who attacked Mary/Melissa prominently displayed on the front page – appeared on the streets at three o'clock, but it was not until a quarter past four that someone rang the incident room to say he recognised the man and the woman.

It was DC Rowley who happened to catch the call.

'Will there be a reward?' the caller asked.

'Before we get onto anything like that, I need to take your name, sir,' Rowley said.

'I mean, if they've done summat wrong and you're looking for them, there's got to be a reward. It stands to reason.'

'This isn't the Wild West, sir,' Rowley said, chuckling softly.

'No,' his caller agreed, mystified. 'It's Whitebridge.'

Well, we've certainly got a rocket scientist on our hands here, Rowley thought.

'What I meant was that in this country, we don't pay bounties. You're supposed to do your civic duty as a . . . well, as a citizen . . . without any thought of reward,' he explained.

'Listen,' the caller said, 'I'm not giving up Frankie Flynn unless there's some money in it for me . . . oh shit!'

'Well, since you've already given me his name, you might as well give me his address as well,' Rowley suggested.

'He's my next-door neighbour. He lives at 17 Navigation Road.'

'That's down by the canal, isn't it?'

'That's right.'

'I really do need your name, sir,' Rowley said.

'Well, you're not having it.'

'As you wish,' Rowley said easily. 'After all, it shouldn't be too hard to find you, now that we know you live at either number 15 or number 19 Navigation Road.'

'Oh shit!' the caller said, for a second time. 'Oh shit, oh shit, oh shit.'

And then he hung up.

Navigation Road was a row of terrace houses with front doors which opened straight onto the street, and backyards which opened onto the canal towpath. Its glory days had been the 1920s and 30s, when the mills had been working full pelt, and countless barges had delivered raw cotton from the Liverpool docks and taken back the finished products which were destined for the colonies. Back in those days, the end two cottages had served as a public house for the bargees, and the rest of them were occupied by mechanics, boat repairers and prostitutes.

With the decline of the mills and the related industries, the houses had been bought up by slum landlords, and rented out to anyone who couldn't afford anything better. Now, they were tottering on the edge of terminal dilapidation, and, on hot days, the stink of the canal seeped through every brick and roof tile.

Meadows and Beresford stood in the street, far enough away from number 17 to be invisible to anyone looking out of the window.

'Frankie Flynn's got form, but when the photo that's attached to his record was taken, he had long greasy hair, a beard and a moustache. Now, he's shaved it all off, and he looks a completely different person,' Beresford told the sergeant. 'That's why we didn't get on to him straight away.'

'What kind of form has he got?'

'Robbery, receiving, assault – the usual sort of stuff you'd associate with toe-rags of his ilk.'

'Is there anything in his record to indicate he's capable of murder?' Meadows asked.

'His level of violence seems to have intensified over the years, as is so often the case. The last time he was arrested, he nearly got done for GBH, but the complainant withdrew the charges, possibly as a result of intimidation. And for a man like him – a big macho shithead – being humiliated by Mary Edwards must have been almost too much to bear.'

'If, that is, he is actually the one who she kicked in the balls,' Meadows pointed out.

'Well, we're about to find out – one way or the other,' Beresford said.

He signalled to the patrol cars (one parked at the top of the street, the other at the bottom) that they should maintain their positions and he and Meadows moved in.

Beresford knocked on the door of number 17, and the knock was answered by a big man with a shaved head, who looked very similar to the sketch the police artist had produced.

'Mr Flynn?' Beresford asked.

'Piss off!' the man replied.

Beresford produced his warrant card, but the man didn't even bother to look at it.

'If you don't mind, Mr Flynn, we'd like you to come down to the station with us, to answer a few questions,' the inspector said.

'What if I do mind?'

Beresford sighed. 'Then, regretfully, Mr Flynn, I'm going to have to arrest you.'

'All right, I'll bloody come with you,' Flynn said, apparently bowing to the inevitable.

Beresford was fit and he was hard, and if he'd been expecting Flynn's fist to smash into his gut, he'd probably have tensed his muscles to cushion the blow. As it was, he was completely taken in by the other man's bluff, and didn't realise what was going to happen until a split second before it did – by which time it was, of course, much too late.

He doubled up – gasping for air – and then collapsed onto his knees.

To both her left and right, Meadows heard the sound of car doors slamming, rapidly followed by the thunder of heavy feet running.

Then someone shouted, 'Get clear, skip, we'll deal with the bastard!'

There was no way that was going to happen, she decided, because Flynn had hurt Colin, and Flynn was hers.

The problem was, it looked as if Flynn might not be *anybody's*. He'd obviously been struck by the enormity of what he'd done, and was gazing down at his fist as if it belonged to someone else.

Another couple of seconds, Meadows thought, and there was a real danger he might just surrender.

'What's the matter, Frankie?' she taunted. 'Have your balls dropped off – or are you just scared of me?'

Flynn took a wild swing at her. Meadows swayed slightly to the right, so that the punch whistled harmlessly past her. Hitting empty air, when he'd been expecting to make contact with muscle and bone, knocked Flynn slightly off-balance. He would have regained that balance in a second or two, but before he could, Meadows scraped the heel of her shoe – hard – down his shin.

Flynn howled with pain, and while he was thinking about how much it hurt, Meadows stepped back, then followed through on her initial attack with a high kick to his jaw.

She aimed the kick with some precision, so that instead of falling on top of Beresford, who was now spewing up his lunch, Flynn toppled over in the opposite direction.

He hit the ground on his back, and just lay there, perhaps trying to work out whether his shin hurt worse than his jaw, or if it was the other way around.

Meadows rolled him over, pulled his arms behind his back, and clicked the cuffs in place.

'That's two fights you've lost against women in just a few days,' she cooed. 'Shame on you, Frankie.'

She became aware that the rest of the team had formed a semi-circle around her, and were clapping enthusiastically.

She smiled. 'Why, thank you, gentlemen,' she said. 'Thank you from the bottom of my heart.'

JOURNAL

Whenever I feel horny in Manhattan, I just pick up the phone and place my order in the same way I would if I wanted a pizza, and a professional, who has been thoroughly briefed on my needs, is knocking on my door within half an hour. But what do you do when the feeling creeps up on you in a foreign country – or, more specifically, in a decaying mill town on the edge of the Lancashire moors?

I had no numbers to call, and no way of finding out what those numbers might be, so I went for a walk around the edge of the Boulevard, just after darkness had fallen. There were plenty of girls there, shivering in the scanty clothes they must wear to advertise their occupation, and there were two or three of them I would really have enjoyed a romp with.

But I had a couple of misgivings.

The first was that I didn't know how they'd react to my proposition. There are girls, I know, who are prepared to do things to the vilest old man that they wouldn't even consider with a young(ish!) attractive woman, and I was not sure I had the nerve to run the risk of being rebuffed. In fact, the very thought of having to walk away with a torrent of abuse following in my wake was enough to bring me out in a cold sweat.

The second misgiving was that I'd begun to wonder if these girls were as clean as their American counterparts.

I know, I know! It's arrogant – and probably bigoted – to assume that foreign whores have lower hygiene standards than American whores.

But there it is – the feeling would just not go away.

Plan B then – find a woman who not only isn't a professional, but isn't even a dyke (or, at least, doesn't yet *know* she's a dyke). I haven't done that very often back home – hey, given the busy lives we all lead, who has the time for seduction – but on the few occasions I *have* done it, it's been really sweet. I suppose, in a way, it must be how men feel when they've talked a virgin into their beds.

So I went to this pub called the Grapes. There were no women sitting alone, but I'd anticipated that, and was on the lookout for girls who looked easily detachable from their friends.

I found one – a pretty little peroxide blonde. I guessed she probably wasn't too educated, and probably not too amusing, but she looked clean and fresh and – most important of all – very suggestible.

The other girl sitting with her was a brunette with a sulky expression, and she just had to go.

I walked over to their table and said, 'Hi, I'm an American, all alone in a strange town. Would you mind if I sat down?'

The other girl – the brunette – said, 'Do you mind, we're having a private conversation here, aren't we, Sheila?'

But my girl said, 'Don't talk so daft, Doris. I'm sure that . . .'

She looked at me for a name.

'Marcia,' I supplied.

'I'm sure that Marcia's very interesting to talk to, and I'd love to hear about what it's like to live in America.'

As I sat down, I noticed that while Sheila's fingernails were beautifully clean, Doris had enough dirt under hers to grow potatoes in.

'What do you do for a living, Marcia?' Sheila asked me.

I thought briefly about saying I worked in television, then decided it would be safer to stick to talk radio.

It was enough.

'Just think of that!' Sheila said, eyes wide at the thought that such fabulous creatures as I could actually exist. 'Working on the radio! In America!'

For the next fifteen minutes or so, I let Sheila ask me questions and ignored the snorts of derision from her increasingly unhappy friend.

Then, when I judged the time was right, I said, 'Something's just occurred to me. I think my station could use you.'

'What do you mean?' she gasped.

And yes, she really did gasp.

'My station has this spot where we bring in guest interviewers from other English-speaking countries,' I told her. 'We've had Australians, New Zealanders, Canadians . . . they come from all over the place.'

'Australians, New Zealanders and Canadians,' Sheila repeated, reverentially.

'The job only lasts for a month, because New Yorkers are notoriously fickle, and by then the novelty has started to wear off – but hey, there's nothing wrong with a month in New York.'

'No,' she said, almost exploding. 'No, there isn't.'

'We fly you out, and put you up at a hotel,' I told her. 'We'd even pay you a wage, but we're only a small station, so it wouldn't be much.'

'How much is not much?' she asked.

'A hundred pounds a week,' I said, figuring she'd be lucky if she took home twenty in whatever job she was holding down at the moment.

'And do you really think I've got a chance?' she asked.

'I'm not promising anything, but I think you've got a very good chance.'

'So what do I have to do?'

'You make an audition tape, and I send it to my boss in New York.'

'Where do I go, and when do you want me to go there?' she asked, positively bubbling with excitement.

'The "where" is my suite in the Royal Victoria Hotel—'

'The Royal Victoria Hotel!' Sheila repeated, with considerable awe.

'Because that's where I keep the recording equipment. As to the "when" . . .' I pretended to think about it. 'My schedule's pretty full for the rest of my time in Whitebridge, so it would really have to be right now.'

'We came out tonight for a good laugh, not to sit in some poxy hotel room,' Doris said.

'Oh, didn't I make that clear, Doris?' I asked, sounding surprised.

'Make what clear?'

'You can't be there when we make the audition tape. I wouldn't mind it personally, but, you see, it's strict company policy.'

'So what happens to me?'

'You arrange to meet Sheila on another night.'

'You're not going to do it, are you?' Doris asked Sheila.

'It's my big chance,' Sheila said helplessly.

'So you're just going to ditch me?'

'Only for tonight. And when I've got the job in New York, you can come and stay with me. That's right, isn't it, Marcia?'

'That's right,' I agreed. 'Once you've got the job, there'll be no objection to having Doris around. We might even find a bit of work for her, too.'

But Doris was not to be bribed, and for a few seconds I thought she was going to be real trouble. I think she thought she was, too. Then she stood up and stormed out of the pub.

As Sheila and I walked back towards my hotel, I promised myself

I'd be fair with her. She'd get her flight to New York and the hotel, and she could even take Doris with her. She'd even get her hundred pounds a week. The only things I'd mentioned that would be missing were the promised job – and me.

Very generous of me, *n'est pas*?

Well yes, in a way, but compared to some of the top hookers I've occasionally engaged, it was still a bargain.

Halfway between the Grapes and the Royal Victoria, Sheila began to get cold feet.

'Doris is my best mate,' she said. 'I should never have treated her like that. You could see she was upset.'

'If she really is your best mate, she'll be fine in the morning,' I told her, 'because best mates don't stand in each others' way when there's a chance of them getting something good.'

'My very best mate,' Sheila repeated.

I decided it was time to take emergency measures, and seeing a pub called the Rising Sun just ahead of us, I said, 'Let's go in there and talk about what's best to do.'

By the time Sheila had downed a couple of strong gin and tonics, her doubts were starting to melt away, and I was just about to suggest we go back to my hotel when the man burst in, saw us together, and blew his stack.

'What are you doing here, Sheila?' he screamed.

'I'm talking to my friend,' Sheila replied weakly.

'It's Doris who's your friend, not this *thing*,' he told her.

It was immediately clear to me what had happened – that bitch Doris had followed us, and then had gone running to Sheila's husband. It was also clear that somebody needed to defuse the situation, and I decided that somebody had better be me.

So I stood up – to reason with him – but before I could say a word, the bastard hit me.

I dealt with him quickly and efficiently – as I'd been taught to – and left the pub. It had been a complete waste of an evening, I thought, and what I'd been planning to have Sheila do to me, I was now going to have to do to myself (which is not half as much fun).

What I didn't anticipate was that there would be any fall-out from the incident. But fall-out is what there has been. I've spotted the man near my hotel twice – and if I've spotted him twice, chances are that he's been there at other times, too. On the second of those occasions, it was dark, and I'd come out for a breath of fresh air. I was walking along the street when he suddenly appeared out of the shadows, on the other side of the road. I don't know what he was planning to do or say, but if a policeman – wearing one of those ridiculous pointy helmets – hadn't turned the corner at that moment, I'm sure he would have done or said *something*.

I'm a fool.

I bring down trouble on myself.

I'm my own worst enemy.

EIGHT

Apart from the twenty-six half-days a year when he sat on the bench, handing down custodial sentences of up to six months and fines of up to five thousand pounds, Brian Chubb worked as a chartered surveyor. He liked to think of himself as a fair man who, once he assumed the mantle of magistrate, carefully weighed up the evidence before reaching his decision. And generally speaking, he *was* fair – as long as he was dealing with men.

It was women who were the problem.

He liked women, but he also liked them to know their place, which – roughly speaking – was either at home or out on the arm of their partners. His own wife, Maureen, had been perfectly satisfactory in this respect, until early one morning – and quite unexpectedly – she had packed her bags and run away with a door-to-door insurance salesman called Derek.

The woman standing before him now clearly did *not* know her place, otherwise, she would never have sought to become a chief inspector. Women did have a role in the police force, Chubb thought – they were much better at breaking bad news than their male counterparts were, for example – but it was quite wrong that they should have the power to order grown men around.

'So what can I do for you, Miss Paniatowski?' he asked, hoping that his expression showed the disapproval he was not allowed to put into words.

'I'd like you to issue a search warrant for 33 Hope Terrace, the home of Mr George Clegg, sir,' Paniatowski replied.

Chubb frowned.

'Is Mr Clegg a known criminal?' he asked.

'No sir, he's—'

'In that case, have you asked the gentleman in question's permission to search his house, and been refused?'

'No sir, we can't—'

'Why haven't you asked his permission? Do you think there's some reason he's *likely* to refuse?'

'He's not in a position to either agree or refuse. He's in a coma in Whitebridge General.'

'You should have mentioned that earlier, then we would have wasted less time,' Chubb said, with some irritation. 'Do you expect to find evidence of the crime you are currently investigating in 33 Hope Terrace?'

'Not exactly, sir, no. But we are hoping to find information relating to the crime.'

'What kind of information?'

'We won't know until we find it.'

'That seems rather vague.'

'Then let me explain, sir. Before he collapsed, Mr Clegg rang the inquiry line and said he knew who killed Melissa Evans, and—'

'Melissa Evans? I thought the woman who was murdered in the Royal Victoria was called Mary Edwards.'

'So did we, sir, but it has recently emerged that Mary Edwards was not, in fact, her real name.'

'I must say, this investigation of yours does seem rather shambolic,' Chubb said.

'The point is that we believe that George Clegg does know the killer's name, and that we will find something in his house which will tell us *how* he knows that name.'

'It sounds to me more a case of woman's intuition than anything with a solid factual basis, Miss Paniatowski,' Chubb said, 'and you can't run a police force on woman's intuition.'

'With respect, sir—' Paniatowski began.

'If you have more tangible evidence, then by all means resubmit your application,' Chubb told her, 'but as things stand, I am certainly not going to sanction the invasion of a law-abiding citizen's home on a mere whim.'

'How did it go?' Meadows asked, as her boss climbed into the passenger seat of the Mini Cooper.

'Not well,' Paniatowski told her. 'I was an idiot. I wanted

to move quickly, so I took it to Chubb. What I should have done was waited until someone else became available.'

'When someone else does become available, you could always try again,' Meadows suggested.

'No point,' Paniatowski told her. 'Most of the others belong to the same funny handshake and bare bollock brigade, and even those who don't would never go against a ruling made by a "brother magistrate". Oh, if I could only meet that bastard Chubb down a back alley one dark night . . .'

'That could be arranged,' Meadows pointed out.

'Kate!' Paniatowski said sharply.

'Only joking, boss,' Meadows assured her. 'Still, it wouldn't do Mr Brian Chubb any harm to realise that even the most self-righteous magistrate has to respect the law.'

'Meaning what, exactly?'

'That if I was in his shoes I'd be careful where I parked from now on – and I'd be *very* careful not to be found behind the wheel of my car with too much alcohol in my bloodstream.'

'I don't want you doing anything rash,' Paniatowski warned.

'I won't do anything at all, boss . . .'

'Good!'

'But I do have friends in the uniformed branch who might consider it advisable to keep an eye on him.'

'Friends?' Paniatowski repeated, as surprised that Meadows should have friends outside the team as she'd been when Meadows had let it slip that she might – possibly – carry photographs around in her wallet.

'Well, not friends exactly,' Meadows admitted. 'More like acquaintances – lads with whom I share a common interest in knots and rubber masks.'

They'd really travelled far enough down that particular road, Paniatowski decided.

'What does the doctor say about Flynn?' she asked.

'That unfortunately I didn't damage him too badly, but that he can't be questioned until tomorrow morning at the earliest,' Meadows said. 'Will you be needing me at the press conference, boss?'

'I shouldn't think so,' Paniatowski said.

Chances were, it would be a rather quiet press conference, because unlike some of the murder cases she'd handled in the past, it didn't have that sensational element which brought the national newspapers and television reporters flooding into Whitebridge. All that would change, of course, once she revealed that the murder victim was, in fact, a famous author, and at the next press conference she gave, it would be standing room only.

'So if you don't need me, would you mind if I took a few hours off?' Meadows asked, casually – far *too* casually for Paniatowski's liking.

'If I do give you some time off, what will you do with it?' she asked suspiciously.

'Oh, I don't know,' Meadows said. 'Take a hot bath. Clean my whips. Maybe watch a bit of television.'

'You're certainly entitled to a break,' Paniatowski conceded, 'but if I say yes, you won't do anything that's likely to cause me a headache, will you?'

'Really, boss!' Meadows said, outraged. 'The very idea!'

Hope Terrace was typical of the rows upon rows of terraced houses in Whitebridge which had sprung up in the nineteenth century to accommodate the workers at the new mills. Each house originally had two rooms downstairs and two rooms up. The rooms at the rear faced an alley, beyond which lay the backs of the houses in Paradise Street. In the back yard there had been a wash house containing a brick boiler and the house's only tap, and a lavatory which was emptied once a week by what the town council liked to call 'sanitary engineers' and the locals referred to as 'shit cart men'.

The character of the street began to change in the middle of the 1960s. There was more money about by then, and as the older residents died off, their place was taken by young families in which the husband wore a tie to work, and the wife never appeared on the street with her hair in curlers. The plumbing was moved indoors, house extensions were built which took up most of the back yards – and for the first time in its long history, Hope Terrace could honestly be described as 'moderately prosperous'.

George Clegg had had a bathroom installed in the back
bedroom, but had gone no further than that. There seemed to
be no need – there was only him and the missus to consider,
and they both liked the house exactly as it was, because it felt
so cosy.

Meadows knew nothing of Clegg's reasoning as she dropped
off the back wall and into the yard. The only thought that
passed through her mind was that less rooms to search meant
less time searching them, which – when you were committing
an illegal act – was a good thing.

Once in the yard, she stood perfectly still and slowly counted
to twenty. There were no lights on in the back rooms close to
number 33 (it was still far too early for bed) and since she
was dressed entirely in black, it was unlikely she'd been seen,
but since she was in the process of doing something which
could cost her her career, it was wise to be careful.

Satisfied that she'd not been spotted yet – yet! – she moved
quickly to the back door. The lock presented her with no
problems, but when she tried to push the door open, it wouldn't
move.

Bolted from the inside!

She'd hoped to get in without damaging the place, but
that was clearly not an option any more. She took a small
crowbar out of her bag, and began the process of prising
open the door.

At first, the bolt held firm, then, suddenly, the retaining
screws surrendered, and it fell to the kitchen floor with a crash.

It sounded loud to her, but then she was right on top of it,
Meadows reasoned. If anyone in neighbouring houses was
talking or watching the television, they probably wouldn't have
heard it.

She could still back out of this, she told herself – but even
as the thought passed through her mind, she knew she wasn't
going to.

What the hell, she thought, as she pushed the door open
and stepped inside. If I lose my job, I can always go back to
being a member of the idle rich.

She closed the door quietly behind her and switched on her
torch. She was in a narrow corridor, just wide enough to store

prams and bikes in. The door at her end of the passage led to the kitchen, the door at the other end to the front parlour.

She decided to check out the parlour first.

In many traditional working-class houses, the family lived in cramped conditions in the other three rooms, only using the parlour on special occasions, and that was the case here. The three-piece suite was old-fashioned, but virtually unused. The display cabinet – highly polished – held souvenirs of holidays by the sea. And the walls were covered with photographs of a woman – starting, to judge from the style of clothes, in the 1930s, and ending fairly recently.

George Clegg's wife, Meadows thought – you couldn't have exactly called her pretty, but she looked very, very, sweet.

She stepped back into the corridor, and closed the door behind her. She had not noticed that though the curtains looked tightly drawn, there was in fact, a small chink in them.

Edna and Jim Atherton were on their way to the local pub when Edna came to a sudden halt and, pointing across the road, said there was someone in the front room of number 33.

'You're imagining things, woman,' Jim said.

And then he saw for himself that there was a beam of light dancing through the air.

'Do you think it's a burglar?' Edna asked.

'Well, at this time of night it's certainly not the gas man,' Jim replied, taking off his jacket, handing it to his wife, and beginning to roll up his right shirtsleeve.

'Just what do you think you're doing?' Edna demanded.

'I'm going across the road to sort yon bugger out.'

'You'll do no such thing. There could be a whole gang of them, for all you know.'

'Oh aye, a whole gang of them,' Jim said. 'It'd need a whole gang to properly burgle George Clegg's front room.'

'You never know,' Edna countered. 'Anyway, what we should be doing is calling the police.'

'I suppose you're right,' Jim conceded.

The duty sergeant who took the call got straight on to the dispatcher.

'There's been a report of a suspected break-in at 33 Hope Terrace,' he said. 'Why does that address ring a bell?'

'It's the home address of George Clegg – the feller who was rushed into hospital this afternoon.'

'It makes you despair of humanity, doesn't it?' the sergeant asked. 'They're like vultures, some people.'

'Would you like me to send a patrol car round to Hope Terrace?' the dispatcher asked.

'Is there only one car available?'

'No, there's three, actually.'

'Then send them all – I want this bastard!'

The sideboard in the kitchen was where George Clegg kept everything he still had left to care about. On the top shelf were Christmas decorations, faded letters tied with a blue ribbon and a box of jewellery. The bottom shelf was devoted to photograph albums, stacked up in neat towers. In fact, the whole sideboard was neatly organised – so neatly that it was hard to believe that the organiser had been a man.

And that was what made the gap particularly significant!

The gap in question was between two of the photograph album towers. There was no need for it to be there. It served no useful purpose at all.

But it *had* served a purpose! Meadows thought. It had held something – and she was prepared to bet that something was a box.

Was there anything she could say about the box?

Yes!

The box had contained something very important, or it would not have earned its place in the sideboard.

And it could have only recently been removed from the sideboard, because that was the only way to explain why the meticulous George Clegg had not rearranged things into a more pleasing symmetry.

There was a loud banging on the front door, and a voice called, 'Police! Open up!'

Meadows glanced out of the kitchen window and saw a dark shape on the top of the wall that could only be a uniformed constable.

They had her hemmed in.

She stood up, and headed for the stairs.

As Paniatowski had predicted, the press conference had not excited a lot of interest, and there were only a handful of journalists and one local camera crew. What came as a surprise, however, was that one of the journalists present was a man called Mike Traynor.

Traynor did not cut an attractive figure. He had the sort of eyes that a hen sees coming out of the darkness, just before she's pulled off her perch by a pair of strong jaws, and he shed so much dandruff that his sloping shoulders could have been used as a ski run for mice. He had been reporting on crime in Whitebridge and the surrounding district for as long as Paniatowski had been on the force, and initially there'd been little to distinguish him from any of the other hacks.

Then – suddenly – his career had taken off. He had filed a series of exclusive stories which had left his competitors feeling dazed and battered. And even when the other reporters had the same stories he did, he supplied extra juicy details which made them seem like incompetent amateurs. Now, he was the regional crime editor for one of the big national newspapers, and though he still lived in Whitebridge, he was rarely there.

So what the hell was he doing covering a local murder which would scarcely raise a ripple of interest in London? Paniatowski wondered.

She stepped onto the podium, and took her seat behind the desk, next to the chief constable.

'Good evening, ladies and gentlemen,' Pickering said. 'I am Chief Constable Keith Pickering, and sitting next to me is Detective Chief Inspector Monika Paniatowski. DCI Paniatowski will issue a brief statement, and then there will be time allotted for a few questions.'

Paniatowski picked up her prepared statement.

'A thirty-four-year-old man was arrested late this afternoon, and is being questioned in connection with the murder in the Royal Victoria Hotel,' she said. 'I'd now like to deal with the question of the identity of the victim. We have suspected, for some time, that the name she was using was not her own, and now we have positively identified her as Miss Melissa Evans. Miss Evans was thirty-eight years old, and lived in New York City.'

'*The* Melissa Evans?' one of the female journalists gasped. 'The woman who wrote those sensational biographies of Frank Sinatra, Elvis and—'

'That is correct. Miss Evans was indeed a biographer.'

'But what was someone like her doing in Whitebridge?'

'We have still to ascertain that.'

Mike Traynor, a broad grin spread across his face, raised a lazy hand high in the air.

'Yes, Mr Traynor?' Paniatowski said.

'It's not her,' Traynor said.

'I beg your pardon?'

'The woman you have in your mortuary isn't Melissa Evans.'

'I can assure you, Mr Traynor, that we do not announce someone's death without first checking out our facts very carefully. The New York police department is certain that the prints of the woman in the mortuary are a perfect match for those of Melissa Evans.'

'It's not her,' Traynor repeated.

'You sound very confident, Mr Traynor.'

'I am.'

'And what do you base this confidence on?'

'I base it on information that I recently received from a thoroughly reliable source.'

Leave it there, Paniatowski ordered herself. Don't let him goad you into saying something you might regret.

But it was too late for that, because the words were already spilling out of her mouth.

'A thoroughly reliable source,' she heard herself say. 'Now that is interesting. I suppose I could, if I wanted to, list the occasions on which your "thoroughly reliable sources" have proved to be thoroughly *un*reliable, but we all have homes to go to, and most of us would rather like to get there before midnight.'

The other journalists, who were no fans of Traynor, laughed appreciatively, but the man himself did not look at all put out.

No more, Monika, Paniatowski told herself. Shut up now!

'Sometime in the next few hours, when you realise you've made a big mistake, you're going to feel very foolish, Mr Traynor,' she said.

'Not as foolish as you'll feel when you discover I was right all along,' Traynor told her.

Constables Kay and Watson had been dispatched on any number of fools' errands as a result of phone calls from over-imaginative neighbours, and they'd half-suspected that their visit to 33 Hope Terrace would prove to be just one more. The jemmied back door suggested otherwise, and the bag of tools, sitting on the kitchen table, absolutely confirmed that this was the real thing.

The burglar was clearly not in the kitchen, and when they checked the front parlour he proved not to be there, either.

'He must be upstairs,' Kay said.

'Forced to be,' Watson agreed.

He wasn't. They searched the bathroom, and they checked under the bed and inside the wardrobe, but there was no sign of him.

'He must have made his escape before we even got here,' Kay said, slightly despondently.

'And left his tools behind?' Watson asked sceptically. 'There isn't a burglar living who'd leave without his precious tools.'

'So where is he, then?' Kay asked.

Watson's eyes scoured the room one more time, and then looked up at the ceiling.

'The loft!' Watson said, with sudden inspiration. 'He's got to be in the bloody loft.'

The press conference ran on for another five minutes, but after the dramatic confrontation between Paniatowski and Traynor, the heart had pretty much gone out of it.

The chief constable waited until the journalists had filed out of the room, then turned to Paniatowski and said, 'You are quite sure that the dead woman is called Melissa Evans, aren't you?'

'Absolutely,' Paniatowski replied. 'Fred Mahoney is a good solid cop, and he would never send me information that was unreliable.'

'Because, you see, if it turns out that Traynor was right and you were wrong, you're going to look a complete bloody fool, especially after the way you went for him.'

'It's Traynor who's got it wrong.'

'And since I was sharing the platform with you, I'm going to look a complete bloody fool as well.'

'It won't happen,' Paniatowski said. 'But even if it did, I don't see why you should take any flak. I was the one who insisted it was Melissa Evans – you didn't say anything.'

'Precisely,' Pickering agreed, 'I didn't say *anything* which could be taken to be a wholehearted endorsement of what *you* said. It's not myself – Keith Pickering – that I'm worrying about, Monika. I have broad enough shoulders to take any amount of ridicule. But as chief constable, I represent the force, and anything that reflects badly on me also reflects badly on the Mid Lancs Police.'

Oh shit! Paniatowski thought.

Most of the terraced houses in Whitebridge had interconnecting lofts, and it should have been possible to get from one end of the street to the other by walking along the rafters.

It wasn't possible on this row. Eleven doors down from number 33 – number 13, unlucky for some – the owner had obviously decided that since he was having an extension built, he might as well have a party wall put in the loft as well, and when she hit this party wall, Kate Meadows could go no further.

She hunkered down on one of the rafters, and gave serious consideration to what she should do next.

There were, as far as she could see, two choices.

She could stay where she was, and hope that the uniformed bobbies, who were now buzzing around like bluebottles, would be too thick to think of looking for her in the loft.

Or she could open the nearest trap door, and then drop in – literally – on the family who called number 13 home.

It was the sound of the trap door at number 33 being raised that decided her. She opened the trap door, and lowered herself into it.

Her legs were already dangling over the upstairs landing when the torch beam hit her.

'I can see him,' Constable Watson shouted excitedly. 'I can bloody see him. Tell the lads on the street.'

Shit! Meadows thought.

She dropped down onto the upstairs corridor. It was a harder – more awkward – landing than she would have liked, but she didn't think she'd done herself any serious damage.

No time to hang about.

No time for subtlety, either.

Hit the stairs running – bang, bang, bang!

If the only way that she could make her getaway was by hurting a civilian, she thought . . . bang . . . then she would give herself up . . . bang . . . otherwise . . . bang . . . she would do whatever she had to do.

She dashed up the hallway and opened the front door.

Down the street – at number 33 – there were three parked patrol cars, their rotating lights cutting orange swathes through the dark night air, and the family who lived at number 13 – mother, father and two children – were standing by the front gate, mesmerized by the display.

Meadows cut across the tiny garden behind the watching family, and jumped the low wall.

'There he is!' she heard someone – probably a policeman – shout from down the street.

The family turned towards her.

'What . . . who . . .?' the man asked.

But she was already gone, dashing down the street.

She was fast, but she couldn't outrun a police car, and she knew it. She could cut down the nearest ginnel, which was too narrow for the cars to follow, but that would only be postponing her inevitable capture.

She turned down the ginnel anyway.

'I lost it in that press conference,' Paniatowski said, after taking a generous slurp of her vodka. 'I completely bloody lost it. How could I be so stupid, Colin?'

'There's no real harm done,' Beresford reassured her, 'and what you said in the press conference is true enough – when Traynor realises he was wrong about the stiff not being Melissa Evans, he's going to look a right pratt.'

'And he must know that, and yet he seemed so confident that he was right. But he can't be, can he?'

'No,' Beresford agreed, 'he can't be.'

Paniatowski turned to Crane.

'Right then, enough of my self-pity,' she said, 'why don't you tell us about your day?'

'There was only one really big story in all the local papers for most of 1924 – and that's the murder of Wilfred Hardcastle and the subsequent trial of John Entwistle,' Crane said.

'Then let's hear about it,' Paniatowski suggested.

'Wilfred Hardcastle owned a mill, in partnership with his younger brother, Oswald. It was, by all accounts, one of the biggest and most successful mills in Whitebridge.'

'I've lived in this town all my life, and I've never heard of Hardcastle's Mill,' Beresford said.

'No, you wouldn't have, sir, because it went out of business long before you were born, but nevertheless, it was a thriving concern before Wilfred Hardcastle was murdered.'

'And how, exactly, *was* he murdered?'

'He was found in his office, with his head bashed in. He'd been known to be on bad terms with John Entwistle, one of his tacklers, and there was a witness who saw Entwistle leave the office just after the murder. Entwistle was arrested, tried at Preston Assizes, and found not guilty. There's a lot more I could tell you – that's just the bare bones.'

'You can't be sure it was the murder that Mary . . . that Melissa Evans . . . was interested in, can you?' Beresford asked.

'Actually, I think I can,' Crane said. 'As well as the microfiche, there were a number of photograph albums in the stacks. Janet says they're part of a "Bring History Alive" project that the library ran a couple of years ago.'

'Who's Janet?' Paniatowski asked.

'She's . . . erm . . . Miss Dobson, one of the librarians,' Crane replied, slightly uncomfortably.

Paniatowski smiled. 'Go on,' she said.

'The idea was that instead of leaving old family photographs rotting away in the attic, people should bring them into the library, and, when their other duties allowed them the time to do it, the librarians would mount them in albums. That way, everyone in Whitebridge could share them. Anyway, I flicked through one of the albums and found a caption which said "The Hardcastle Mill's Day Excursion to Blackpool, 1924." But the photograph it referred to wasn't there!'

'Are you sure it was *ever* there?' Beresford asked. 'Maybe the librarian wrote the caption but never got round to mounting the photograph.'

'It was there, all right,' Crane said. 'Janet – Miss Dobson – remembers mounting it herself, and she swears that none of the library staff has removed it, so who did? It has to have been Melissa Evans.'

'Maybe it was, but now we know who she was, the "why" she was here suddenly doesn't seem very important anymore,' Paniatowski said regretfully. 'In all probability, she was researching a book – a different kind of book to the one's she's famous for, but a book nevertheless. I really can't see how we can tie that in with her murder.'

'With respect, boss, I think we can,' Crane said. 'I think the two murders are connected, and that if there'd never been the first, there wouldn't have been the second.'

The ginnel led to the broader alley which ran behind the houses. Meadows could see another patrol car parked by the back gate of George Clegg's house, but she was banking – she *had to* bank – on the bobbies who'd arrived in it now being on the main street.

She stripped off her gloves, overalls and ski mask, and dropped them in the nearest bin. That done, she sprinted fifty yards down the alley, came to an abrupt stop, punched herself hard in the face, and fell to the ground.

She'd only just made it in time. A patrol car appeared at the end of the alley, and there was the sound of heavy footfalls emerging from the ginnel.

It was one of the officers on foot who reached her first.

'There's somebody here – it's a woman!' he shouted. He bent down over her. 'Can you hear me, love?'

'Of course I can hear – how could I not, when you're screaming in my ear?' Meadows said. 'Help me to my feet, will you?'

The constable straightened up, and offered her his hand.

'I know you,' he said, shining his torch in her face.

'I'm DS Meadows,' she said.

'Did you see which way he went, sarge?'

'He went that way,' Meadows said, pointing to a ginnel on the other side of the alley.

'The bugger's heading for Paradise Street,' the constable shouted to the other officers. He turned his attention back on Meadows. 'Are you going to be all right, sarge?'

'I'll be fine,' Meadows said. 'To be honest with you, I'm a bit shaken up right at this moment, and tomorrow I'll have a bruise the size of a goat's bollock on my cheek, but that's about it.'

'What were you doing here, anyway?' the constable wondered.

'I heard what was going down here on the radio, and since I happened to be nearby, I thought I'd come down to see if I could help. I knew you'd have Hope Terrace well covered, so I parked on Paradise Street. I thought the burglar might come this way. And guess what – he did.'

'And he hit you, did he?' the constable asked.

'No,' Meadows said, 'I hit myself.'

The constable grinned. 'Sorry, sarge, that was a pretty stupid question. Do you have any idea what he looked like?'

'I didn't really see his face, but I'd say he was about four inches taller than me, with a medium to heavy frame.'

'He didn't look that big when we saw him running down the street,' the constable said dubiously.

'Then maybe you're right and I'm wrong – after all, you did get a closer look at him than I did.'

'Fair point, sarge,' the constable said. 'Medium to heavy frame it is.'

'Will you do me a favour?' Meadows asked.

'What?'

'I wouldn't ask this if we were dealing with a major incident here, but this is little more than petty thieving, and you'll probably never catch the feller who committed it anyway, so when you write up your report, can you leave me out of it?'

'Why?'

'Partly because, if you don't, I'll have to write a report myself, and I'm up to my neck in a murder at the moment.'

'Yes, I can see that might be an annoyance.'

'But mostly,' Meadows grinned, 'it's because if my team find out I've let a toe-rag of a burglar knock me down, they won't stop taking the piss out of me till Christmas.'

'And you wouldn't want that,' the constable said.

'No,' Meadows agreed, 'I wouldn't. Hadn't you better join your mates now, constable?'

'If you're sure you're all right . . .?'

'I am.'

'So what will you do?'

I'll retrieve the gloves, overalls and ski mask and take them somewhere I can burn them, Meadows thought.

'I'll just go and sit in my car until I feel confident about driving home,' she said aloud.

'You're attempting to link two murders that are fifty-four years apart,' Beresford pointed out to Crane. 'Surely, everyone who was involved in that first case will be dead by now.'

'No, not everyone,' Crane said. 'The detective sergeant who worked on the case was called Stan Addison, and he's still very much alive. In fact, I was talking to him on the phone, not half an hour ago. And there may be others – but I haven't had time to look into that yet.'

'If the killer from the first murder was still alive, he'd be in at least his late seventies. You're not saying that a man like that could have killed Melissa Evans?'

'No.'

'So what's the link?'

'I don't know,' Crane confessed, 'but it's there. I can feel it in my gut.' He shrugged helplessly. 'I know that sounds stupid . . .'

'Your gut instinct may be wrong, but it's never stupid,' Paniatowski said. 'It's something every really good detective needs to have. Yet sometimes you just have to accept that there's absolutely nothing to support what your gut's telling you, and call it a day as far as going off in that particular direction is concerned.'

'But there is something to support it,' Crane said.

'What?'

'This morning, George Clegg rang up and told us that he knew who the killer was – and you're prepared to accept that he *does* know, aren't you, boss?'

'I didn't quite say that,' Paniatowski replied. 'What I did say was I believe that *he* believes he knows who the killer is.'

'But you're taking him seriously enough to have to give him a round-the-clock babysitter, in case he wakes up and says something useful.'

'True.'

'So on the one hand we've got *George* Clegg, who thinks he knows who killed Melissa Evans, and on the other we've got *Tom* Clegg, who was the only witness for the prosecution at John Entwistle's trial.'

'Clegg is a common enough name around here,' Colin Beresford said dismissively.

'Tom Clegg was George Clegg's uncle,' Crane countered, 'and I think George knew about Melissa's death because of what he'd been told about Wilfred Hardcastle's death.'

'It really is a very tenuous connection,' Paniatowski said.

'Give me one more day on it, boss,' Crane pleaded.

Paniatowski thought it over. She could spare Crane, certainly, and he had done a good job of finding out what Melissa Evans was doing in Whitebridge, so he was certainly entitled to some leeway. Besides, an important part of training was recognising when your gut was telling you something important, and when it was just having a laugh.

'You can have one day,' she said, 'but no more.'

'Thanks, boss.'

For quite a while – though he had no idea of how long it actually was – George Clegg had seriously thought that he was dead. There was good reason for this. He couldn't move, he couldn't see, and he couldn't speak.

He didn't even know that he could hear, until a woman's voice said, 'It's time to change your drip.'

That was when he had realised that he must be in hospital, and that the woman who had spoken was a nurse.

Now there were two voices in the room.

One of them said, 'Will he be able to hear me if I talk to him?'

And the other replied, 'It's possible. Some patients do wake up from a coma and say they've known what's been going on all the time, but others know nothing about the time they were unconscious.'

'But it won't do him any harm, will it?'

'It can do no harm at all, as long as you don't say anything that might upset him.'

'I would never do that.'

There was the sound of footsteps leaving the room, then the first woman who'd spoken said, 'Hello, Mr Clegg, my name's Detective Sergeant Katherine Meadows, but you can call me Kate.'

Hello Kate, he thought.

'And would you mind if I called you George?'

I wouldn't mind at all, Kate.

'You're an exceptionally brave man, George,' Meadows said. 'Did you know that?'

No, he thought, I didn't.

'Shall I tell you why I said that?'

Yes, please.

'You're a very brave man because you put your own life at risk to help catch Melissa Evans' killer.'

You've got it wrong, he thought. Her name's not Melissa Evans – it isn't that at all.

'I've been to your house,' Meadows said. 'It's all very neat and tidy. It's a real credit to you.'

I always was tidy, he thought. Ellie used to say that all her mates were jealous of her having such a tidy husband. 'You respect our home just like you respect me, Georgie,' she'd say, 'and don't think I don't appreciate it, because I do.' I miss her – I miss her so much.

'But there's a gap on the shelf in the kitchen sideboard,' Meadows continued. 'It's a very neat gap, and that's because, until recently, there was something there. I think it was a box, George. Am I right?'

Yes, yes, you're right.

'And I think that the box has something to do with the case I'm working on. Am I right about that, too?'

Yes.

'I have to go now,' Meadows said, 'but I can come back again some other time, if you'd like me to.'

Oh, please come back, he thought. Please, please, come back.

'Right, that's settled,' Meadows said, as if she actually could hear him. 'I'll be back as soon as I can.'

He listened to her retreating footsteps. If he'd had control over his own body, then perhaps a single tear would have trickled down his cheek. But he had no such control.

JOURNAL

I have just spent a day in Preston Crown Court. From the moment I arrived, it was like I had blundered into the pages of a history book. The attorneys (barristers, they call them over here) wear wigs made of horsehair, with curls at the sides and two little tails hanging down behind (I swear I am not inventing this!) and the judge wears an even longer (and maybe even stupider) wig.

What else?

Oh yeah, the prisoner does not sit at his attorney's table, but stands in a square box (the dock or bar) behind him, with a police officer on each side to make sure he behaves.

It may not have been exactly like this when John Entwistle stood trial for the murder of Wilfred Hardcastle, but since nothing much seems to have changed in hundreds of years, I'd put money on it being pretty damned close.

When I left the court, it was with a real prize under my arm – a copy of the transcript of Rex v. John Entwistle. I intend to study it carefully. This will not be a case of collecting rumour and innuendo and fashioning it into some kind of narrative. This will be real research, and even if nothing ever comes of it, I am proud of myself for undertaking it.

Transcript.

> Sir Reginald Bower KC (Prosecution): Where do you work, Clegg?
>
> Tom Clegg: At the mill, sir.
>
> Bower: And which mill might that be?
>
> Clegg: Hardcastle's Mill, sir.
>
> B: So why didn't you say so in the first place, instead of wasting the court's time?
>
> C: Sorry, sir.
>
> B: What do you do at the mill?
>
> C: Mr Hardcastle calls me the odd job wallah.

> B: And what does that entail?
> C: Beg pardon, sir.
> B: For what?
> C: I don't know . . . I don't understand what enter . . . entre . . .
> B: Entails?
> C: Yes, that. I don't know what it means.
> B: Oh, for God's sake! What kind of work do you do?
> C: All sorts. Sweep up, run messages, make the tea . . .

To be honest, I'm shocked by the way Bower talks to Tom Clegg. I was trying to think what it reminds me of, and now I know – it's the way the prosecuting attorney talks to Tom Robinson in *To Kill a Mockingbird*.

But at least in the book, Robinson was the one on trial. Tom Clegg is Bower's witness, the cornerstone of his case, and yet he treats him with contempt. And why? I think it is because he's from the lower orders, and must be kept down and reminded of his place even when he's doing exactly what you want him to do. Bower makes no attempt to get into Tom's head – never tries to see things from Tom's perspective – because it's not worth the effort.

In so many ways, I hate Tom Clegg, and yet, reading this, I feel nothing but pity for him.

Transcript.

> Bower: Were you at the mill at seven o'clock on the evening of the fifteenth of May?
> C: Yes, sir.
> B: Who else was there?
> C: Mr Wilfred—
> B: That would be Mr Wilfred Hardcastle.
> C: Yes, sir.
> B: Who else?
> C: Me and John Entwistle.
> John Entwistle (from the dock): That's a lie. I'd gone fishing in the canal.
> Judge: One more interruption like that, and I'll have you taken down, Entwistle.
> JE: Sorry, m'lud.

Judge: You may proceed, Sir Reginald.

B: Apart from yourself, Entwistle and Mr Hardcastle, was there anyone else, Clegg?

C: No, sir.

B: But what about the weavers? I thought they worked all the hours that God sends. That's certainly what they claim, every time they demand more money.

C: There's a bit of a slump on at the moment. We don't weave cotton unless we've got firm orders on the books.

B: We've got firm orders? Don't you mean unless Messrs Hardcastle have got firm orders?

C: Yes, sir. Sorry, sir.

B: Why were the three of you there?

C: Mr Wilfred always works late, and I'm not allowed to go home in case he needs something doing.

B: And Entwistle?

C: He was there because Mr Wilfred was giving him a rocket.

B: A rocket?

C: A telling off – a talking to.

B: And do you know why Mr Hardcastle was giving Entwistle a rocket?

C: Yes, sir.

B: Then – for goodness sake – tell me, man!

C: John's a tackler, sir, and—

B: By John, are you referring to Entwistle?

C: Yes, sir.

B: Then call him by his name. You're not in the pub now, you know.

C: John – Entwistle's a tackler and—

B: Am I supposed to know what a tackler is?

C: He's the feller what makes sure the looms are running smoothly, and this particular day, two of them had broken down.

B: And was it Entwistle's fault?

C: Mr Wilfred thought it was.

B: I see. So what happened next?

C: They were in the office. I was outside in the corridor, scrubbing the floor. I could hear Mr Wilfred shouting at John – at Entwistle – for what must have been at least half an hour. Then Entwistle started shouting back.

B: Let me get this clear. Entwistle, a common working man, had the temerity to shout at his employer.

JE (from the dock): I never went to see him. Why would I have gone to see him when I knew he was going to sack me?

Judge: Bailiffs, take the prisoner down – and don't bring him back up again until he promises to behave himself. You may proceed, Sir Reginald.

B: Thank you, m'lud. You were saying, Clegg, that Entwistle was shouting at Mr Hardcastle.

C: Yes, sir.

B: And what happened then?

C: I heard like a thudding sound. Then John – then Entwistle – came out of the office and dashed down the corridor. I went into the office to see what had happened, and Mr Wilfred was lying on the floor, and there was blood everywhere. He was dead.

NINE

On nights when Paniatowski was unsure about what time she would be getting home, the twins slept in their nanny's room. And it was as well that this was one of those nights, because if they'd been sleeping with their mother, they would undoubtedly have woken when the telephone began screeching its incessant demand to be answered at three a.m.

Paniatowski groped for the phone.

'DCI Paniatowski,' she mumbled.

'Hey, lady, how come it took so long to pick up?' demanded a voice that Paniatowski thought should rightfully belong to a mature grizzly bear. 'Don't you get your people trained?'

'Who is this?'

'Harvey Morgan.'

'Well, Mr Morgan, none of my people are here – probably because it's three o'clock in the morning.'

'Boy, are you confused,' Morgan said. 'It's only just ten p.m.'

'It's three o'clock in England,' Paniatowski insisted.

'You sure about that?'

'Yes.'

'OK,' Morgan said dubiously. 'Anyhow, my secretary tells me we need to talk, so let's talk.'

'I wanted to ask you about Melissa Evans.'

'You mind if I ask you a question, first?'

'I don't mind at all.'

'You're a chief inspector, right?'

'Yes.'

'What rank would that be in a real police force?'

In a real police force! Paniatowski thought.

'I suppose I'd be a captain.'

'Good, 'cos I'm too busy a man to talk to anybody but the top honcho,' Morgan said. He sighed. 'Melissa Evans! Yeah, it's a great loss. She's got God as her agent now. I only hope He handles her right.'

'So what *can* you tell me about her?' Paniatowski asked.

'Melissa is – Melissa was – the queen of the unauthorised biography. She did books on all the big names – Elvis, Teddy Kennedy, Sinatra . . . You've heard of those people in England, right?'

'Right,' Paniatowski agreed.

'They were big thick books she wrote – eight or nine hundred pages – and they always created a sensation because they revealed tons of things about the celebrities that nobody had before.'

'Bad things?'

'Sure, bad things sometimes! Nobody wants to read a book about little Peter Perfect.'

'What made her so good at her job?'

'The woman was an instinctive genius. She was like Albert Einstein or . . . what's the name of the guy who got hit by an apple falling from a tree? . . . she was like William Tell.'

'I think you mean Sir Isaac Newton.'

'You sure about that?'

'Yes.'

'OK, then she was like Sir Newton. An apple falls on your head and you think, "Jesus, how dumb was I to sit under that tree?" An apple falls on her head and it starts her thinking.'

'Do you mean she was very good at making connections?'

'Yeah, ain't that what I just said? And another thing about her – you remember that Thomas Edison said genius was one per cent inspiration and ninety-nine per cent perspiration?'

'Yes?'

'For Melissa, it was one hundred and ten per cent perspiration! And determined? She was like a big old alligator – once she'd got her jaws clamped around something, there was no way she was gonna give up until she'd chewed right through it. Plus – and maybe this is the real secret of her success – there was something about her that made all kinds of people want to please her, so when she asked a question, she usually got an answer.'

'How did the people she wrote her books about feel about her?'

'Not too good. After her book on Sinatra came out, there was a rumour going round that Frank himself had called his friends in the Mob and asked them to teach her a lesson, but if anybody asks me if I believe that's true I say no, because (a) there's no proof he ever did that, and (b) I've got my family to consider.'

'Was she ever threatened?'

'All the time. There were dozens of death threats in her mail every day of the week.'

'From the people she'd written about?'

'Since most of the letters were anonymous, that's kind of hard to say, but my guess is that only a few were from the "injured" parties, and the rest were from their fans. You see, fans invest in their heroes – worshiping the guy is really all they have to live for – and when some bitch of a writer suggests that hero isn't perfect, they really lose it. And that's why Melissa had two bodyguards.'

'*Full-time* bodyguards?'

'Sure. They went everywhere she did – her condo in Florida, her ski lodge in Aspen, her ranch—'

'They weren't with her on this trip, were they?'

'No, they weren't.'

'Why not?'

'I don't know. Maybe she thought she'd be completely safe, back in the old country.'

'Her family came from England, did they?'

'With a name like Evans, the family had to have come from England, don't you think? Or maybe even Walesland. But my guess is that was a long time ago – maybe last century – and Melissa herself was about as New York as they come.'

'She was working on a book here in Whitebridge, wasn't she?'

'Yeah, I tried to talk her out of it – hell, Clint Eastwood's so hot right now he's hanging there like some big juicy fruit, and she was just the gal to pick him, but she wouldn't listen.'

'Did she tell you what kind of book she was going to write?'

'Sorta.'

'Sorta? What do you mean by that?'

'I mean that she told me, but I was no wiser when she finished than I'd been when she started.'

There is something different about Melissa this early January morning, but Harvey Morgan is still trying to put his finger on exactly what it is.

And then he has it!

It's defensiveness! he decides. There's something she wants to do that she knows I won't like, and she's come here to slug it out with me.

'Have you seen the reviews of my Sinatra book?' she asks.

'I don't read reviews, Melissa, honey-child,' Morgan tells her, 'and neither should you.'

'You're a liar,' she says.

He grins. 'I'm an agent – and a good one. I don't lie – I say what people need to hear.'

'The Chicago Tribune *calls it trash. The* New York Times *says it takes unauthorised biography to a new low.'*

'And if you look in the bestseller list of that very same newspaper, you'll see that Albert *is at number three – and next week it will be number one. So screw all of them.'*

'I'm a good writer,' Melissa says.

'You're the best.'

'I'm a good writer up here,' she taps her forehead, 'but I've never *written down* anything that is good. *I've never put it on the page.'*

'You're raving now,' Morgan tells her. 'You think John Updike wouldn't like your sales figures? Or Philip Roth? They'd kill for them.'

'That doesn't work for me anymore,' she says. 'It's not enough to know that what I do, I do much better than most people ever could. It's not enough that the books have made me rich. I want to do something better – something more worthwhile.'

'There's no money in authorised *biographies,' Morgan tells her. 'They're snow jobs. Everybody knows that – and who's going to lay out hard cash just to read a snow job?'*

'It's not a biography that I want to write,' she says.

'Then what? A novel?'

She shakes her head. 'I don't think I could write a novel. I don't think it's in me.'

Morgan groans. 'Please don't tell me you're going to start writing poetry,' he says. 'I don't think my heart could stand it.'

'It's not poetry either. I want to do a literary historical reconstruction,' Melissa says.

'I don't even know what that is, but already I know it's not going to sell,' Morgan says.

'I want to do it both for myself – and to pay off some old debts.'

'You've got debts?' Morgan explodes. 'You earned more last year than most people make in a dozen lifetimes – and you've got debts!'

'Not those kind of debts,' Melissa says, almost pityingly. 'I'm talking about debts of gratitude. I'm talking about duties and obligations.'

Morgan shakes his head. 'You've lost me, kid,' he says.

'No,' she tells him, 'you've lost me, because whatever happens to my literary historical reconstruction – even if it sinks without trace – I won't be writing any more unauthorised biographies.'

'And she was right about that, poor kid,' Morgan said to Paniatowski. 'She sure as shit won't be writing any more of them.'

There had been a heavy frost overnight, and when Jack Crane arrived at the Alderman Crick Retirement Home at nine o'clock, the lawn in front of the home was still silver-spiky.

The home was located on the edge of Whitebridge, close to the abattoir. It had once been the Whitebridge Workhouse, where paupers had spent their final days at the tedious and soul-destroying task of unpicking old tarry ropes, strand by strand, so that they could be recycled.

An attempt had been made to brighten the place up since those long-gone dark days. The windows had been enlarged, and the walls had received liberal applications of pastel-coloured paint, but you couldn't obliterate history entirely, Crane thought, as he walked in through the main door, and to him it was still a grim, forbidding building which reeked of carbolic soap and Victorian moral rectitude.

The man he'd come to see – Stan Addison – was already waiting for him in the supervisor's office. Addison was well over eighty years old, and had prominent veins on both hands, with liver spots largely filling in the gaps between them. His hands shook slightly, and his eyes, although still alert, were covered with a light milky film. Until his retirement, he had been a member of the Mid Lancs police force, and he had moved into the home five years earlier, when his wife had died.

'I don't get many visitors these days, lad,' he told Crane. 'Me son's in Australia, me daughter's in Canada, and most of me old mates popped their clogs long ago. So it's nice to see you, even if it is only police business what's brought you here. What can I do for you?'

'Do you remember a murder in 1924?' Crane asked.

'Are you talking about the Wilfred Hardcastle murder?'

'Yes.'

'That was my first case as a detective sergeant, so naturally, I remember it very well.'

'Could you tell me about it?'

'Wilfred Hardcastle and his brother Oswald ran one of the biggest mills in Whitebridge. Well, I say *they* ran it, but it was really just Wilfred, because Oswald was a bit of what you might call a wastrel, and had no interest in the mill beyond the dividends it paid him.'

'What sort of a reputation did Wilfred have?' Crane asked.

'He was what, back then, they used to call "firm but fair". He knew what was right, and there was no point in arguing with him, because he had a direct line to God. Folk used to say that him and God agreed on almost everything most of the time, and that if they ever did have a bit of a falling out, that was only because God had got it wrong.'

Crane laughed, and then, seeing the puzzled expression on Addison's face, realised that he'd just heard an example of the kind of deep Lancashire humour that you weren't *supposed* to laugh at. He wondered if, as an outsider, he'd ever really understand the North.

'He wasn't a man for giving second chances, Wilfred Hardcastle,' Addison continued. 'If you made one mistake, you were out. That said, if you kept your head down, and did things just the way he thought they should be done, he was a better boss to work for than most of the mill owners round here.'

'Tell me about the day of the murder,' Crane said.

'It was after the mill had shut down for the day, and there were only three of them there – Hardcastle, Tom Clegg and John Entwistle. Hardcastle had called Entwistle into his office, so that he could give him a bollocking about the looms breaking down. Anyway, Tom Clegg comes running into the police station to tell us he's found Wilfred Hardcastle dead, and that it's John Entwistle who's killed him. My inspector sends somebody to Entwistle's lodgings, but he's not there, so we institute a general search, and we find him down by the canal, where he's gone to try and establish an alibi.'

'Can we go back a bit?' Crane asked.

'Yes, all right.'

'On the stand, Entwistle said the looms didn't break down at all, but had, in fact, been sabotaged.'

'How do you know that?' Addison demanded.

'It was in the transcript, which I read last night.'

'You're a keen young bugger, aren't you?' Addison asked, in a voice which made it quite clear he was not exactly paying Crane a compliment. 'Yes, he claimed the looms had been sabotaged, all right. Well, he had to say something, didn't he?'

'And did you have it checked out?'

'What do you mean?'

'Did you send an expert to look at the looms, to try and ascertain if they *had* been sabotaged?'

'No.'

'Why not?'

'We didn't need to – we had more than enough evidence to convict John Entwistle, so why go to all the trouble of uncovering a lie that could have no real effect on the case?'

But if it wasn't a lie, it *would* have an effect, Crane thought, because if somebody had deliberately sabotaged the looms, then you needed to ask yourself *why* he'd sabotaged them, and the reason could have been that—

'Are you still with me, lad?' Addison asked.

'Sorry,' Crane said. 'You were talking just now about having more than enough evidence to convict Entwistle. What was the evidence that you were referring to?'

'Well, we had Tom Clegg, who was virtually an eye-witness . . .'

'Tell me about Tom Clegg,' Crane said.

'Tell you *what* about him?'

'What was your impression of him?'

'He wasn't quite right in the head, if you ask me. I'm not saying he was a loony, or anything like that, but he was slow on the uptake, and you got the impression he didn't see the world in quite the way everybody else did.' Addison paused. 'Have you got a cigarette, son?'

'Sure,' Crane said, offering the packet and lighting the old man's cigarette for him.

'The other thing about him was, he was a bit girly,' Addison said.

'Girly?'

'You know, sensitive – and a bit timid.'

'Is that right,' said Crane, who liked to think he was rather a sensitive soul himself.

'You couldn't imagine him in the middle of a rugby scrum, or trying to talk a girl out of her knickers. He was the sort of lad who'd be bullied at school, and would end up begging one of the bigger lads to protect him.' Addison stopped speaking, as if he'd just realised that he'd been running down someone he should have been building up. 'But he was a good witness – a *very* good witness,' he continued, clearly trying to compensate. 'He knew exactly what he'd seen, and he stood in that witness box and gave his evidence like a good Christian should.'

'He retracted that evidence later, though, didn't he?'

'No, he didn't – you're quite wrong about that!' Addison said, his voice suddenly aggressive. 'Tom Clegg gave his evidence – under oath – in the witness box, and the only way he could have retracted it properly was to stand in that same witness box a second time – under oath again – and say that he'd been lying. *That* would have been a retraction – all we got was a note.'

The trial is due to re-start at ten o'clock, and at five to ten Stan Addison is summoned to the judge's chambers.

'Thomas Clegg is due to be cross-examined on his testimony in fifteen minutes,' the judge says.'

'Yes, My Lord, I know,' Addison agrees.

'But Clegg isn't here. Why is that?'

'I don't know, My Lord.'

'How is he supposed to get to court?'

'I gave him a travel voucher and told him to catch the eight o'clock train from Whitebridge.'

'But you didn't travel with him?'

'No, My Lord, I came by car.'

'I hold you personally responsible for this delay, sergeant.'

'But My Lord—'

'You are to drive back to Whitebridge, pick Clegg up, and bring him to me. Is that clear?'

'Yes, My Lord.'

By the time Addison reaches Clegg's house, there are already four constables standing out on the pavement, and another two in the kitchen, at the table, interrogating Tom's weeping mother.

'Where is he, Mrs Clegg?' one of them is shouting.

'I don't know – I've told you a thousand times, Constable Walker, I just don't know.'

'What pubs does he use regularly?'

'None – he's not much of a drinker.'

'Who are his friends?'

'He doesn't really have any. He's always found it hard to make friends. Besides, he doesn't have the time. Mr Wilfred works him very hard, and if Mr Wilfred doesn't want him, then Mr Oswald finds him jobs to do.'

'You're lying to me,' the constable says. 'You know exactly where he is, don't you?'

'No, I don't. I swear I don't.'

This is getting us nowhere, Addison thinks, and sometimes the best way to get what you want quickly is to slow
down a little.

He gestures to the constable to stand up, and he takes the
man's place at the table.

'Good morning, Mrs Clegg,' he says. 'I'm Detective Sergeant
Stan Addison.'

The gentleness of his tone surprises her.

'Good . . . good morning, Mr Addison,' she stutters.

'You look like you could use a cup of tea,' he says.

'Yes.'

'Shall I get one of my lads to make you one?'

She stands up.

'That you'll not, sergeant. I'm not having no man making
the tea in my kitchen.'

Addison smiles.

'Then would you like to make it?'

'All right.'

'Just for you and me,' Addison says, because he guesses he
has more chance of learning something useful if there are just
the two of them there.

'Won't the constables . . .?'

'They've already had their tea.'

He forces himself to wait patiently while Mrs Clegg
boils the kettle over the open fire, pours the boiling water
into the teapot, and lets the tea brew. Only when she is back
at the table does he speak.

'Does Tom have any favourite places, Mrs Clegg?'

'I don't know what you mean.'

I can see now why your son's so thick, Addison thinks. He
obviously takes after you.

'Is there somewhere he likes to go when he's upset, or needs
time to think things over?'

'He's always liked the woods,' Mrs Clegg says.

The woods are a mile and a half from the edge of Whitebridge,
on the other side of the river. In the summer, they are lush
and green, the ground is springy underfoot, and the clean air

offers a welcome relief from the soot-filled atmosphere of the town. But now it is winter, the trees are stark and dark and skeletal, and the ground is as hard as rock.

It is from one of these skeletal trees that they find Tom Clegg hanging. The noose he has fashioned for himself is a clumsy one, but it has done its job and he is quite dead.

There is a note pinned to his shirt. It reads: I DINT SEE JOHN LEAF THE OFFICE. I LIED IN COURT.

'Maybe he lied in court, and maybe he lied in the note,' Addison said. 'Who can say for sure which it was? The judge advised the jury to believe what he'd said in court, because that was under oath – and that was good enough for me.'

'On the other hand, his suicide note could be regarded as a dying declaration,' Crane said.

'Now you're just splitting hairs,' Addison said uneasily.

'Why did he hang himself?'

'I don't know.'

'And didn't you bother to find out?'

'No. Who knows why people kill themselves? Maybe his girlfriend wouldn't open her legs for him, and he found out that she was opening them for some other feller.'

'I thought you said you couldn't ever imagine him trying to talk a girl out of her knickers.'

'That was probably going too far. Every young lad wants to get his end away, doesn't he? You know what they say about a woman's thingy – when you're being born you can't wait to get out of there, and then you spend the rest of your life trying to get back in.'

This was the sort of comment that Crane was expected to laugh at, and if it had been someone else, he might have faked it, but he didn't like the kind of policeman Stan Addison had been, and – for the purposes of this interrogation – he had no wish to put the other man at his ease.

There was an uncomfortable silence which Addison finally broke by saying, 'Or maybe he'd convinced himself he'd got some incurable disease. There could be dozens of reasons he decided to top himself.'

'But before he kills himself, he goes to all the trouble of

writing the note, and then pins it on his shirt so you couldn't miss it?' Crane asked.

'There could be reasons for that as well. Maybe he hated Wilfred Hardcastle, but liked John Entwistle, and was feeling guilty about shopping him. Well, he'd decided to kill himself anyway, so he thought he might as well do what he could to get John off.'

'Even though he knew him to be a killer?'

'Could be.'

'What was the other evidence you mentioned?'

'Wasn't that in the transcript?'

'Yes, but I'd rather hear it from you.'

Frankie Flynn rubbed his chin gingerly, then shot a hostile look across the interview table at Meadows and Paniatowski – but mainly at Meadows.

'I've been a victim of police brutality,' he complained.

'Police brutality?' Paniatowski repeated. 'Wherever did you learn a phrase like that, Frankie?'

'He's maybe been watching some of those American cop shows on the telly,' Meadows suggested.

'Yes, that'll be it,' Paniatowski agreed.

'You think it's all just a big joke, don't you?' Flynn asked sullenly. 'Well, let me tell you, you won't be laughing when my solicitor gets here. Then, you'll be in real trouble.'

Meadows chuckled. '*I'll* be in trouble, will I?' she asked. 'That's hysterical coming from a feller who punched a detective inspector in the gut.'

'You almost broke my jaw,' Flynn said.

'Nonsense,' Meadows countered. 'I gave you the gentlest of taps – as has been confirmed by the police doctor. I wasn't even trying to hurt you. If I had been, you'd have spent the next half hour chasing your rolling head down the street.'

'Speaking of solicitors, where *is* yours, Frankie?' Paniatowski asked. 'He should have been here by now.'

'He's probably tied up with another case – one in which the client's prepared to pay him what he thinks he's worth,' Meadows said.

'Yes, I think you're right about that,' Paniatowski agreed.

'And what that means is that even if he does eventually turn up here, he'll probably cut the quickest deal he can, so that he can get back to the client who's paying him real money as soon as possible.'

'I think we should use the time before he gets here constructively,' Meadows said. 'Don't you agree, Frankie?'

'I've no idea what you're talking about,' Flynn told her.

'It was a huge blow to your pride when Mary Edwards kicked you in the balls, and you knew you'd never be able to look yourself in the face again unless you did something about it,' Meadows said. 'So you went up to her suite in the Royal Vic, didn't you? I don't think you wanted to kill her – you were just looking for an apology – but she was probably very provocative, and you lost your temper, and hit her with the poker.' Meadows shrugged. 'These things happen.'

'I didn't go anywhere near her,' Flynn said.

'Now that's not entirely true, is it?' Meadows suggested. 'It can't be true, because the doorman at the Royal Vic – who, I have to tell you, will be a very credible witness – saw you walking back and forth in front of the hotel on Saturday. Now you're not going to deny that, are you?'

'It's a free country,' Flynn said. 'I can go where I like.'

'Yes, but why would you want to walk up and down in that bloody awful weather? It was cold enough to freeze the balls off a brass—' Meadows stopped abruptly. 'Sorry, Frankie, I forgot that balls are a particularly sensitive subject with you at the moment. But you get the point? It was so cold that nobody was outside unless they absolutely had to be – yet there you were.'

'It's a free country,' Flynn repeated, stubbornly.

'The thing is, Frankie, if you help us, we'll help you,' Meadows said. 'I'm more than willing to stand up in court and tell the judge that she was more-or-less asking for what she got. We think she was a lesbian—'

'She was! She was! When I found her in the Grapes, she was trying to talk my missus into bed.'

'And nobody likes lesbians, do they? I don't like them, juries don't like them, and judges don't like them. So that can only be to your advantage, can't it? But if we're going to do a deal, Frankie, then we really do have to do it before your solicitor arrives.'

The door swung open, and Arthur Tyndale – leaning heavily on his stick – entered the room.

'Sorry I'm late,' he said. 'I had a certain amount of difficulty getting out of bed this morning.' He turned to his client. 'Not another word, Frankie – until we've had a little chat, you're not to say another word.'

'You asked for the other evidence,' Stan Addison said to Crane. 'Well, for a start, there was the fact that Hardcastle and Entwistle had had a big argument.'

'But the only reason we know about that argument is because Tom Clegg told us. And we've already established that he lied at least once.'

'There will have been an argument,' Addison said confidently. 'Two looms had broken down – and that, we *do* know for a fact, because it was confirmed by the weavers. Well, that kind of disruption costs money, and Wilfred Hardcastle would have been wanting his pound of flesh.'

'But Entwistle said he never went to the office, because if he was going to be fired – and knowing Hardcastle's reputation, he was sure he would be – he didn't see why he should have to put up with a half-hour bollocking first.'

'He went to Hardcastle's office,' Addison said stubbornly 'He's bound to have gone there.'

'Why is he bound to have gone there?' Crane asked. 'Is it because your whole case was based on him going?'

'And then, of course, there was the money,' said Addison, ignoring the question.

'Ah yes, the money,' Crane said.

'We found fifty pounds under Entwistle's mattress. That's a handy sum even nowadays, but it was one hell of a lot of money back then.'

'You think he stole it from Hardcastle, do you?'

'I'm convinced he did.'

'Why?'

'He needed money to run away.'

'But he didn't run away, did he? Despite the fact that he

knows Tom Clegg has seen him running from the office, he leaves the money where it is bound to be found – and goes fishing.'

'Maybe he thought his bluff would work, that we'd believe him and not Tom, and there'd be no need to run away.'

'Did you check how long he'd been down at the canal?'

'No, we bloody didn't!' Addison said.

He's getting angry now, Crane thought, and the only reason he's not telling me to piss off is because if I do, he'll be alone again – and that's the last thing he wants.

'Why didn't you check how long John Entwistle had been down at the canal?' he asked.

'Because it just wasn't bloody necessary. The whole business was in the papers.'

'So?'

'So say I'm a fisherman, and I'd been down at the canal that day, and seen Entwistle. I read in the papers that he's been arrested, and I think to myself, "Hello, that can't be right, because at the time the murder occurred, I was talking to him myself." So what do I do? I get myself off to the police station, and I give Entwistle an alibi. But nobody did that because nobody saw him. And the reason nobody saw him was because he wasn't there for long.'

'There are any number of reasons why a witness won't come forward voluntarily,' Crane said.

'Like what?'

'Like he'd been skiving off work and didn't want his employer to find out. Like he had a criminal record, and didn't want to draw attention to himself in case the police started taking a new interest in him. Like—'

'You're a real armchair bobby, aren't you, son?' Addison sneered. 'Well, let me tell you, I was a real policeman, working in the real world.'

'Were you in the court yourself when the jury brought in its verdict?' Crane asked.

'I was.'

'And how did you feel?'

'I was shocked. Everybody was shocked.'

* * *

Nearly the entire Hardcastle family is sitting on the front row.

There is Sarah Hardcastle, the dead man's widow, dressed from head to foot in black, and as stern and unyielding as her late husband had been.

There is Anne, her daughter, heavily pregnant – and a very useful prop for the prosecutor.

'Think of the damage John Entwistle has caused,' he'd said in his closing remarks. 'What he has done means that a grandchild will be denied the love of his grandfather. What he has done means a grandfather will never experience the joy of holding his little grandchild in his arms.'

Next to Anne is her husband, Simon, who is a competent enough barrister, but will never be impressive enough to command high fees.

The only one who is not there is Oswald Hardcastle. He has no real feelings of family obligation. For the first few days of the trial, he was a reluctant attendee at best, and for the last few days he has been wholly absent.

The trial has not gone as well as it might have done since John Entwistle's barrister insisted that Tom Clegg's suicide note be read to the jury. The family know that. Yet they are confident the right verdict will be arrived at, because the jury is made up exclusively of ratepayers – members of the middle class. This jury, they feel, will have known even before the trial started that John Entwistle was guilty, because if he wasn't guilty, the police would never have arrested him. Besides, they appreciate the damage that the wrong verdict could do. It would be seen as a defeat for the police, and anything which damages the police damages them, too, since the forces of law and order are all that is preventing the workers from rising up – as they have so recently done in Russia – and murdering their betters in their beds.

The jury is led in, and the clerk of the court asks the foreman of the jury if it has reached its verdict, and if it is the verdict of them all. The foreman says that it is, and – ominously – looks straight at the prisoner in the dock.

'Then on the charge of the wilful murder of Wilfred

*Hardcastle, do you find John Entwistle guilty or not guilty?'
the clerk of the court asks.*

*The foreman of the jury fingers his tie nervously, as if he
knows he is about to do the right thing, yet wishes he didn't
have to do it.*

'Not guilty,' he says.

*Though all the signs had been there that he was going to
say exactly that, a collective gasp still fills the courtroom.*

*Sarah Hardcastle turns to face the dock, and gives John
Entwistle a look of pure hatred.*

*And Entwistle himself – standing there open-mouthed –
seems hardly able to believe his luck.*

'Hardly able to believe his luck,' Addison said, 'because he
knew he was guilty, and he'd got off.'

'Or perhaps because, although he was innocent, he knew
the odds were stacked against him and never really expected
to get off,' Crane countered.

'He was guilty,' Addison said wearily. 'He was as guilty as
sin. Your problem, lad, is that you don't know which facts are
important, and which facts don't matter a damn – so instead
of seeing the bigger picture, you get bogged down in a thousand petty details.'

'And your problem is that you refuse to see that you made
a monumental mistake,' Crane said. 'You expected to get a
conviction on the basis of one discredited witness and the
money you found in John Entwistle's room. But if he'd stolen
the money in order to run away, he'd almost certainly have
done just that. At the least – the very least – he'd have found
a better hiding place for it. The money was planted. It simply
had to have been.'

'So who did kill Wilfred Hardcastle?' Addison screamed.
'I know – it was Tom Clegg. Tom wasn't very bright, and
nobody but Hardcastle would even think of giving him a job,
so by killing his boss he would lose his livelihood. That's a
perfect motive for murder, isn't it? No, I'm wrong – it wasn't
Tom, it was Oswald. You see, Oswald didn't like it that his
brother was earning him a lot of money, and all he had to do
was spend it. So he thought he'd kill Wilfred and let the mill

go bust. Except that Oswald was so upset about what had happened to his brother that within three years he'd drunk himself to death. Hold on – maybe it was a passing tramp who thought he'd kill Hardcastle for fun, and then take fifty quid and then leave it under the mattress in John Entwistle's room.'

Addison fell silent, clearly exhausted by the effort.

'It could have been worse,' Crane said. 'The guilty man got away with it, it's true, but at least you didn't hang an innocent one.'

Addison opened his mouth to speak, but no words came out, and in the end, he made do with gesturing towards the door.

Crane nodded, and left. He didn't say goodbye, because there didn't seem to be much point.

TEN

Once the interview had resumed, it hadn't taken long to work out what advice Arthur Tyndale must have given to Frankie Flynn during their private consultation.

'No comment,' Flynn had said to the first question – and the second, and the third.

Paniatowski and Meadows had put on their best double act in an effort to draw him out, but Flynn had stuck to his guns, while Tyndale had watched the whole proceedings with an amused smile occasionally playing on his lips.

Now, with the interviewing suspended for the moment, Paniatowski and Tyndale were sitting in the chief inspector's office.

The solicitor looked around the office with what seemed to be genuine interest.

'You really don't have much of a flair for interior decoration, do you, DCI Paniatowski?' he asked, when he'd finished his inspection.

'What do you mean by that, Mr Tyndale?'

'There's nothing here in this room which casts any sort of light on your personality – nothing which proclaims the passions and feelings which fuel the engine that drives you.'

'Do you think I should have my walls covered with newspaper articles, like you've covered yours?'

'Why not? You've made plenty of headlines in your time – and most of them have been very complimentary,' Tyndale said. 'So what's wrong with nailing your colours to the mast?'

And then he began coughing – and this coughing fit, Paniatowski thought, was harder and even bloodier than the last one she'd witnessed.

'Why don't you go home now, and have a good rest, Mr Tyndale?' she suggested.

'Oh, you'd like that, wouldn't you, chief inspector?' Tyndale replied. 'With the Lone Ranger completely out of the picture, the men in black hats can do whatever they want.'

'Is that really how you see us – as the men in black hats?' Paniatowski asked.

'Yes, that's exactly how I see you.'

'Isn't that view of the world a little lacking in subtlety?'

Tyndale laughed. 'The police have come a long way since I started out in this trade. The bobbies I was up against in the early days would never have used the word "subtlety". They wouldn't even have known what it meant.'

Paniatowski smiled. 'Nicely sidestepped, Mr Tyndale,' she said. 'You won't answer the question I've just asked, and you've instructed your client not to answer *any* of my questions. That's right, isn't it? That *is* what you've done?'

'I have not *instructed* my client to do anything,' Tyndale said. 'What I have done is to make him aware of his options – *one of which* is to answer no more questions.'

'Yeah, right,' Paniatowski said. 'And what were the other options that you presented him with?'

'Why should he answer?' Tyndale replied, ignoring the question. 'You can't place him in Melissa Evans' suite – and without that, you haven't got a case.'

'You know for a fact that we can't place him in Melissa Evans' suite, do you?'

'No, but I really believe that if you *could* place him there, you'd have brought it up during the interrogation. So what have you actually got, when all's said and done? You have a motive of sorts – but *only* of sorts – and an alleged sighting by one of the hotel's employees.'

'The doorman will be a very good witness,' Paniatowski told him. 'You'll see that for yourself, when you talk to him.'

'The doorman has been arrested twice for being drunk and disorderly,' Tyndale countered. 'Did you know that?'

Of course she knew. Before dealing with a slippery character like Tyndale, she'd made certain she'd found out all she could about everyone involved.

'That was years ago,' she said, 'back in the days when he was a professional boxer.'

'True,' Tyndale agreed, 'but if this comes to trial – and I

seriously doubt that it ever will – I'll make sure the counsel for the defence mentions that fact to the jury. We may even suggest that the doorman had been drinking on the day in question – and the chances are that the jury will believe us.'

'I can offer you manslaughter, which is as good an offer as you're ever going to get,' Paniatowski said.

'I don't want any kind of offer,' Tyndale countered. 'What I want is that my client – who is innocent – be released.'

'Don't you have a conflict of interest here?' Paniatowski wondered.

'In what way?'

'Both the victim, and the man we strongly suspect of killing her, are your clients. That seems like a conflict to me.'

Tyndale laughed. 'Frankie Flynn has been my client ever since he was old enough to throw a punch or steal a bar of chocolate – the silly boy is always getting himself into trouble. Melissa Evans was never my client. I was retained by Mary Edwards.'

'You're splitting hairs,' Paniatowski said.

'It's what lawyers do,' Tyndale told her. 'It's what they are *supposed* to do. But even if I accept that there is no distinction to be made between the two, Mary Edwards/Melissa Evans is dead, and since she gave me no instructions as to what to do after her demise, there is simply no way I *can* represent her, which is why, the moment I have the address of her estate's executor, I will send him the advance that she paid me.'

'If Flynn really didn't do it—'

'Trust me, he didn't.'

'Then why won't you advise him to give an alibi for the time Melissa Evans was killed?'

'It is not up to him to prove his innocence – it is up to you to prove his guilt,' Tyndale said. 'If he says anything at all, you will immediately twist his words to make them mean what you want them to mean. If he says nothing, you will be denied such ammunition.'

'All I want is the truth,' Paniatowski said.

Tyndale studied her face for a moment, then said, 'I believe you. I do truly believe that left to run the investigation your own way, you would produce an honest, decent result. But you are caught up in a system which is corrupt down to its very bowels, chief inspector – an organisation which is committed firstly to its own convenience and secondly to its own survival, which means that justice comes in a very poor third.'

'That's simply not true,' Paniatowski said.

'Why don't you let my client go, chief inspector?' Tyndale urged. 'We both know you have nowhere near enough evidence to charge him with the murder of Melissa Evans.'

'No, we don't,' Paniatowski agreed, 'but we will be charging him with attacking a police officer – and we will be opposing bail.'

'From what I've heard, Inspector Beresford sustained no real damage as a result of my client's actions, and all-in-all I think it might be wiser not to charge him,' Tyndale said.

'And why is that?'

'Because if you charge him with the attack on Beresford, I will demand that you investigate Sergeant Meadows' attack on him.'

'You've got to be joking,' Paniatowski said. 'Flynn attacked her. She was only defending herself.'

'So you say.'

'So say the four other officers who witnessed the incident.'

'We both know that police officers will lie to protect their colleagues. And we're not the only ones who know it – judges and juries know it, too. Besides, once Meadows had damaged his shin, my client was helpless. There was absolutely no justification for her attempting to break his jaw.'

Paniatowski laughed. 'If Kate Meadows had wanted to break his jaw, she would have broken it. Flynn was out of control, and Meadows used no more than necessary force to restrain him.'

'That is a matter of opinion.'

Paniatowski shook her head. 'You're clearly not going to bend even a little, and neither am I,' she said. 'There isn't really much point in prolonging this conversation, is there?'

'No,' Tyndale agreed, 'I don't suppose there is.' He stood up with some difficulty. 'This case is probably my swansong, chief inspector, and while I have always done my best for my clients, it is particularly important to me that I get it right this time.'

Detective First Grade Pete Franco was on the phone to the South Carolina Department of Health and Environmental Control's Vital Records Office.

Franco had always been highly regarded within the police department – he was generally acknowledged to be a good detective and all-round nice guy – but the simple courage and dignity he had shown when his wife died of breast cancer had raised him to almost heroic status in many people's eyes.

No one had been the least surprised when Franco had volunteered to trace Melissa Evans' family, because he was not a man to run away from death. On the contrary, with his own bereavement, he had developed a strong empathy for others who had suffered a loss, and now he sought out such cases with an almost priest-like dedication.

Franco had been making notes while he'd been talking on the phone, and when he hung up, he slid those notes across the desk to Detective Third Grade Ted Henning, his partner.

'The captain's not going to like this,' he said.

Henning read the notes and nodded.

'It's not exactly going to have them dancing in the streets over in England, either,' he replied.

Every time a new customer opened the door to the public bar of the Drum and Monkey, the howling gale – which had been banging against the windows and rattling their frames – seized the opportunity to rush in. It did not come alone, but brought with it some of the sheets of discarded newspaper, cigarette packets and plastic bags it had collected as it roared around the town. It was a foul night, and, according to the weather forecast, the next day promised to be no better.

The gloom at the corner table had little to do with the climate.

There were always frustrating days during any investigation, but this seemed to be one of the worst any of the team could remember.

Melissa Evans had almost definitely been intending to write about the Hardcastle murder, but they still had no idea what had attracted her to it. It was possible, of course, that there was a family connection, but Evans was a Welsh name, and there had been no Evanses living in Whitebridge – or Accrington or Burnley for that matter – in 1924.

Frankie Flynn, encouraged by his solicitor, was still refusing to say anything but 'no comment'.

They had now, finally, managed to trace Melissa's port of entry – Manchester Ringway Airport – but that got them no closer to finding the killer than if they hadn't known at all.

So where did they go from there?

'What we're left with is two possible directions in which we can go,' Paniatowski said. 'The first is that the murder had everything to do with what Melissa Evans did in the past, and nothing at all to do with her being in Whitebridge. In other words, we accept the idea that she was killed on the instructions of someone who didn't like what she'd written about him. In support of this theory, she employed full-time bodyguards back home, and her conversation with Arthur Tyndale suggests she was worried about someone following her from the States and getting his hands on a gun. Theory two is much simpler: Frankie Flynn did it because she'd publicly humiliated him. Which one of those are you all inclined to go for?'

'Flynn,' Beresford said, without hesitation. 'If you examine his record over the years, it's clear that he's been growing increasingly violent, and it was only a matter of time before he killed somebody.'

'I agree,' said Meadows – who almost never agreed with Beresford. 'If Flynn had an alibi – even a tenuous one – his solicitor would have advised him to present it by now.'

'That might well be true if we were dealing with any other solicitor, but in this case it's Arthur Tyndale, and he believes that if Flynn says anything at all, we'll just twist his words round in order to fit him up.'

'But that's paranoid!' Meadows said.

'Yes, it is,' Paniatowski agreed. 'But there's always been a hint of paranoia in the way Tyndale's acted, and the closer he gets to death, it seems to me, the more paranoid he becomes.'

'I still think Flynn's our man,' Beresford said.

'And I think we haven't been taking the hitman theory seriously enough because, given our own experience, it seems so unlikely.' Paniatowski countered. 'But that's a failing on our part. Americans don't always think like we do. Over there, violence is often seen, by many people, as the solution to a problem. In recent years, John F Kennedy, Robert F Kennedy, Martin Luther King and Malcolm X have all been assassinated. When was the last time an important political figure was assassinated in England, Jack?'

'In 1812,' Crane said. 'The prime minister, Spencer Perceval, was shot in the Houses of Parliament.'

'So what I'm saying is—' Paniatowski began.

'Phone call for you, chief inspector,' the barman shouted across the bar. 'Shall I switch it through to the other phone?'

Paniatowski nodded, and headed for the corridor.

'Monika, that you?' said the voice at the other end of the long-distance line.

'It's me,' Paniatowski confirmed. 'You'll have to stop ringing me here, Fred, or people are going to start thinking I've got a secret lover.'

It was Mahoney's cue to slip into their 'were-we-lovers, weren't-we-lovers' routine, but all he said was: 'Yeah.'

'Is something wrong, Fred?' Paniatowski said, although there was no real need to ask, because her stomach had already informed her that she was about to hear something that she really wouldn't like.

'We've finished checking out Melissa Evans,' Mahoney said heavily. 'We've looked through her social security record, her driving licence form and her passport application, and they seem to indicate that she was born in a small town in South Carolina on June 7, 1940.'

That made her thirty-eight, which was just about right, Paniatowski thought.

So what was Fred so worried about?

'Have you talked to the family?' she asked.

'We can't. Her only immediate family were her parents, and they both died in a car crash in 1942.'

'Then who brought her up?'

Mahoney sighed regretfully.

'Nobody brought her up, Monika, because she was in the car with her parents, and she was killed, too.'

The Fox and Hounds sounded like an old pub, but it wasn't. Ten years earlier, there had been a row of terraced houses on the site, but when that terrace – along with all the terraces surrounding it – had been demolished in order to create an executive estate, the Fox and Hounds had risen from the ashes as a watering hole for the assistant bank managers and junior accountants who had moved into the area.

It was the kind of pub which had coloured lights around the windows even when it wasn't Christmas. Its walls were covered with traditional hunting prints (imported from a small factory in Thailand), and its bars were made of a solid oak which somehow managed to look like a veneer.

Paniatowski hated it, but not as much as she hated the thought of what she was going to have to do once she was inside.

She found Mike Traynor at a round copper-topped table in the saloon bar. He was alone – but that was pretty much par for the course.

Traynor was watching her from the moment she entered the pub, and when it became obvious that she was heading for his table, he grinned.

'Why if it isn't Detective Chief Inspector Paniatowski,' he said. 'What an unexpected pleasure. Do sit down.'

Paniatowski sat. 'Murder isn't funny,' she said. 'It's not something you treat as a game.'

'Do let me buy you a drink, DCI Paniatowski,' Traynor suggested. 'What would you like?'

'I'd like you to be honest with me,' Paniatowski told him. 'You were playing with words at the press conference. You said the body in the mortuary wasn't Melissa Evans. It is – it's just somebody else as well.'

'You'll get no argument from me about that,' Traynor said.

'Why did you do it? What was the point?'

'Listen, chief inspector, the reason that I said what I did say at the press conference was that it serves to enhance my reputation. There's me on the one hand – a simple journalist working with just a notepad and a telephone – and there's you on the other – a senior police officer with a huge organisation to back you up – and it's me who gets to the truth first. The next article I write will cost fifty quid more than the last one – and the newspaper will pay up willingly.' He took a drag of his cigarette. 'But it was a purely professional decision to make you look an idiot in front of the cameras – there was absolutely nothing personal in it at all.'

'Liar!' Paniatowski said.

Traynor grinned again.

'Well, maybe there was just a *little* bit of malice in it,' he admitted. 'After all, you and me don't really get on, do we?'

'You must have a lot of faith in your source to have gone out on a limb like that,' Paniatowski said.

'I have *tremendous* faith in him. You said in the press conference that my sources have sometimes fed me a load of old cobblers, and so they have. But not this one! He's no manky old river, washing up the odd bit of detritus at my feet. He's a bubbling fresh mountain spring. He's been giving me information for years, and he's never once let me down.'

'I need to talk to him,' Paniatowski said.

'You can't.'

'You're refusing to give me his name?'

'Yes.'

'Do you want me to arrest you?'

'I'd *love* you to arrest me – it will only add to the reputation of Fearless Mike Traynor, the crusading journalist.'

'I wonder if you'll still be feeling as brave when you hear the judge pass sentence on you,' Paniatowski mused.

'That would be even better,' Traynor said. 'I wouldn't get more than six months, and I'd be out in three – and when I was released, I'd be fighting off offers for a film of my life.'

He was right, she thought.

'Could you, at least, tell me what Melissa Evans' real name is, Mr Traynor?' she asked.

'I'm afraid not.'

'Why?'

'If anybody else asks me for the name, I'll say I promised my source I'd never reveal it.'

Sally Spencer

'Whereas, in fact . . .?'

'Whereas, in fact . . .' Traynor paused. 'I'm in a good mood, so I'll tell you what you want to know, but on the strict understanding that not only is it off the record, but you don't pass it on to anyone else.'

'All right,' Paniatowski said, hating herself for agreeing to his demand.

'I can't tell you what her real name is because my source didn't tell me, and however much I grovelled – and I can do a very good grovel for the right people – he simply wouldn't budge.'

'If I knew who the dead woman really was, that would probably help me to catch her killer,' Paniatowski said.

'Yes,' Traynor agreed, 'it probably would.'

'Don't let him get away with it,' Paniatowski urged. 'Give me the name of your source.'

'No chance!'

'Don't you have an ounce of human decency in you, Mr Traynor?' Paniatowski asked.

Traynor frowned, as if he was really considering the matter.

'Nope,' he said finally, 'I don't think I do.'

As Paniatowski drove home, the skies opened and the rain lashed her windscreen with a fury to match her own.

Sometime in the next few hours, when you realise you've made a big mistake, you're going to feel very foolish, Mr Traynor, she'd said at the press conference – even though she'd done dozens of press conferences before, and knew she should be circumspect; even though she'd seen the camera lenses winking at her!

And what had Traynor said in reply?

Not as foolish as you'll feel when you discover I was right all along.

But she could live with looking foolish – could even live it down, in time – because everybody made mistakes.

What was really getting to her was that there was one very important question that she simply had no answer to.

'I wish I knew how Traynor's source knows Melissa Evans' real name,' she said aloud.

And her windscreen wipers, battling against the storm, went 'swish, swish, swish' as if to mock her.

How *could* this source – whoever he was – possibly know the name? she asked herself for probably the twentieth time.

How could any one person – and a person, furthermore, in little Whitebridge, for God's sake! – know what the combined might of the Mid Lancs Constabulary and the New York City Police Department didn't know?

As she pulled into the driveway, she was surprised to see that the lounge light was still on, because Elena was normally in bed by that hour, and the nanny, coming from a Spanish family where money was tight, was almost fanatical about not wasting electricity.

She parked the car, and entered the house through the side door. Elena was sitting on the sofa. She looked miserable, and her eyes were red, as if she'd been crying.

'What's happened?' Paniatowski asked in a complete panic. 'Is it one of the boys?'

'The boys are fine,' Elena assured her.

'Then why are you looking so unhappy?'

'Mrs Green, the lady from next door . . .'

'I know who Mrs Green is.'

'She bring her puppy round, for the boys to stroke.'

'And did it bite one of them?'

'No, it was very good – very friendly.'

'Then what, for God's sake?'

'Philip grab hold of the puppy's tail. He pull it very hard. The puppy is crying and Thomas is crying. I say, "Philip, let go of the puppy," but he only laugh and pull harder. He only let go when Mrs Green shout very loud at him.'

'He's only a baby,' Paniatowski said. 'He was just playing. He didn't know he was hurting the puppy.'

'I tell him . . .'

'You can't expect a baby to understand the concept of inflicting pain on others. It's far beyond their mental reach.'

Elena looked as if she was about to argue, then she said, 'Mrs Green is very angry.'

'I'll deal with her in the morning,' Paniatowski said. 'Thank

you for staying up so late, Elena. It was very thoughtful
of you. But you can go to bed now.'

As Elena climbed the stairs, Paniatowski allowed her body
– which was as weary now as she could ever remember it
being – to sink down into the sofa.

Is this how it begins? she thought. Is this how the bad seed
starts to emerge?

ELEVEN

When Detectives Franco and Henning were ushered into Harvey Morgan's office by Linda, his secretary, Morgan himself was on the phone.

'Listen Hank,' he was saying, 'you need to clear the presses, because you got to have the capacity to reprint her books . . . yeah, all of them, even the early ones . . . I don't know . . . fifty thousand, maybe a hundred thousand copies of each . . .' He looked up and seemed to notice the two detectives for the first time. 'Give me a number between twenty and thirty,' he mouthed.

'Uh . . . twenty-four,' Henning said.

'I shouldn't need to be telling you this, Hank, because you're the publisher, and you should already have the figures at your fingertips,' Morgan said into the phone, 'but when Vladimir Nabokov died last year, his sales went up twenty-four per cent! That's right. Twenty-four per cent! And *he* died of natural causes!' He paused for a moment, then continued, 'Yeah, it makes a difference how she died. You're gonna have one surge in sales at her funeral, and you're gonna have a second surge when the guy who killed her goes on trial. And you'd sure as hell better be ready for both of them.'

When he hung up, Franco said, 'It didn't take you long to cash in on Melissa Evans' death, did it, Mr Morgan?'

'You're damn right it didn't,' Morgan said, with evident satisfaction. 'That's why I'm at the top of the tree. That's why I have writers queuing up to have me represent them. Besides,' he added, perhaps finally detecting a hint of criticism in what Franco had said, 'it's what Melissa herself would have wanted.'

'Sure she would,' Franco said, not even bothering to try and hide his scepticism.

'Sure she would,' Morgan echoed, 'because fifteen per cent of what she makes goes directly into the foundation.'

'What foundation?'

'The Melissa Evans Foundation – it's some kinda charity.'

'Does the foundation *really* get fifteen per cent of her income – or is that another figure you've just made up?' Franco growled.

'Steady, Pete,' Henning cautioned.

'*Did* you make it up?' Franco persisted.

'I'm thinking about it,' said Morgan, apparently impervious to Franco's anger. 'Yeah, it was fifteen per cent. The reason I remember is because I had to talk her down from twenty – and boy, was that hard work.'

'How well did you know Melissa Evans?' Henning asked, in an attempt to steer the conversation into safer waters.

'How well did I know her? I was like a father to her,' Morgan said.

'So tell us about her,' Henning said quickly, before Franco had the chance to say something which was almost bound to be unhelpful.

'About six or seven years ago now, she comes in here with a biography of John Lennon she's written,' Morgan told him. 'What it has to say is God awful boring, because all she's done is collect up information that's already been published – but the *way* she says it is just great. It's like Lennon leaps off the page and he's there with you in the room. I sign her up on the spot, and give her $5,000 dollars – out of my own pocket – so she can do some research.'

'What exactly do you mean by research?' Franco asked.

Morgan sighed, as if he'd just realised that he was dealing with a numbskull here.

'Research is when you pay people to tell you things.'

'And by "people" you mean post-graduate students and recognised experts in their field?' Franco asked.

'Yeah, people like that,' Morgan said, unconvincingly. 'But also chauffeurs and maids, and doormen at nightclubs – especially doormen at nightclubs.'

'Did you see her very often?' Henning asked.

'Sure, we were both in the loop, so we were always meeting at parties and receptions.'

'I meant socially.'

'Like I said, we were always meeting at—'

'Did you ever get together just as friends?'

'Get together as friends? Who the hell has time for that?' Morgan asked dismissively.

'I'd like the names and addresses of her family and all her friends,' Franco said.

'I don't know anything about the family,' Morgan admitted.

'What about the friends?'

Morgan thought about it for a moment.

'I can't help you there, either,' he admitted. 'Now, if you'll excuse me, I just gotta—'

'Do some more cashing in?' Franco suggested.

'Move some more product,' Morgan corrected him.

They stepped into the outer office, and Linda looked up from her desk and smiled at them.

'He's not always as crass and insensitive as he seemed today,' she told the two detectives.

'He couldn't be,' Franco replied. 'No one could.'

The secretary held out a piece of paper for Henning to take. 'This is the name and address of Melissa's best friend.'

Once they were back out on the street, Henning turned to Franco and said, 'You're getting too involved in this investigation, Pete – *way* too involved.'

Franco sighed. 'You're right,' he agreed. 'Maybe I'd feel better if we could find just one person who was really mourning Melissa Evans' death.'

Patricia Courtney, who lived in a loft in the middle of SoHo, was about the same age as Melissa Evans had been, but was a little shorter, slightly stockier and had spiky purple hair. She was a painter, and several of her works were hanging on the bare brickwork walls.

Henning supposed that her paintings must be art, because that was what paintings were, but he himself could not relate to the display of female body parts which any decent woman would only uncover in the dark.

Franco, on the other hand, displayed no such embarrassment, but instead studied the pictures with interest.

And while he was studying them, Patricia Courtney was studying him, her body language saying that she knew he was about to launch an attack on her work, and she was more than ready for it.

'Do you sell your paintings, Miss Courtney?' Franco asked.

'Yes, I sell them,' Patricia Courtney replied aggressively. 'I'm an artist. It's what artists do.'

'But you don't *need* to sell them,' Franco said.

'What do you mean by that?'

'I'm no expert on the acrylic painted vagina market – I'm much more into Roy Lichtenstein—'

'That phoney!'

'But I'd be willing to bet your paintings – which I rather like, as a matter of fact – didn't earn you nearly enough to buy this loft.'

She could go one of two ways, Henning thought – she could explode, or she could smile.

She smiled, and – not for the first time – Henning was impressed by his partner's skill in reading people.

'You're right, of course,' Patricia Courtney agreed. 'I bought the place with money from my trust fund.'

'According to Harvey Morgan's secretary, you were Melissa Evans' best friend,' Franco said. 'Is that right?'

'Yes . . . and no,' Patricia Courtney told him. 'I enjoyed her company a great deal, and I spent a lot of my free time with her when we weren't both working. She was intelligent and amusing, and sometimes we'd even hop into bed together, though that was mostly for old times' sake.'

Henning looked down at his shoes, and wished he was somewhere – anywhere – else.

'What you've just said sounds like a description of best friends to me,' Franco told her.

'You'd think so, wouldn't you? But what really makes best friends, in my opinion, is that they tell each other everything.'

'And Melissa didn't tell you everything?'

'Melissa told me practically nothing – she played her cards real close to her chest.'

'So what *do* you know about her?'

'I know Melissa Evans wasn't her real name, because that's one of the things that she *did* tell me.'

'But she didn't go any further than that, and tell you what her real name actually was?'

'Nope.'

'What else?'

'I know that her father died a couple of months ago. He's the reason, incidentally, that she changed her name.'

'Could you explain?'

'Sure. She always believed she was going to be famous – although some people might prefer to call her infamous—'

'Is that what you'd call her? Infamous?'

'I wouldn't call her anything. Hey, I'm an artist. I create things of beauty. And if Melissa wanted to churn out dross to pay the bills, then that was absolutely no business of mine.'

'I'm sorry, I interrupted you,' Franco said. 'You were telling us about why she changed her name.'

'Yeah. She knew that when she was famous, the tabloids would try to dig up dirt on her, in pretty much the same way as she was digging up dirt on the subjects of her books.'

'And she didn't want her father to be bothered?'

'That's right – but there was more to it than that. It seems that he had his own skeleton in the closet . . .'

'What kind of skeleton?'

'That I don't know, but I got the impression that it related to something that happened a long, long time ago. Anyway, the skeleton was there to be found, and she didn't want it brought out into the daylight and given a thorough rattling in front of the cameras.'

'Did her father live here in New York?'

Patricia Courtney shrugged. 'She didn't tell me he didn't, but I don't think that he did.'

'What leads you to that conclusion?'

'When he died, she dropped out of sight for about a week. If she'd have been here, I'd have seen her, because New York is a big city, but the New York that Melissa and I shared is just a village.'

'Is there anything else you can say that might help me, Patricia?' Franco asked.

'Maybe this. When she came back from his funeral, she said, "I'm really going to miss Dad. The one consolation I have is that I'm now free to do something I've wanted to do for a long, long time." And I said, "Honey, you're a free spirit. If you really wanted to do it, how come you let your father stop you?" And that's when she came over all strange, like she wasn't really with me anymore. "I know you think nothing good can come from opening old wounds," she said, "but sometimes you have to do it, so the wounds have a chance to heal properly." I think she was talking to her father at that point.'

'I think so too.'

'And maybe that had to do with the skeleton.'

'Yes, maybe it did.'

Patricia stepped back a couple of paces, and ran her eyes critically up and down Franco's body.

'You wouldn't like to come around and model for me sometime, would you?' she asked.

Franco smiled. 'I don't think I've got the right sort of equipment, Patricia,' he said.

'I can see that for myself,' Patricia Courtney agreed, 'but I've fallen into a bit of an artistic rut, and I think it's time to branch out.'

Franco's smile became a little sadder.

'I'm a recent widower,' he said.

Most people would have grown all embarrassed and regretful at this point, Henning thought, but it didn't look to him as if Patricia Courtney was about to become either of those things.

He was right.

'You're a widower and I'm a dyke,' she told Franco. 'But sometimes you have to leave the past behind, and set off in a new direction.'

'The widower and the lesbian,' Franco mused. 'Nah – that kind of thing only works out in the movies.'

Brad Jones, the more senior of Melissa Evans' bodyguards, lived in Brooklyn, and agreed to meet the two detectives in a bar just off Utica Avenue.

Jones was around six feet two inches tall and tightly muscled. But he also had a pair of brown eyes which revealed both compassion and intelligence. Franco guessed he was an ex-marine, and decided that he could trust the man, and probably might even like him.

'The reason I didn't invite you up to my crib is that it's a shit-box,' Jones explained, when they'd ordered their drinks. 'Hell, I don't need anything better, 'cos I'm hardly ever there.'

'Every man should have a place that he can call home,' Henning said solemnly.

'You're right,' Jones agreed, 'and mine, my friend, is a log cabin in the Catskills.'

'Are you working at the moment?' Franco asked.

Jones shook his head. 'No. I've got a good name in the business, and the second it was announced that Melissa was dead I started getting offers, but she paid me till the end of the month, so I reckon I'm still working for her.'

'She's dead,' Henning pointed out.

'But not buried,' Jones countered. 'I won't consider my job finally over until she's laid to rest.'

'You sound like you were quite fond of her,' Franco said.

'Yeah, she was a real nice lady. We weren't friends – I was the hired help – but we got on well.'

'Did she really need a bodyguard, or did she just keep you around because famous people have to keep proving to themselves that they really are famous, and having a bodyguard is one of the ways to do it?'

'She really needed a bodyguard,' Jones said. 'Most of the time, it was just little things that I prevented – people screaming abuse in her face or throwing ink at her. You know the kind of shit that goes down.'

'Yeah,' Franco agreed, 'we get plenty of shit of our own.'

'But there've also been a couple of more serious attacks. I don't say the guys who went for her wanted to actually kill her, but they sure-as-shit meant to hurt her a lot.'

'And what happened?'

Brad Jones shrugged his heavy shoulders. 'I intervened.'

'And what does that mean?'

'I had to break the guy's arm both times.'

'Did you report it to the police?' Franco asked.

Brad looked him squarely in the eye.

'Nope, I didn't report it to the police – and neither did the guys with the broken arms. That kinda tells you something, doesn't it?'

It certainly does, Franco thought – but I've no idea *what* it tells me.

'So you went everywhere that Melissa went, did you?' he asked.

'Mostly.'

'What does that mean?'

'I went with her to the condo, the ranch and the chalet. I went with her on book tours and talk show tours. Where I didn't go with her was New Mills.'

'Where's that?'

'It's a little town in Massachusetts. She visited it maybe three or four times a year.'

'How long did she stay there?'

'Except for the last time, it was just for a day or two.'

'And what *about* the last time?'

'Then she stayed for six days.'

'When was this?'

'A few weeks ago. Maybe late January. I've got the details written down in my log.'

'So let me see if I've got this clear – you never went with her to New Mills,' Franco said.

'That's right.'

'And why was that?'

'She said no, and she was the boss.'

'And you were happy about that?'

'No, I was very *un*happy, but she wouldn't be moved. The best I could get her to agree to was that I would stay in a motel about ten miles from New Mills, so she'd know where I was if she needed me.'

'You were never tempted to slip quietly into New Mills to make sure she was all right?'

'Sure, I was tempted, but she must have figured that out for herself, because she said, "If I catch a whiff of you in New Mills, Brad, you're out. There'll be no second chances. Have you got that?" And her voice was real cold – it didn't sound like her at all – so I knew she was serious. So what I did was,

I taught her a few basic combat moves, so that if she had to, she could defend herself.'

'Was she a quick learner?'

'Very quick – and very good. She was one determined woman.' Jones took a reflective sip of his beer. 'Most of the time, she was very direct and clear, you know, but there's one thing she said that still puzzles me.'

'And what's that?'

'She said, "Don't lose any sleep over me when I'm in New Mills, Brad. I'm quite safe there, because nobody knows who I am." And I said, "You're fooling yourself, Miss Evans. You've been on dozens of TV shows, and your picture is on the back of like a couple of million books. There isn't anybody in America who doesn't know who you are." "The people who live in New Mills *don't* know who I am," she told me. "They *think* they know, but they're wrong." Then she laughed. "Although, in a way, they are right – and everybody else is wrong." Do you know what that means?'

'I haven't a clue,' Franco said.

Although he was beginning to think that maybe he had.

According to *A New History of Massachusetts* (revised edition), which Franco had consulted at the library, New Mills had once been a small city, but had been in decline for years, and now, on even the most optimistic evaluation, it could not have been called anything but a large village. The community college was long gone, as was the Howard Johnson's, but the police department had survived, and it was the police department that Franco rang.

Since they'd said goodbye to the bodyguard, he had been grappling with the puzzle that Brad Jones had set him – had been trying to explain how was it possible that the people of New Mills didn't recognise Melissa Evans – and he thought he had come up with an answer which, though it seemed highly unlikely, was the only one that worked.

When the chief of police came on the line, Franco identified himself and the chief said, with something like awe, 'I sure never thought that I'd ever get a call from a New York City detective. What can I do for you, detective?'

Henning and Franco exchanged a glance which said that what he *should* have done – what they *would* have done in his place – was to ring the precinct in order to establish that they were, in fact, the genuine article.

'I'd like to ask you a few questions about New Mills,' Franco said. 'It probably won't make a lot of sense to you at first, but hopefully it will by the time I've finished. Are you OK with that?'

'Is this what they call "collecting background material"?' the police chief asked.

'Sort of,' Franco said.

'Never done that kind of thing myself – there's not much call for it in New Mills, where everybody knows everything anyway – but I've seen it on cop shows on the TV, so I guess it's fine.'

'Were there any funerals in the town in late January?'

'Sure – two or three. There was Sarah Dunn . . . no, wait a minute, that was in December—'

'Maybe I can narrow it down a little for you,' Franco interrupted. 'Was one of the people who was buried towards the end of January an old man with a daughter who lives in New York?'

'OK, now I know where we are – you're talking about John Entwistle.'

'What can you tell me about him?'

'He was an Englishman, you know. Came over here some-time in the Twenties, and worked in the old Pine Valley Mill, down by the river. I was a kid back then, and I remember thinking at the time that it was great to have an Englishman in New Mills – it gave the town some kind of distinction. Course, I also thought that having an elephant would have been better.'

'Yes, there really is no competition,' Franco said, with a smile. 'The elephant wins hands down, every time.'

'John married Hester Cockburn, sometime in the late Thirties, I think, and their daughter Maggie was born around 1940,' the chief continued. 'Then the war broke out, and Hester went to work in one of the big munitions factories that had sprung up round Boston. She said it was just till she'd built up a decent stake for the family, but she never came back. Well, that was no surprise to anybody but John, because none of the Cockburns have ever been exactly what you might call reliable.'

'Tell me about Maggie,' Franco said.

'John brought Maggie up all by himself, and I have to say he did a pretty good job of it. She was a good student – always winning prizes. She won the county essay competition one year. We were all so proud of her, but to be honest with you, I just can't remember what that essay was all about.'

'It doesn't matter,' Franco said. 'Carry on with the story.'

'Well, when she graduated from high school, she went to work in the mill with her father. We all thought that was a bit of a waste, but mill work was the only kind of work there was round here – and now even that's gone.'

'What did she do when the mill closed down?'

'She took herself off to New York City to seek her fortune.' The chief paused. 'I haven't thought of this before, but now Melissa Evans has been murdered, Maggie will be out of a job again. Poor girl – it just don't seem fair, does it?'

'Did she work for Melissa Evans?' Franco asked.

The chief chuckled. 'Well, yes, in a manner of speaking, she did,' he said. 'She's a Melissa Evans lookalike. She makes personal appearances at charity events and state fairs. And she's damn good at it, too. You see the real Melissa on TV, and you couldn't tell her and Maggie apart.'

'I hate to be the one to break this to you, chief,' Franco said, 'but she isn't a Melissa Evans lookalike – she *is* Melissa Evans.'

'This is some kind of sick joke, isn't it?' the chief asked angrily. 'It just *has to be* some kind of sick joke.'

'I'm sorry, chief – I'm *really* sorry – but it isn't,' Franco said.

'You're sure?'

'I'm sure.'

There was silence from the other end of the line for at least half a minute, then, in a cracked voice, the chief said, 'Everybody liked Maggie. She was the sweetest girl you could ever hope to meet. The whole town's gonna be . . .

it's gonna be . . . I'm sorry, detective, but I have to hang up now.'

'No problem,' Franco said. 'I'm sorry for your loss.'

Melissa's agent saw her death as a way of selling more of her books. Her 'best friend' would simply move on to a new best friend. Even her bodyguard would wipe her from his mind once she was buried. But in New Mills, Massachusetts, there were any number of people who would grieve for her – who, in remembering her life, would ensure that her light didn't quite fade.

When Franco put the phone back on its cradle, he was feeling strangely at peace.

TWELVE

I t was six o'clock in the morning, and Ruth Tyndale stood in the kitchen, making up a breakfast tray, and thinking about the fact that after over thirty years of marriage, she no longer shared a bed with her husband.

She had moved out of the master bedroom some months earlier, when Arthur's condition had begun to worsen. She hadn't done it because she suddenly loved him less than she had, or because she now found him repulsive. In fact, on the long dark nights when she lay in her narrow single bed in what had once been their daughter's room, she positively *ached* to return to the marital bed.

But it just wasn't practical, she told herself, because either Arthur had a bad night and she got no sleep, or she had a bad night (she'd been sleeping very badly since his diagnosis) and disturbed him.

She had completed laying the breakfast tray, and now it contained a very mild herbal tea, a softly boiled egg, and some lightly buttered toast. She hoped that this would be one of his better days, when he'd be able to keep most of it down, and picking up the tray, she began to walk to the stairs.

She so wished that he'd stay at home and get more rest, she thought as she climbed the stairs, but he was who he was – and she had married him for just that reason – so if carrying on working kept him sane, then she supposed she could learn to put up with it.

At the top of the stairs, she manipulated the door handle with her right elbow, and gently pushed the door open with her hip.

'Time to get up, sleepyhead,' she called out in a cheery voice.

She was acting as if it were a game – as if staying in bed was only wilfulness on her husband's part.

And he usually played along with it.

'I know I'm being a lazy boy, Ruth, but if you'll just give me another ten minutes, I'll come downstairs all bright-eyed and bushy-tailed.'

But it was nothing to do with laziness and it was nothing to do with sleepiness – it was to do with dying – and there were some mornings when he didn't get up because he *couldn't* get up.

The light streaming in from the landing behind her provided Ruth with sufficient illumination to cross the room, so it wasn't until she'd put the tray on the bedside table that she switched on the lamp and got her first good look at her husband's face.

But when she *did* get a look at him – when she saw that his chest was hardly rising and falling, and that though his eyes were open, there was no sign of life in them – she almost fainted.

It was around seven o'clock that Philip started vomiting.

'What should I do?' Paniatowski asked Elena. 'Do you think I should call the doctor?'

'Why would you do that?' the Spanish girl asked. 'Felipe is just being sick. It is what little babies do – if the *mierda* is not coming out of one end of them, then it is *vómito* coming out of the other.'

It's easy for you to be so calm, Elena, Paniatowski thought. According to Louisa, you were brought up in a house absolutely jam-packed with children, so you've seen it all – but the whole thing is new to me.

Her gut still told her to call the doctor, but her mind advised her that was a bad idea.

Don't forget the story of the boy who cried wolf, the mind said. If the doctor comes and there's nothing wrong with Philip, he's going to be pissed off with you, isn't he? And the next time one of the twins is ill – and that might *really* be serious – he may decide that their mother's just being hysterical, and there's no real hurry to see them at all.

She rocked Philip very gently on her knee.

'That was why you pulled the puppy's tail yesterday, wasn't it?' she cooed, reassuringly. 'It wasn't that you were being a bad boy – no, no, it wasn't – it was just that you weren't feeling very well.'

At around half past seven, Thomas started to throw up, and Paniatowski, who had been working hard to keep a lid on the panic that was bubbling up inside her, realised she was heading for a major meltdown.

It wasn't only that Thomas was ill now, she told herself – it was that Philip was *still* being sick. And while it was true that Philip's puking was not as violent as it had been – how could it be, when the poor little mite must have nothing left in his stomach? – he was still retching, and he had turned very pale.

She phoned the doctor, and described the symptoms.

'I'll be round right away, Miss Paniatowski,' he said.

When she put down the phone, she was trembling. On the one hand, it was a great relief that he was coming round immediately; on the other, she would have been much happier if he'd felt able to say there was no urgency and he'd drop in later in the morning.

The doctor arrived five minutes later. He took one look at the babies, and clapped his hands.

'Right, clear the room,' he said.

'Can't I stay, Dr McCloud?' Paniatowski asked meekly.

'You most certainly cannot,' the doctor replied sternly, 'the boys and I have work to do here, and the last thing we want is any mothers or nannies getting in the way.'

Paniatowski slowly and reluctantly descended the stairs.

Thank God Louisa slept over at her friend's house last night, she thought – because if she was here, she'd be in a worse state than I am.

She paced the lounge for two minutes, then picked up the phone and called Beresford.

'The twins are sick,' she moaned. 'For all I know, they may be *very* sick. I've called the doctor, and he's here now.'

'Then he'll make them better, won't he?' Beresford asked. 'It's what doctors are paid to do.'

'But Philip looked so poorly, Colin. He—'

'They'll be all right,' Beresford said, soothingly. 'They're big strong lads, and they'll be fine.'

'Do you really think so?'

'I *know* so.'

The magic was working. If solid, reliable Colin Beresford – who had not lied to her in all the years she'd known him – said that everything was going to be all right, then everything was going to be all right.

'Thank you, Colin,' she said. 'Listen, if the doctor says that what's wrong with the twins isn't serious—'

'Not *if* he says it, *when* he says it,' Beresford interrupted her. 'Repeat after me: when the doctor says that what's wrong with the twins isn't serious . . .'

'When the doctor says that what's wrong with the twins isn't serious . . .' Paniatowski said dutifully.

'You'll have to fill in the rest of the sentence yourself, Monika, because I've no idea what you'll do.'

'I'll leave Elena in charge, and come down to headquarters for a couple of hours.'

'You've absolutely no need to do that,' Beresford told her. 'I've got everything under control here.'

'You're sure . . .?'

'I'm sure,' Beresford said firmly. 'Call me when they're *so much* better that you look like a complete silly cow for ever having been so worried.'

'I will,' Paniatowski promised.

The man waiting in the public reception area at police head-quarters was in his early forties, and was wearing a smart charcoal grey suit, white shirt, neutral tie and beautifully polished black shoes. Kate Meadows – who was very good at making instant assessments – guessed that he'd probably attended a minor public school and a major provincial university, and was either a chartered surveyor or a solicitor – though, given that he was in the police station so early in the morning, it was much more likely to be the latter.

She walked up to him, and held out her hand.

'Good morning. I'm Detective Sergeant Meadows,' she said.

They shook hands.

'I'm Paul Robinson,' the man said, 'and the reason that I'm here is because your chief constable has asked me to speak to DCI Paniatowski.'

'The boss isn't in,' Meadows told him. 'She's been detained at home with a domestic crisis.'

'I see,' Robinson said. 'Then I suppose I'd better ring her, so if you'd like to give me her number . . .'

'I'm afraid that won't be possible,' Meadows said.

'I'm not sure you quite understand the situation, sergeant,' Robinson replied. 'Your chief constable, Keith Pickering, wants me to—'

'Sorry!' Meadows said firmly.

She meant it, Robinson thought. He could easily bypass her, of course. All he had to do was ring Pickering, because the chief constable was bound to have Paniatowski's home number. But that would probably get Meadows into trouble, he told himself, and he didn't want to do that. Besides, there was something about the sergeant which said that even the Prince of Wales or the Archbishop of Canterbury would think twice before getting on her wrong side.

'Well, if it's not possible to speak to DCI Paniatowski,' he said, 'who *should* I speak to?'

'That depends,' Meadows said. 'What was it that you wanted to talk to the boss about?'

'I wanted to discuss a man called Frankie Flynn. He's been detained and, as I understand it, he's being questioned this morning.'

'He certainly is,' Meadows agreed, 'and I'll be the one wielding the rubber hose.'

'I beg your pardon!'

Meadows smiled. 'Don't worry, Mr Robinson, I'm only speaking metaphorically.'

Robinson returned her smile. 'Well, that is a relief,' he said.

'I much prefer to use a piece of lead pipe, for the simple reason that it's very hard to jab someone in the kidneys with a rubber hose,' Meadows told him.

There were probably any number of smart and witty answers he could make to that, Robinson thought, but since he couldn't come up with a single one at that moment, he settled for saying, 'Do you think we could possibly get back to the reason I'm here?'

'Absolutely,' Meadows agreed, with the apparent enthusiasm of a small puppy.

'Up until now, Frankie Flynn has been represented by Arthur Tyndale, hasn't he?'

'Yes – the Lone Ranger rides again.'

'But he's not been well for some time, and it seems that early this morning, poor old Arthur collapsed and had to be rushed to hospital. He's in a pretty bad way, by all accounts, and apparently, they're not expecting him to last the day.'

'Which leaves our poor little Frankie without anyone to wipe his bottom for him,' Meadows said.

'I . . . err . . . wouldn't have put it quite like that,' Robinson said.

'I know you wouldn't – you'd have said it leaves him without anyone to wipe his *arse* for him,' Meadows replied, 'but, you see, I'm a lady.'

'No, that's not it at all,' Robinson began, before deciding to give up on this particular strand of the conversation and move on. 'The point is that the chief constable – who, for wholly understandable reasons, wants this matter over and done with as soon as possible – has asked me to come here and proffer myself as an alternative.'

'Yes, you could certainly do that – and you could take over Tyndale's job, as well.'

Robinson smiled again, because – really – there was no choice in the matter.

'Do you always take the mickey out of . . . out of . . .?' he asked, before finding himself lost for the right words.

'Out of people like your good self?' Meadows supplied.

'Yes.'

'Only when the opportunity presents itself.'

Had he been flirting? Robinson asked himself.

No that was impossible, because he was an upstanding pillar of the community and upstanding pillars of the community simply didn't flirt.

'What do you think the chances are that Flynn will agree to me representing him?' he asked, in a deliberately dry, solicitor-like voice.

'He's a bit of a conservative – I find that most mindless

thugs are,' Meadows said, 'and he won't like changing horses mid-stream at all, but if I explain to him that the one he was riding has gone under, I'm sure he'll come round to the idea.'

'And you're willing to do that, are you?'

'I'd do *anything* for a friend of the chief constable's,' Meadows said, in mock sex-siren voice, which somehow managed to override the parody and still be quite sexy anyway. 'By the way, which are you – golf or Masons?'

'I'm not quite sure what you mean?'

'If the chief con thinks he can get away with ringing you at this time of the morning, you've either got to be a golfing buddy or a fellow Mason. I was just wondering which it was.'

'It's both,' Robinson said.

Paul Robinson had only spent a little over twenty minutes talking to Frankie Flynn, but when he returned to the visitors' reception area, the look on his face said it had been the longest twenty minutes of his life.

'What's the matter?' Meadows asked.

'Have you got a cigarette?' Robinson asked.

'I don't smoke.'

'I didn't think that I did any more, but I could really use one now,' Robinson said.

'I'll see what I can do,' Meadows said.

She disappeared into the bowels of the station, and re-emerged a minute later with a packet of Embassy Filter and a box of matches.

Robinson took the cigarettes gratefully and reached into his inside jacket pocket for his wallet.

'They're on the house,' Meadows said. 'What seems to be the problem? Doesn't Frankie want you to represent him? He seemed perfectly happy with the idea when I suggested it to him.'

Robinson lit a cigarette, sucked on it greedily, and then began to pace the room.

'Flynn seemed perfectly happy about it then, and he's perfectly happy about it now,' he said. 'I think he's quite relieved, in a way, because he could see with his own eyes that Arthur wasn't at all a well man.'

'So if Frankie's agreed to the change of solicitor, then there's no problem, is there?'

'Not from his side, no.'

'But from yours?'

'Yes.'

'Do you want to tell me why you think there's a problem?'

'I'm not sure I can,' said Robinson, still pacing.

'Why not?'

'Because of who I am, and because of the standards laid down by the society to which I belong.'

'Well, that's as clear as mud,' Meadows said.

Robinson lit a second cigarette from the glowing butt of his first, then stubbed the butt out in the ashtray.

'On the other hand,' he said, 'if I withdraw, I'll just be shunting the dilemma I find myself facing over to one of my colleagues – the thought of which is already making me feel extremely uncomfortable.'

'Or to put it another way,' Meadows said, 'you're playing pass the parcel, and you hear the parcel ticking and realise it's a bomb. You don't want to be blown up yourself, but you don't want any of your mates blown up either, so you start to think about ways you can defuse it.'

'Eloquently put,' Robinson said. He stopped pacing and locked eyes with Meadows. 'Could I give you a hypothetical example of the sort of problem I might possibly be facing?'

'If it helps to do it that way, I don't see why not,' Meadows agreed.

'Hypothetically, I might be called in, at the last minute, to take over a case from another solicitor, and I might discover that that solicitor had served his client very badly indeed. Note my wording carefully, Sergeant Meadows – I did not say he had served him incompetently – which is regrettable, but not morally reprehensible – the words I actually chose were that he had served him badly.'

'So noted,' Meadows agreed.

'But the simple truth is that by the rules and standards that bind me as a solicitor, I am not entitled to make any such judgement, unilaterally, on one of my peers.'

'In other words, you're not allowed to say he's a useless dickhead – even if he is?'

'Exactly. Were such a hypothetical situation to arise, I would have to report the facts to the Law Society, which would then conduct an investigation, and that investigation would, in turn, decide whether or not any action needed to be taken against that solicitor. The result of the investigation would be honest and fair, but it would also take some time. "The wheels of justice grind slow, but they grind exceedingly fine" as the old quotation has it.'

'I don't see—' Meadows began.

'I haven't finished, Sergeant Meadows,' Robinson said. 'Let us say, in this hypothetic example of ours, that the police were investigating a murder, but had arrested the wrong man. Are you still with me?'

'Yes.'

'There'd be a danger, don't you think, that while they were so distracted with this false trail, the murderer might get away?'

'That certainly is a possibility,' Meadows agreed.

Robinson hesitated before speaking again.

'If I were to do something which was *right*, but not necessarily *legal*, could I trust you not to reveal it to any third party?' he asked.

'We've stopped speaking hypothetically, haven't we?'

'Yes, we have.'

'It would depend,' Meadows said.

'On what?'

'On whether *I* thought it was right, too.'

'You would. I'm sure you would.'

'Then you can trust me.'

Robinson reached into his pocket, pulled out a slip of paper, and handed it to Meadows.

'Now that I've explained to my client his situation as it truly is, you will probably find him much more amenable than he has been previously,' Robinson said, 'and if you were to ask these questions during the interview, I think you might well be surprised by some of the answers you get in return.'

*   *   *

'It's a nasty virus Philip and Thomas have had, so you were quite right to call me,' the doctor said, when he finally came downstairs, 'but fortunately it's a virus which doesn't linger long once it's begun its retreat.'

'So . . . so are they going to be all right, Dr McCloud?' Paniatowski asked, tremulously.

'They're going to be fine.' The doctor walked over to the front door. 'They're big strapping lads, and they're over the worst of it now. They'll probably sleep for most of the day, and then they'll be almost back to normal.'

Paniatowski rushed up the stairs, but forced herself to slow down once she reached the landing, and entered the sick room on tiptoes.

The twins were sound asleep, and their breathing was almost back to normal. She wanted to pick them up and hug them to her, but she knew it was rest – not desperate, gushing love – that they needed.

'I will watch them now,' said a voice from the doorway.

'No, it's all right, I want to do it,' Paniatowski said.

'You are a – how do you say it? – a nervy wreck,' Elena told her. 'It is not good for you – and it is not good for the babies – for you to stay. Go and get a little rest, Mrs Monika.'

'All right,' Paniatowski agreed, meekly.

She had rushed up the stairs, but now her body felt very heavy, and she descended them like an old woman.

Once she was back in the lounge, she sank gratefully into her armchair, and closed her eyes.

'I'll have a sleep,' she said softly. 'Just a short one.'

But suddenly she was wide awake – suddenly she was thinking about how things *could have* gone.

She pictured herself, dressed from head to foot in black on a frozen March morning, walking between two rows of yew trees in the wake of two tiny coffins. She could hear the priest, standing by the open grave and promising everlasting life for her babies, and though she believed in that herself, it gave her no comfort.

Paniatowski jumped up, and paced the room. This was no good. She had to find something to absorb her.

But she didn't want to go back to work.

Not yet.

Not until she was feeling a little stronger.

'It's about time that I gave Charlie a ring,' she told herself.

She'd started these once-weekly phone calls when Woodend had announced that he had cancer, and the habit had continued even after the doctors had given him the definitive all-clear.

It was no chore to ring Charlie, she thought, as she dialled the number, because she was really very fond of him.

No – it was more than fond. They had been through so much together during the years he had been her boss that they had developed a bond which was intangible as a summer breeze, but as strong as steel.

She was glad he had eventually retired, since it had allowed her to take on the job he had trained her for, and yet there were moments when she wished he was still the DCI and she his sergeant.

The phone stopped ringing and she heard the voice she knew so well say, 'Woodend.'

'How are you, Charlie?' she asked.

'I'm getting stronger every day, lass,' Woodend said. 'I managed to walk nearly all the way to the beach yesterday.'

'That's brilliant!'

'Me hair's started growing back, too, which is a bit of a nuisance, really, because I don't know what I've done with me comb.'

Paniatowski giggled. God, it felt so good to be talking to Charlie.

'You could always buy another comb,' she suggested.

'I don't know about that,' Woodend said dubiously. 'It's a big investment, is a new comb.'

'What's the weather like there, Charlie?' she asked.

'Well, it's not like what it is back in Lancashire, and that's for damn sure,' he said. 'I'm sitting on me terrace at the moment – and I'm wearing me shorts.'

She pictured him sitting there, – a big man who had worn a hairy sports coat and cavalry twill trousers for most of his adult life – gazing out to sea and living the Mediterranean dream.

They chatted about Louisa and the twins, about Joan,

Charlie's wife, and Annie, his daughter, who was a nurse in London.

Then Paniatowski said, 'I didn't know that you were a mate of Arthur Tyndale's.'

'I wouldn't say that me and the Lone Ranger were exactly mates,' Woodend replied, 'but I enjoyed talking about Dickens to someone who knew almost as much on the subject as I did. Mind you, having said that, he was dead wrong on the subject of Martin Chuzzlewit!'

'He says that you're the one who's got it wrong.'

'Aye, well he would, wouldn't he? So how did you happen to be talking to him, anyway?'

'He's involved in my latest investigation. Before she was killed, he was representing the victim, but when we made an arrest, it turned out he was also the prime suspect's solicitor. He says his duty is to serve the client he had first, which is the prime suspect.'

'Oh aye,' Woodend replied. 'Well, watch him, because, as you've just demonstrated with that particular bit of sophistry, he can be a very tricky bugger when he wants to be.'

'I'll watch him,' Paniatowski promised.

'Having said that, I'm not sure he ever really earned that reputation of his – at least, not properly,' Woodend said reflectively. 'I mean, he had a few spectacular successes – I'll give him that – but were they ever more than a flash in the pan? And there are bobbies in Whitebridge who've had much more to do with him than we ever did – like Bill Stokes, who used to head up the Serious Crime Squad – and they certainly don't call him the Lone Ranger. In fact, what Bill used to call him was the Jinx.'

'Why's that?'

'Well, because things often seemed to go wrong for his clients. Just when Bill was considering releasing one of Tyndale's clients because of lack of evidence, the very evidence he needed would miraculously appear. DCI Stokes told me that on a few occasions, he even got an idea about how to refocus the investigation from something he read in the newspapers.'

'That can happen to all of us,' Paniatowski said. 'At least, it's certainly happened to me. You just never know what's going to give you a new perspective on a case.'

'You're missing the point entirely, lass,' Woodend said. 'Yes, it does happen with everybody – but it happened much more often with Tyndale's clients than with any other solicitor's – that's why Bill Stokes called Tyndale the Jinx.'

'Still, you've got to give him credit for self-promotion,' Paniatowski said, thinking of the newspaper articles hanging on his office wall.

'Aye, bullshit overshadows logic every time,' Woodend said. 'So tell me about this latest case of yours.'

It always came back to the cases, Paniatowski thought, with a rueful smile. They could talk about anything and everything else under the sun, and have a really enjoyable time doing it, but ultimately – inexorably – they'd somehow find their way back to crime.

'The victim is an American woman,' Paniatowski said. 'She was murdered in the Royal Vic.'

Woodend chuckled. 'Bloody hell, a murder on sacred ground – that'll have set the cat among the pigeons,' he said. 'Still, I bet you've had no difficulty getting authorisation for overtime.'

'None at all,' Paniatowski agreed.

'So have you got any leads?'

'Several. She might have been killed by someone who took offence at what she wrote about him.'

'Was she a reporter?'

'No, she was a biographer – and not a very academic one.'

'Eee, you shouldn't go using big words like "academic" with a simple Lancashire lad like me,' Woodend said.

Paniatowski grinned again.

'Not to mention "biographer",' she said.

'Aye, that's another big word we're best steering clear of,' Charlie Woodend agreed.

'Another possibility is that she might have been killed by a man who she kicked in the balls in the Rising Sun.'

Woodend chuckled again. 'That should stop *his* sun rising for a while,' he said. 'Was he trying to pick her up?'

'No, *she* was trying to pick *his wife* up.'

'That's two motives for you, then – damage to his pride, and damage to his goolies.'

'And then there's the line that Crane's following. You remember Crane, don't you? You met him once in the Drum.'

'Aye, I think so. Is he the lad who looks like a poet?'

'He *is* a poet.'

'Is he, by God! Well, it takes all sorts to make a world, I suppose, and he seemed a bright lad, so he'll probably go far.'

'Anyway, just before she died, our victim was doing research on a murder that happened in Whitebridge in 1924.'

Woodend sighed. 'When I were but a nipper,' he said.

'Yes, when you were but a nipper – with your bare arse hanging out of your short pants, and a slice of bread and dripping held firmly in your tiny right hand,' Paniatowski said.

'Aye, it were just like that,' Woodend said nostalgically.

'Now where was I?' Paniatowski wondered.

'You were saying that your victim was researching this murder that happened in 1924.'

'That's right, and Crane had a gut feeling that that murder is somehow connected to the one we're investigating now, so—'

'Don't tell me, lass, let me guess,' Woodend interrupted her. 'You don't think much of the theory yourself, but you're letting him run with it because it's all part of his education.'

'That's right,' Paniatowski agreed.

'You're a good boss, Monika,' Woodend said fondly. 'Mind you, you bloody-well should be, considering you were trained up by a feller who was a pretty good boss himself.'

'You were the best, Charlie,' Paniatowski said.

'Nay, I wasn't – but I was better than most,' Woodend said. 'It's been nice talking to you, Monika.'

'It's been nice talking to you, Charlie.'

They didn't say goodbye – they *never* said goodbye – and Paniatowski had almost returned the phone to its cradle when she heard Woodend shouting, 'Monika! Don't hang up, Monika!'

She put the phone to her ear again, and said, 'Is something the matter, Charlie?'

'That murder you were just talking to me about – the one that happened in 1924 . . .?'

'Yes?'

'Was the victim called Wilfred Hardcastle, by any chance?'

'Yes, as a matter of fact, he was.'

Paniatowski heard a sharp intake of breath from the other end of the line.

'Are you all right, Charlie?' she asked worriedly.

'I'm fine,' Woodend assured her. 'It was just a bit of shock, that's all. You do know who Wilfred Hardcastle's grandson is, don't you?'

'No,' Paniatowski admitted. 'I don't.'

Frankie Flynn was walking almost normally when he entered the interview room, but the moment he saw that it was Meadows who was sitting there, he began to exaggerate his limp.

He might be a tough man on the street, Meadows thought, but take him out of his comfort zone and he was like a puppy, looking at the world through big sad eyes which said he'd been treated cruelly, and pleading for kindness and understanding.

Flynn and Robinson sat down, the formalities were gone through for the record, and then Meadows said, 'You've been seen hanging around the Royal Victoria Hotel in the last few days, Frankie. You don't deny that, do you?'

Last time he had been asked the question, he'd answered it by saying it was a free country. This time, he merely shook his head.

'You have to say "no", Frankie, because this is being recorded,' Meadows told him.

'No, I don't deny it,' Flynn said.

'Did you have any special reason for loitering there?'

'I was trying to find out more about that woman.'

'What woman?'

'The one what kicked me square in the knackers, in the best room of the Rising Sun.'

'Mary Edwards?'

'Yes, that's her.'

'What kinds of things were you trying to find out about her?'

'What her address was over in America. What family she's got. Things like that.'

'And how did you hope to find these things out?'

'I was going to see who she talked to, and then I was going to have a quiet word with them myself.'

'*Just* a quiet word?'

'Yes.'

'Are you sure?'

Flynn looked at his solicitor for guidance, and Robinson nodded.

'It might have got a bit rough if I'd thought they were hiding something from me,' Flynn admitted.

'There, you see, it's much better if we're straight and honest with each other,' Meadows said. '*Why* did you want to know where her family lived in America? Were you planning to visit them?'

'No.'

'So what was the reason?'

'I wanted to let her know that I knew where she lived.'

'Again, why?'

'Because she's a lezzie, and she's got plenty of money.'

'How do you know she's got plenty of money?' Meadows asked.

Flynn gave her a look which said she must be the stupidest woman he'd ever met.

'She was staying in the Royal Vic, wasn't she? An' on the top floor, an' all, which is where the *really* posh people stay.'

'Forgive me, I know I'm being a bit thick here, but I still don't see why you needed her address,' Meadows said, although she was beginning to think that she just might.

Flynn checked with his solicitor again, and got another quick nod.

'Why would a woman like her ever want to come to a dump like this?' Frankie asked.

'I don't know.'

'She came for sex. She'd have had her nasty way with my missus if I hadn't stopped her.'

Oh, you stopped her, all right, Meadows thought. You hurt her foot so much with your balls that she was quite incapable of getting her end away.

'Go on,' she said.

'But why would she come here at all? There are lezzies in America, aren't there?'

'Yes, there are.'

'So why didn't she just have sex where she lived?'

'You tell me.'

'You really are thick, aren't you?' Flynn asked. 'She didn't want to get her end away in America because her family didn't know she was a lezzie, and she was frightened that if she did, they'd find out.'

It was not a very sophisticated – or even clever – theory, Meadows thought, but then Frankie Flynn wasn't a very sophisticated man.

'I think I'm finally getting it now,' she said. 'Once you'd got her address, you were planning to go up to her, and say something like, "If you don't give me some money, I'm going to tell your family that you're a lesbian." In other words, you were going to blackmail her.'

'My client saw it more in terms of demanding compensation for the damage she'd done to his crown jewels,' Robinson said smoothly. 'The strategy he's just outlined was merely a negotiating tool.'

'Yeah, that's right,' Flynn agreed. 'I wanted some compensation, and it was a nego . . . nego . . . it was a tool.'

Meadows consulted the note Robinson had given her.

'Where were you the afternoon that Mary Edwards was killed, Frankie?' she asked.

'I was at the hospital.'

'Why were you there?'

'When I woke up that morning, it hurt me to pee, and my thing kept dripping, so I went to the hospital to see if she'd done any permanent damage.'

'And had she?'

'No, it wasn't what she'd done that was causing the problem – I've got the clap.'

'You were at the hospital all afternoon?'

'Yeah, it was one o'clock when I went in, and six o'clock when I came out. They did a lot of tests. They . . . they stuck things in my . . . in my . . .'

'Penis?' Meadows suggested.

'No, they stuck them in my dick.'

'So why didn't you tell us that you'd been at the hospital when we first arrested you?'

'Mr Tyndale said I shouldn't.'

'Did he give you a reason?'

'He said if I gave you an alibi, you'd realise you could never pin the murder on me, so you'd do me for the blackmail, just out of spite. He said my best plan was to keep quiet until you found the real murderer, 'cos once you'd done that, you'd be so busy with him that the blackmail wouldn't even seem worth bothering about.'

'Had you actually asked anyone for Mary Edwards' address in America?' Meadows asked.

'No.'

'Had you talked to Mary yourself?'

'No.'

'And did Mr Tyndale know all this?'

'Yes.'

'I want to make sure I've got this absolutely clear,' Meadows said. 'You didn't talk to anyone about Mary, you didn't talk to Mary herself, and you made Mr Tyndale aware of both these facts. Is that right?'

'Yes.'

'You can't be charged with something you haven't done, you know,' Meadows said.

'Mr Tyndale told me I could. He said you'd do me for intent. He said what I'd done was exactly like a burglar loitering outside a house with his tools in his pocket, or a robber parked in front of a bank, with a sawn-off shotgun and a ski mask in the boot of his car.'

'Jesus!' Meadows said.

She turned to Mr Robinson, but the solicitor was focussing his attention on the upper part of the wall opposite him.

THIRTEEN

The watery winter sun had made a valiant attempt to warm up the earth in the late morning, but around noon, a massed army of heavy grey clouds had blocked it. The temperature had begun to drop almost immediately, causing sparrows perched on telephone lines to shiver, and stray dogs to search for exterior walls which interior heating had warmed up just a little.

Ice had begun to form in the dips in the Whitebridge General visitors' car park, and one of the porters had spread a thin layer of sand over it, because the last thing anybody wanted was for a visitor to slip and be transformed – via an unlucky fracture – into a patient.

Paniatowski, with Crane just behind her, followed the sandy path to the main entrance of the hospital. From three different sources, she had learned three things that morning. The first was the victim's real name, the second that Frankie Flynn had a rock solid alibi for the time of the murder, and the third was the identity of Wilfred Hardcastle's grandson. They all pointed her in the same direction – and that direction led to a room on Whitebridge General's second floor.

Arthur Tyndale had been taken straight to intensive care when he'd first been admitted, but had shown some improvement during the morning, and after lunch he had been moved to a private room.

It was there that Paniatowski and Crane found him – propped upright in bed by several pillows, and with a morphine button in his hand.

'It appears I'm going to live to fight another day, chief inspector,' he said, with a weak smile. 'I confidently expect that will be about my limit.'

It should have been difficult not to be affected by such cheerful courage in the face of death, but – given what she already knew – Paniatowski found it the easiest thing in the world.

'Is that true?' she asked.

'It could be true,' Tyndale told her, 'but – though this is highly unlikely – I could hold out for another six months.'

'We've let Frankie Flynn go,' she said.

Tyndale sighed. 'I expected as much. Without me there to control the situation, it was almost bound to happen.'

'You manipulated him for your own ends,' Paniatowski said accusingly.

'Yes, I did,' Tyndale agreed. 'Over the years, I've manipulated most of my clients.'

'Why? What did you get out of it?'

'I got nothing out of it personally. Not a thing! It was a question of duty. The police seemed unable or unwilling to do their job, so I felt obliged – as a responsible citizen – to do it for them.'

'Does this have something to do with John Entwistle's trial?'

'It has *everything* to do with John Entwistle's trial. Because of police incompetence, the killer walked free.'

'Have you ever read the transcript of John Entwistle's trial?' Paniatowski asked.

'No. I've never seen a need to. I was brought up on that trial. It was my bedtime story from before I even learned to speak. Other children had Peter Pan and Tinkerbell, but I had Rex v. Entwistle at Preston Crown Court. It destroyed the family, you know. My great uncle Oswald was so devastated by the death of his brother that he let the business go to pot, and drank himself to death.'

'I've heard Oswald wasn't much of a businessman, even without the drink,' Paniatowski said.

'Perhaps,' Tyndale conceded, 'but drowning his sorrows certainly didn't help. After Uncle Oswald's death, we had to sell the mill for a pittance. My father was never a very successful barrister, and without the Hardcastle family money, we simply could not afford to go on living where we were. We sold the mansion – again for a pittance – dismissed most of the servants, and moved to a much smaller home. Sometimes, when my father was going through a particularly lean patch, things were so bad that Mother had to get down on her knees and scrub the floors herself. It broke her heart to do that. And none of it would have happened if John Entwistle hadn't killed my grandfather. That was why we were so bitter! That was why we wanted to see justice done! And it wasn't done!'

'I'm still surprised that someone with your legal training hasn't even bothered to read the trans—' Paniatowski began.

'My father wanted me to follow in his footsteps, but I knew that was not the way, because by the time a case gets to court – by the time a John Entwistle is standing in the dock – the damage has already been done. But I am a solicitor – I can attack the evil at the root.'

'And how exactly do you attack it?'

'If I had a client who I knew to be guilty, I'd gently guide him towards self-incrimination, so that no matter how stupid the prosecutor, he would not be able to wriggle out of getting his just deserts. Sometimes, I'd use what my client had told me to uncover evidence which was previously hidden. And sometimes I used the press to plant ideas. I have used a number of journalists over the years.'

DCI Stokes told me that on a few occasions he even got an idea about how to refocus the investigation from something he read in the newspapers, Charlie Woodend had said.

That can happen to all of us, Paniatowski had replied. *At least, it's certainly happened to me. You just never know what's going to give you a new perspective on a case.*

You're missing the point entirely, lass. Yes, it does happen with everybody – but it happened much more often with Tyndale's clients than with any other solicitor's clients – that's why Bill Stokes called Tyndale the Jinx.

'You used Mike Traynor, didn't you?' Paniatowski asked.

'Oh yes, I used him. He was one of the best reporters I ever worked with – because he had absolutely no morals at all.' Tyndale gave himself a shot of morphine, and grinned weakly. 'Do you want me to tell you how I've got away with it all these years?'

'Since you're the prime suspect in a murder case, your wisest course would be to say nothing,' Paniatowski told him. 'But I can give you that advice without any fear that you'll follow it, because you want to tell us how clever you've been – in fact, you're *bursting* to tell us.'

'When I got one of my clients off, I was a bit like those gambling machines which we call one–armed bandits, and the Americans – less imaginatively, but more accurately – call slots. When they have a big payout, it's all bells and whistles, and people talk about what a good machine it is for days after. What they forget, of course, is that for there to be one big winner, there have to be a lot of small losers.'

'Hence the newspaper headlines so prominently displayed on your office walls,' Paniatowski said.

'Hence the newspaper headlines on my office walls,' Tyndale agreed. 'But you see, though those headlines talked about the innocent, it wasn't about them at all – it was about the guilty. I was never Jay North – the Lone Ranger.'

'Then who were you?'

'Can't you guess?'

'He thinks that he was Steve McQueen – the bounty hunter,' Jack Crane said.

'That's right,' Tyndale agreed. He smiled again, and this time it was a smile of triumph. 'There are two reasons why you won't be arresting me for the murder of Melissa Evans. Shall I tell you what they are?'

'Why not?'

'The first is that your whole case is built on circumstantial evidence – at best – and you'd stand virtually no chance of getting a conviction, even if I lived long enough to stand trial. But it's the second one that's the really important one – if you arrested me, then everything I've just told you would be public knowledge, and every convicted toss-pot I've ever represented – and, believe me, there are literally hundreds of them – would be launching an appeal. The Lancashire judicial system would grind to a halt – and everyone would blame you. I know how hard you've worked to get where you are now, Detective Chief Inspector Paniatowski, but that would just about finish you.'

Paniatowski took her handcuffs out of her bag.

'Arthur Tyndale, I am arresting you on suspicion of the murder of Margaret Entwistle, who was also known as Mary Edwards and Melissa Evans,' she said. 'You do not have to say anything, but anything you do say may be taken down and used in evidence against you.'

'Are you insane?' Tyndale demanded. 'Or is it that you don't believe me when I tell you that it will ruin you?'

'Oh, I believe you,' Paniatowski told him, 'but I still have to do what I have to do.'

'And are you going to handcuff one of my wrists to the bed frame, as if I were a common criminal?' Tyndale asked, clearly in a panic now.

'I certainly am,' Paniatowski confirmed, 'because you *are* a common criminal, and it's standard operating procedure.'

'But I couldn't possibly escape.'

'There have been numerous cases of men in your condition who've suddenly found the strength to do a runner,' Paniatowski said, 'and anyway, as I've just told you, it's standard procedure.'

'But don't you understand – my wife will be arriving soon. She can't possibly see me like that.'

'I'm sorry, but she'll have to,' Paniatowski said. 'And just in case you get the wrong idea – it's her I'm sorry for, not you.'

'I'd like to make a deal,' Tyndale said.

'What do you want, and what have you got to offer in return?' Paniatowski said.

'I'll tell you everything I know – things you'll never find out about if you don't get them from me – and, in return, you promise not to handcuff me.'

It would mean posting a constable on permanent duty, Paniatowski thought, but it just might be worth it.

'Agreed,' she said. She took a tape recorder out of her pocket, and switched it on. 'Interview with Arthur Tyndale at 2.30 p.m. on the 16th of March, 1978. I am Detective Chief Inspector Monika Paniatowski. Also present is Detective Constable Jack Crane.'

She placed the tape recorder on the bedside table.

'When did you first learn that your client's real name wasn't Mary Edwards, Mr Tyndale?' she asked.

'When did *you* learn it?' he countered.

He was trying to save a little of his pride by taking control of the interview, Paniatowski thought. Well, that was all right – for the present.

'I learned yesterday that she was, in fact, Melissa Evans,' she said, 'but it wasn't until an hour or so ago, when the New York Police Department contacted me, that I found out her original name was Entwistle.'

'I knew right from the start,' Tyndale said, with a strange and totally unjustified pride. 'She told me.'

They have just signed the documents which will allow Tyndale to draw on a bank account in New York whenever Mary needs money.

'*You will notice that the signature I have used on the permission forms is not the same as the name I gave you when I walked in here,' she says. 'Mary Edwards is an alias, and the name I have signed is my real one.'*

'*Melissa Evans,' he reads.*

'*Yes. Does it bother you that I am using two different names?'*

'*I'm not sure,' he admits. 'There is nothing illegal about using two different names* per se, *but there may be concerns about the nature of the activities which require the use of those two names.'*

'*I am doing nothing wrong,' she assures him. 'I'm a writer, and I'm in Whitebridge to research the murder of Wilfred Hardcastle, which occurred over half a century ago. I don't want to use my real name, because if people realise that a best-selling author is asking the questions, they won't respond to them in the same way as they would if the question was put by an ordinary person.'*

I was at that trial, Tyndale thinks. I was not even born at that point, and yet I was there on the front row.

And then, fight it as he might, another thought comes into his mind – he'd had a womb with a view!

He giggles. He can't help himself.

'*Is something wrong, Mr Tyndale?' Melissa Evans asks.*

'*No,' he says, 'I'm sorry, that was very unprofessional of me, but I was thinking of something else entirely.'*

She has suddenly grown very serious. It is almost as if his levity has driven her in the opposite direction.

'*I have a secret,' she says. 'I thought I could keep it to*

*myself, but I know now that if I do, I'll explode. Can I trust
you with that secret, Mr Tyndale?'*

'*Of course,' Tyndale says. 'I'm your solicitor. You can trust
me with anything.'*

'*I was born in America, but my father was not,' she says.
'He was from Whitebridge. His name was John Entwistle, and
he is the man who was tried for killing Wilfred Hardcastle.'*

'How did you feel when you realised who she was?' Paniatowski
asked. 'Did you hate her?'

'Not at all,' Tyndale said, pressing on the morphine button
again. 'In fact, I felt rather sorry for her.'

'Why?'

'Which of the two questions would you like me to answer?
Why didn't I hate her? Or why I felt sorry for her?'

'Both.'

'I had no reason to hate her. Nearly two decades had passed
between her father killing my grandfather and her entry into
the world. She could not be held responsible for anything he
had done.'

'And why did you feel sorry for her?'

'It was clear to me that she had been indoctrinated from an
early age into the belief that her father was innocent. It would
have become one of the central pillars of her being, and she
had come to Whitebridge to shore up that pillar by proving
that her father didn't kill my grandfather. Imagine how she
would have felt, then, when she finally accepted the truth. The
poor girl would have been absolutely devastated.'

'She never said all that crap about being afraid of a New
York hitman tracking her down in Whitebridge, did she?'

'No, she didn't, but after my conversation with her, I did a
little research of my own and discovered that she was fabu-
lously wealthy, that she had offended a great many important
people with her writings, and that she had a bodyguard. It
seemed to me, after her death, that to tell you the story I did
tell you would be a perfect smokescreen.'

'That's why you told Mike Traynor that her name wasn't
really Melissa Evans, wasn't it?'

'Yes. I couldn't tell him her real name – that would have led you straight to me – but I thought that even knowing she wasn't really Melissa would be enough to confuse you for a while.'

'It did confuse me initially,' Paniatowski admitted, 'but in the end, it did more to help me, because once I knew that Mary's solicitor was also Wilfred Hardcastle's grandson, it was pretty obvious who the source of the information was.'

'Ah yes, it might have been wiser for me not to pull that particular trick,' Tyndale admitted.

Paniatowski remembered something Dr Shastri had said about Mary's injuries.

'There is this pattern of damage which is diagonal, and runs from near the top of the right-hand side of the frontal lobe to near the bottom of the left-hand side.'

'Tell me when it was that you lashed out at Mary with your walking stick,' she said.

'All in good time,' Tyndale replied. 'Before we get to the actual act, I'd like to put things in context,' he smiled, 'if you don't mind, that is.'

He had so very little power left, she thought, but he did have the power to keep her waiting, and he was relishing it.

Well, let him!

'By all means put things in context,' she said, indifferently.

'The morning Mary died, I paid a visit to the specialist who had been treating me for cancer,' Tyndale said.

The specialist, Henry Stewart, is an old friend of Tyndale's, and there is genuine sadness in his eyes as he greets him at the door.

'I'm so sorry, Arthur, but I've got some rather bad news,' he says.

'I'm already dying of cancer, so how bad can it be?' Tyndale asks.

'It's about the treatment I was going to put you on,' Stewart says. 'The hospital's turned it down.'

'But you said it would help me.'

'And so it would. It's impossible to say anything with any degree of accuracy in cases like yours, but I believe the drugs

would have prolonged your life by between twelve and eighteen months.'

'Would have *prolonged,*' Tyndale exclaims. 'There's no "would have" about it. Tell the petty bureaucrats who run this hospital that I simply have to have those drugs.'

'It wouldn't do any good, Arthur. They won't budge, and though it upsets me personally, if I look at the matter from a professional perspective, I can quite see their point.'

'What are you talking about?'

'The hospital only has limited resources, and the drugs are very, very expensive.'

'I'll pay for them myself,' Tyndale says.

The specialist shakes his head. 'Unless you're very much richer than I take you to be, you can't possibly afford them,' he says.

'So how much will they cost?' Tyndale asks.

The specialist tells him.

'But you'd have to be a millionaire to afford that,' he says.

'Yes,' the specialist agrees, 'you would.'

And this is when Tyndale gets his idea.

'You went to see Mary,' Paniatowski said.

'I went to see Mary,' Tyndale agreed.

He makes no attempt at subterfuge as he enters the hotel. Why should he? He has not done anything wrong, nor is he planning to do anything wrong, but a great many of the staff are deployed in the restaurant at that time, and there is some kind of crisis being dealt with at the reception desk, so he reaches the lift to the Prince Alfred suite without being noticed.

Mary is surprised to see him, but quickly recovers and invites him in. He notices how opulent the suite is, and that only increases his resolve.

'I have come both to confess something to you, and to make a request,' he says.

She looks at him quizzically. 'Please go ahead.'

'I am the grandson of Wilfred Hardcastle. I realise that I should have told you that when you told me who you were, but I held back because I didn't want you to hate me.'

'Why should I hate you? Do you hate me?'

'Of course not. I rather like you.'

'And I like you. There is no reason why what happened in the past should in any way affect the way we react to each other now.'

'No, there isn't,' he agrees.

'You said something about a request.'

'I am not a well man, Mary. You must surely have noticed that.'

'Yes, I had. I just assumed, because you were still at work, that it was not as serious as it seemed.'

'It's very serious. I'm dying.'

'Oh, I'm so sorry,' she says.

'With the right drugs, I can live a little longer,' he tells her, 'but these drugs are very expensive.'

This is the point at which she should say, But you must have them, and since I am a millionairess, I will gladly pay for them.

She doesn't. Instead, she looks very sad – sad for him, sad for herself, sad for the whole situation that they find themselves in.

He forces himself to say, 'I was wondering, Mary – Maggie – if you'd give me the money.'

She shakes her head regretfully.

'I can't do it. If I gave you what you wanted, how could I – in all conscience – turn down the next person who asked me, and the one after that, and the one after that? It would simply never stop.'

'But my situation's desperate,' he protests.

'There are millions – perhaps billions – of people in the world whose situation is desperate,' Mary says. 'There are children who are slowly starving to death. There are young men who are going blind for want of a simple operation. Is their need any less than yours?'

'No, but you don't help them, either.'

'I don't help all of them – you're quite right about that – but I do help some. I have a foundation into which I put a percentage of my earnings. I don't administer that foundation myself, but I could write to the trustees, and ask them if they'll consider you.'

'*And would you recommend me?*'

'*If I could, I would. But the deeds of covenant prohibit me from recommending anyone.*'

'*You owe me!*' *he screams.*

She is startled by this, but quickly recovers herself.

'*What do you mean – I owe you?*' *she asks.* '*I've only known you for a little over a week. How can I possibly owe you anything?*'

'*If your father hadn't murdered my grandfather, the mill wouldn't have gone bust,*' *he says.* '*If your father hadn't cold-bloodedly murdered my grandfather, I'd have plenty of money, and I wouldn't need to humiliate myself by coming to you, cap in hand.*'

'*My father didn't murder your grandfather,*' *she tells him, and now she is angry, too.* '*I've got some evidence which presents quite a different scenario. Would you like to know who I think killed him – and why he had to die?*'

'*No,*' *he says.*

'*Well, I'm going to tell you anyway, because it really is time you faced the truth.*'

He swings his stick almost before he realises it. It catches her across the forehead, and she collapses into the chair.

'*I'm sorry,*' *he says.* '*I didn't mean to do that. But it's partly your fault, too. You should never . . .*'

He realises he's wasting his time talking, because she can't hear him. But she's not dead – her chest rises and falls as her unconscious body takes in, and expels, air.

He wonders what will happen when she wakes up.

Will she want him arrested?

Of course she will.

What a stupid question to ask himself.

So it all boils down to this – if she lives, he will go to prison, and if she dies, he won't.

She has to die.

He searches around for a weapon, and finds the poker.

Perhaps, after all, this is only natural justice, he tells himself – an Entwistle has killed a Hardcastle, why then shouldn't one of the Hardcastle clan kill an Entwistle?

He is amazed by the force with which he is able to wield the poker, but when the skull splits open, it still comes as a surprise.

If the police know who she really is, and what she is doing in Whitebridge, it will not be long before the trail leads back to him, he realises. He picks up her smart leather briefcase, which already contains her passport, and puts into it all the notes he can find. As an afterthought, he adds the poker.

He uses the back stairs to leave. The effort nearly kills him, but at least he meets no one who will remember him later. By the time he reaches the street, he has already come up with the red herring of American hitmen.

'I only hit her to stop her talking,' Tyndale told Paniatowski. 'I didn't mean her any harm. If she'd just have shut up when I asked her to, she'd still be alive today.'

'What did you do with her notes?' Paniatowski asked.

'I burned them.'

'Why?'

'I should have thought that was obvious – because they would have connected me directly to her death.'

'To her *murder*,' Paniatowski corrected him. 'They would have connected you directly to her *murder*. Did you read them before you burned them?'

'No.'

'Why not?'

'Because there wasn't time.'

'There was plenty of time,' Paniatowski said scornfully. 'How long would it have taken to skim them. Ten minutes? Fifteen minutes?'

'Fifteen minutes max,' Crane said.

'All right then, I didn't read them because I had no wish to enter her fantasy world,' Tyndale said.

'Interview ends at 3.10 p.m.,' Paniatowski said, switching off the tape recorder.

'Is that it, boss?' Crane asked.

'No, it's not it,' Paniatowski said, and suddenly there was real anger in her voice. 'You didn't read her notes, Mr Tyndale, for the same reason that you lashed out at Mary when she was about to tell you what was in them – for the same reason you've never read the transcript of the trial. Your whole life had been built on an injustice done to your family in 1924.

But what if there was no injustice? What if John Entwistle was innocent?'

'I . . . don't know what you mean,' Tyndale gasped. 'I don't understand what you're saying.'

'Of course you do,' Paniatowski said contemptuously. 'Your whole life – everything you've ever been and everything you've ever done – is just a bad joke. And deep inside yourself, you know that as well as I do.'

'Why . . . why are you doing this?' Tyndale asked, amazed by the ferocity of the attack.

'I'm doing it because you took another human life, and it doesn't really bother you at all,' Paniatowski said. 'I'm doing it because the last thing I want is for you to die at peace with yourself.'

It was eight o'clock in the evening. Paniatowski had been home and spent a few hours with the twins – both of whom were well on the way to recovery – then entrusted them to the tender care of Louisa and Elena, and slipped down to the Drum for a celebratory drink with her team.

Crane was the last one to arrive.

'Arthur Tyndale died at half-past six,' he said. 'I think our interview with him may have pushed him over the edge.'

'I feel sorry for his wife, but he's no loss to anyone else,' Paniatowski said. She took a sip of her vodka. 'So that's one murder out of the way, now let's turn our attention to the other one. Who did it, Jack?'

'My best guess is Tom Clegg,' Crane said.

'Why him?'

'Because it's clearly an inside job – somebody sabotaged the looms and somebody took the fifty pounds from the office – and Clegg's the only one left when you've ruled out John Entwistle and Oswald Hardcastle.'

'And why would you rule them out?' Paniatowski wondered.

'I'd rule Entwistle out because any man who's bright enough to go across to America and build a new life up from nothing would not be stupid enough to hide the money he'd stolen under his own mattress.'

'And Oswald?'

'It's like that old copper in the retirement home said – he was sitting pretty, getting the money without doing the work. And his brother's murder did seem to devastate him, because within three years, he'd drunk himself to death.'

'And so we're left with Tom,' Meadows said.

'Exactly,' Crane agreed. 'We know that Wilfred worked him very hard – keeping him there till all hours of the night – and maybe he finally snapped. He kills Wilfred in a rage, and when the red mist has cleared, he realises that if he's not going to hang for it, he has to blame someone else. He chooses John Entwistle, who is known to be a bit of an awkward bugger. But when he gives his first day of evidence at Preston Crown Court, one of two things happens – he either gets scared at the thought of the defence counsel questioning him, or he starts to feel guilty that he's landed John in it. Whichever it is, it's enough to make him hang himself.'

'So when he left his suicide note, why didn't he say that he'd killed Wilfred?' Beresford asked.

'Ah, that's the weakness in my theory,' Crane admitted. 'Maybe he was too ashamed to admit to what he'd done, even though he knew he'd be dead before anyone read the note.'

'And your "red mist" theory doesn't work. The murder was premeditated, and we know this because the looms were sabotaged earlier in the day, which means that the killer had planned to frame Entwistle hours before he killed Hardcastle,' Beresford pointed out.

'OK, I give up,' Crane said, holding up his hands. 'Chances are, we'll never know now.'

The conversation drifted, as it always inevitably did on these occasions, into reminiscences of old investigations, but Paniatowski noticed that while Beresford and Meadows were enjoying reliving the past, Crane seemed to be withdrawing more and more into himself.

Finally, when half an hour had passed and it looked as though Crane would soon disappear into a whirlpool of introspection, Paniatowski put a five-pound note on the table and said, 'Could you go up to the bar and order the next round of drinks for us, Colin?'

'We can just call the waiter,' Beresford pointed out.

'I'd rather you bought them at the bar,' Paniatowski said. She turned to Meadows. 'And I'd like you to go and help him.'

She waited until the sergeant and the inspector were out of earshot, then said, 'What's bothering you, Jack? Are you feeling guilty about pushing Arthur Tyndale over the edge, because you've no need to – if that is what happened, then it was all my doing.'

'No, it's not that,' Crane told her. 'You said he was no loss, and you were right.' He hesitated for a moment, then continued, 'What are you going to do about Tyndale's confession?'

'It's on tape,' Paniatowski said.

'I don't mean the confession that he killed Maggie Entwistle. I mean the other thing that he said he'd done – setting his own clients up for years.'

'There's no record of that,' Paniatowski pointed out.

'No, there isn't,' Crane agreed, 'but we both heard him say it, and if you chose to, you could make a statement to that effect.'

'Best to let sleeping dogs lie,' Paniatowski said, 'because Tyndale was right, it would tie up the judicial system for years, as well as effectively torpedoing my career – and possibly yours as well.'

A look of real disappointment came to Crane's face.

'What's the matter?' Paniatowski asked. 'Have I failed to live up to your expectations of me? Am I not the shining example you thought I was?'

'I wouldn't put it quite like that, boss,' Crane said uncomfortably. 'I can see things from your point of view – you've worked hard to get where you are, and it would be unfair that you should be punished for doing the right thing, so no one can really blame you if you don't.'

'But . . .?' Paniatowski said.

'But there have been serious miscarriages of justice, and that doesn't sit easily with me.'

'Have there been any miscarriages of justice?' Paniatowski asked. 'What was it Tyndale said, exactly?'

'He said that when he knew one of his clients was guilty, he made sure the police found enough evidence to convict him.'

'So how could he be so sure they were guilty – and how did he know where to find the evidence?'

'They confessed to him!' Crane said.

'They confessed to him,' Paniatowski agreed. 'They trusted him enough to tell him that they'd done it, and he used that. The way they were convicted was wrong, and went against all the fundamentals of British justice – but there's no doubt that the people who were sent down were guilty. And do you want to give those same people a "get out of jail free" card?'

'No,' Crane said, 'I don't think I do.'

FOURTEEN

24th March, 1978

Harvey Morgan only glanced at the thick manila envelope that his secretary, Linda, had just placed on his desk, before looking up at her and saying, 'What's this?'

'It's a manila envelope,' Linda replied.

'That, I can see for myself. The question I'm asking is, what's it doing on my desk?'

'It could be waiting to see whether or not you decide to open it?' Linda suggested.

Morgan leant back in his expensive leather chair.

'Let me ask you a question, Linda,' he said. 'Would you describe me as a successful man?'

'Sure.'

'Would you say that I'm the most successful literary agent in New York City?'

'You're in the top five, certainly.'

Morgan frowned. 'But not *numero uno*?' he asked.

'No.'

'Who is number one then?' Morgan asked. 'Is it Harry Conner? Is it . . . No, forget that,' he added as he realised that he was getting distracted. 'What I was going to say, before this pointless discussion began—'

'It's *your* pointless discussion,' Linda reminded him.

'Was that as a man of some consequence, I do not open envelopes myself. What I expect is that every envelope which appears in front of me has already been opened.'

'Look at it closely,' Linda told him.

I shouldn't do everything she tells me to do, he thought – but by then it was too late, and his eyes were already on the envelope.

'It's got English stamps on it,' he said, 'which would be great if I was still in the business of selling stamps, but I

moved out of that – and into much more profitable ventures
– when I was nine years old.'

'Look who it's addressed to,' Linda said.

'It's addressed to Melissa Evans, care of the Harvey Morgan
Agency. So some no-hoper in England has sent Melissa a book
to comment on. That happens all the time.'

'Except that it's not some no-hoper, because that's Melissa's
own handwriting.'

'You're sure?'

'I'm sure.'

'Then this must be the last thing she ever wrote.'

'That would appear to be the logical conclusion.'

'So, you wanna open it for me?' Morgan asked hopefully.

Linda shook her head quite firmly. 'You're Melissa's literary
executor – you open it.'

'Am I also the executor of the . . . the—' Morgan waved
his hands in the air – 'of all the other stuff?'

'Of the estate?'

'Yeah.'

'No, you're not.'

'Then who is?' Morgan asked, sounding rather hurt.

'Somebody else,' Linda said.

'That I could have figured for myself,' Morgan told her.
'Does this somebody have a name?'

'Yes.'

'And what is it?'

'Linda Kaufmann.'

'But that's you!' Morgan exclaimed.

'So it is,' Linda agreed.

'She made a *secretary* her executor?'

'She did indeed,' Linda confirmed. 'What a crazy lady she
must have been.'

It was nearly an hour before Harvey Morgan called Linda
Kaufmann back into his office.

'I've read it,' he said. 'It's sort of a diary, describing her
investigations into this old murder over in England. She must
have sent it to herself here for safe keeping.'

'Yes, that would make sense,' Linda agreed.

'It's not like anything she's done before, but I think we could sell it. The only problem is that it's nowhere near eight or nine hundred pages, but if we could bring in an editor with a good imagination, and add some background articles—'

'Before we do anything else with it, I think we should let the police have a look at it,' Linda said.

'And by the police, you don't mean New York's finest, you mean that Captain Panovski in England?'

'That's right, I mean Detective Chief Inspector Paniatowski.'

'I'm not sure we should do that,' Morgan said.

'Aren't you?' Linda asked. 'I am.'

JOURNAL

It seemed to me, when I had collected all the evidence together, that two things happened that afternoon. The first was that Mr Wilfred Hardcastle was killed, and the second was that someone went to a great deal of effort to frame my father.

But why was my father framed – because the killer hated him, or because the killer merely wished to distract attention away from himself?

To begin at the beginning: two looms were sabotaged that afternoon. The motive behind that was obvious. The killer wanted John to have an argument with Wilfred, or at least be able to claim, with some plausibility, that such an argument occurred.

And what does this tell us? It tells us that the killer belonged to the mill, because no one from outside could have sabotaged those looms.

Actually, that's not quite true. Someone from outside – say, a rival mill owner – could have bribed one of the workers in Hardcastles' mill to do it. But would that rival mill owner have risked putting himself in the power of the lowly mill worker in that way? I think not.

Then there's the money found under my father's bed. Fifty pounds was nearly as much as the average mill worker earned in a year back then, so there is no way one of them could have saved up that much. Of course, the killer could have stolen the money, but he would have had to know where to find it first, and Wilfred Hardcastle does not strike me as the kind of man who would just leave money lying around.

Could Tom Clegg have been the killer? He came into close contact with Wilfred, and lied about seeing my father. But surely, if Tom had done it, he would have confessed as much when he hanged himself, rather than just leaving a note which said that he had lied.

So what conclusions had I come to? That Wilfred was killed by someone from inside the mill, and that that someone had to be at management level. And that was where I hit the problem of a motive. No one who is benefiting from it wants to kill the goose that lays the golden eggs, and Wilfred was, by all accounts, a prodigious layer.

I was going round and round in circles, and getting dizzier and dizzier.

And that was when I went to see George Clegg.

George is one of those people you like at first sight. He's in his early sixties, but he suffers from very poor health, and most people probably think he is much older. But what he does have – and I noticed this the moment he opened the door to me – is the kindest eyes I've ever seen in my life.

I said, 'I'm investigating the murder of Wilfred Hardcastle,' but looking into those eyes, I discovered that I couldn't be even the slightest bit disingenuous with him, so I added, 'Actually, I don't care who killed him. My only concern is to prove that my father, John Entwistle, didn't do it.'

For a moment, he looked as if he didn't quite know how to react, but then he smiled and said, 'In that case, you'd better come inside, lass.'

I followed him in through the front door.

'I'd invite you into the front parlour, but there's no fire in there, so it'll have to be the kitchen,' he said, as he led me down the corridor.

'The kitchen will be fine,' I said.

And it was. It had one of those old-fashioned ranges, where the fire heats the oven, and toast is cooked over a naked flame.

He saw me looking at it.

'There's not more than a dozen of these left in Whitebridge,' he said. 'It's all electric now. But I like the old ways.'

'You're Tom Clegg's nephew, aren't you?' I asked him, when we'd sat down at the table.

'I am.'

'Do you remember him well?'

'Very well, even though I was only a nipper when he hung himself in the woods.'

'So what can you tell me about him?'

George frowned. 'I hope I'm not speaking ill of the dead, but Uncle Tom was a bit slow. I don't mean he was a nutter or anything, but he didn't always catch on very quick. But he was a nice man – a kind man – and both me and me dad loved him.' He paused. 'As far as I know, we were the last people to see him alive.'

I didn't know why that fact should have made me go all tingly, but it did.

'Tell me about it,' I said.

'The morning he hung himself, he came round to see us. Me dad says, "Shouldn't you be in Preston, giving evidence again, Tom?" Uncle Tom says, "They don't need me anymore," but even a kid like me could see he was lying. Anyway, he had this old shoe box in his hands, and he handed it to me dad and says, "Will you look after this for me, Raymond?". "What's in it, our Tom?" me dad asks. And Uncle Tom says, "My life", which struck us both as bloody odd. He didn't say no more, just turned and walked away, and a couple of hours later, they found him hanging in the woods.'

'And what was in the shoe box?' I asked, doing my best not to wet myself with excitement.

'I don't know,' George said. 'Me dad never opened it.'

'Why not?'

'I can't say. All I know is that when it was passed down to me, after me dad died, I didn't open it either. It were as if it held some dark secret that should never see the light of day again. I know that's a bit fanciful, but that's the way it felt.'

'Have you still got the box?' I asked.

'I have.'

'And can I see it?'

He thought about it, long and hard.

'How important is it to you to clear your dad's name?' he asked, finally.

'It's very important,' I said. 'Now my dad's dead, it's the only thing I can still do for him.'

George nodded, then went over to an ancient sideboard and produced an even more ancient cardboard box.

He placed it on the table, then said, 'I think I'll go for a bit of a walk, if you don't mind.'

I waited until I heard the door click closed, then opened the box.

On the top layer, there was a Sunday school attendance certificate, several payslips from the mill, and a collection of cigarette cards of famous footballers.

The letters were underneath. There were half a dozen of them. Tom's name was on the front of each envelope, written in a hand which showed a degree of education far beyond what he would have acquired, but there was no stamp.

With trembling hands, I took the first letter out of the envelope. At the top of it was written, in block capitals: BURN THIS AS SOON AS YOU'VE READ IT.

But Tom hadn't been able to bring himself to burn it, not even when he'd been on the point of taking his own life.

I started to read the letter.

'My dearest Tom, I know it is foolish of me to write to you, but I am helpless to resist. When you came into the office this morning, it was all I could do to prevent myself from touching you, from running my hands over your beautiful slim body . . .'

Was it that Tom was Wilfred's lover, I asked myself. Had the upright, self-righteous mill owner a penchant for young men? And had they had a lover's argument at the end of which, Tom had killed Wilfred?

'. . . running my hands over your beautiful slim body, exploring your mouth with my eager tongue . . .'

There were three pages of it, and it got more fervid – and frankly, more pornographic – as it went. Even the handwriting began to deteriorate from page two onwards.

And then I got to the end, and saw the signature.

'I will always love you, Oswald.'

And now, finally, we have reached the point at which I can postulate my grand theory. It is not perfect – there are gaps in it, there are questions unanswered – but it is the best I can do.

Tom and Oswald were lovers, and somehow Wilfred found out about it. I don't know what he told Oswald, but it will not have been comforting, because Wilfred knew what was right – and this definitely wasn't – and Wilfred gave no second chances.

Would Wilfred have reported it to the police? I believe he would have, because Oswald had disobeyed both the laws of God and the law of the land, and even if it brought shame down on the whole family, he would have to be punished for it.

So why didn't he go to the police immediately?

I think it was because he wanted to give Oswald a little time alone – a little space in which he could repent of his sins!

But Oswald is not prepared to go to prison, and so, as he sees it, he has no choice but to kill the golden goose. He gets Tom to sabotage the looms, thus putting my father – a good worker, but well-known to be a man who won't take shit from anybody – in the frame. He kills his own brother, then either plants the money himself or gets Tom to do it.

Why does Tom go along with the killing, and why is he prepared to lie in court?

Because he too, is afraid of going to gaol?

Perhaps, but I believe that this is not his driving motivation.

This is the man who cannot bear to burn Oswald's letters, even though that is what Oswald himself has instructed him to do. Even more tellingly, he can't even bring himself to do it on the morning he hangs himself – when he knows he will no longer be around to see them.

So what is driving him is not fear, but love. He loves Oswald, and he tells himself that he will do whatever Oswald asks him to.

But then he finds himself facing a dilemma which a quicker brain would have seen coming much earlier. He must either send an innocent man to the gallows, or betray the man he loves. He cannot do either, and chooses to sacrifice himself – to face a lonely death in the woods.

And what about Oswald himself?

He drinks himself to death – because he finds life without Tom unbearable.

EPILOGUE

George Clegg, lying there immobile, heard the voice of an angel.

'Hello George, it's me – Kate,' the angel said.

Hello, Kate, he thought.

'I've been talking to some of your neighbours, George, and they told me that you and Ellie were the happiest couple they'd ever seen, and that it almost destroyed you when she passed on.'

It *did* destroy me. I've never been strong, but I was healthy enough while she was alive. After she went, there seemed no point to anything.

'It was Arthur Tyndale who killed Maggie, George, but then you knew that already, didn't you?'

I didn't know for certain, but he was Wilfred Hardcastle's grandson, and I couldn't think of anybody else who would want to kill that beautiful girl.

'Maggie never told you what was in the shoe box, did she, George?'

No, she didn't. When I got back from me walk, she'd gone – and so had the box. I don't think she could face me after what she'd found in there. I didn't blame her. And the next morning, the florist delivered this huge bouquet of flowers. It was lovely. There was a card with it. It just said 'Thank you'.

'We've all read Maggie's diary, so now we think we know who killed Wilfred, too. It was his brother. Oswald was your Uncle Tom's lover, and they really did love one another. Does that shock you?'

It might have done once upon a time, but not anymore. Now I think that if you've a chance of happiness – any kind of happiness – you should grab it while it's there.

'I'm going to hold your hand now, George,' the angel said. 'I don't think you'll be able to feel it, but at least you'll know I'm doing it.'

You're a lovely girl, Kate. I wish I could see you, if only for a second, George thought.

'Do you believe in God, George?' Kate Meadows asked.

Yes, yes I do.

'I think you do, and that means you probably also believe in the afterlife as well.'

Yes, that too.

'You've been very brave. Maggie Entwistle probably never had a champion in life, but you were her champion after she died, and you were a wonderful one.'

I did my best.

'But she doesn't need you anymore. Your work is done. You can let go, George. Ellie's been waiting for you, and now you can go and join her.'

Thank you, Kate, George Clegg thought.

And then he died.